THE
HOUSE
ON
RYE LANE

SUSAN ALLOTT grew up on the English south coast, moved north to study English Literature at Leeds University, and later lived and worked in Sydney. South London is the only place she has ever called home, and she lives there today with her family. Susan's debut, *The Silence*, was longlisted for the 2021 New Blood Dagger Award. *The House on Rye Lane* is her second novel.

Also by Susan Allott

The Silence

THE
HOUSE
ON
RYE LANE

SUSAN ALLOTT

THE BOROUGH PRESS

The Borough Press
An imprint of HarperCollins*Publishers* Ltd
1 London Bridge Street
London SE1 9GF

www.harpercollins.co.uk

HarperCollins*Publishers*
Macken House,
39/40 Mayor Street Upper,
Dublin 1
D01 C9W8

First published by HarperCollins*Publishers* 2024
1

A catalogue record for this book is available from the British Library

Hardback ISBN: 978-0-00-856715-6
Trade Paperback ISBN: 978-0-00-856716-3

This novel is entirely a work of fiction.
The names, characters and incidents portrayed in it are
the work of the author's imagination. Any resemblance to
actual persons, living or dead, events or localities is
entirely coincidental.

Typeset in Adobe Garamond Pro by Palimpsest Book Production Ltd, Falkirk, Stirlingshire

Printed and bound in the UK using 100% Renewable Electricity by CPI Group (UK) Ltd

For Sam and Lauren

1

14 December 1994

It was the day of the murder, a dark Wednesday in south London, and Diana was listening to the lodgers. They were on the staircase, all three of them. She couldn't see them from the ground floor, but she heard them clearly; she felt their shock. Lee Delaney was shouting orders at his wife and child. There was fear in his voice, in the quiet of the house. One of them whimpered and puked on the carpet.

'Do you hear me?' Lee said. Ruth and Cookie replied that they did. He ran up to the next floor, told them not to move.

Diana listened. She located the mother and son from their voices: they were together on the stairs, halfway up. Out on the street she heard rain bouncing off the tarmac, a car horn on the far side of the Rye. A door slammed at the top of the house. Cookie spoke, frightened words that Diana didn't catch. But she knew his voice, with its adolescent tremor. She pictured him, stooped and awkward in his school uniform, all at odds with himself. That strange boy.

'Let me think,' Ruth said to her son. 'Be quiet a minute.'

Diana wished she had never let them into her house, this family with all their problems, but you couldn't pick and choose lodgers in this part of town. And the house put most normal people off. She had lived here all her life, as had all the Lloyds before her, not because it was a beloved family home but because no one had ever managed to sell it. It had been grand once, apparently. But nothing had ever gone right in the house on Rye Lane. It was a house of mistakes, of luck turned bad, of love gone cold. Most people knew that before they got through the door.

Ruth stepped down into the hallway. Diana heard her shoes on the tiles, the skim of her shower-proof coat. Ruth despised her; Diana had cottoned on to this too late. She'd thought Ruth was reserved. A bit surly. But it ran deeper than that, and stronger, more poisonous for being suppressed. It had scared her when it rose to the surface.

'Don't look down,' Ruth said to Cookie as he followed her.

But Cookie looked. His face was the last face Diana would see: his pale fright at the sight of her. She caught the smell of vomit on his socks. Her left foot dropped from the bottom stair as he stepped over her, and her head rocked back. She saw a different patch of ceiling then, before her vision darkened.

Ruth Delaney stifled a scream.

Diana was not scared now. It was too late for that. But she was angry at this old lady's death she'd been given: a bag of old bones at the foot of the stairs. She knew that when she was found there would be sympathy, and she would not be able to refuse it. There would be questions, but she would not get to ask them. This was the thing that really got her. She would die without answers, without knowing which of the Delaneys had given her that shove. Whose hands she had felt at her back.

She died in the minutes before the ambulance arrived, before the house was searched and the Delaneys were pushed into police cars. She heard the rain and the shouting. Then only rain. She thought that the house might rest now, with the last of the Lloyds gone. She thought, surely now there can be happiness here; people will bring love inside and it will live.

The house heard this last thought of hers, swallowed it into its history, and buried it.

2

12 September 2008

Maxine pushed open the gate and led the way up the steps to the front door. Seb was slow to follow. He was on the phone, telling someone he would call them back. She felt his reluctance, the bad mood that fell over him whenever they came to the house. The renovations bored and frustrated him, whereas she would happily spend the day watching it all happen, planning colour schemes and room layouts, discussing where they might move a door or a light fitting. She thought about it constantly, when she couldn't be here. From the first viewing she had loved this place, and if you'd asked her why she would have said it had bags of potential, with its original Georgian fixtures and fittings, its aspect looking out across the Rye at the morning sun; its location at the good end of Peckham, which was on the up. She would have said it was cheap, even when you factored in the cost of the work they'd need to do, which was considerable. It was a project, but she loved a project. She had the optimism of a woman who badly wanted everything to be fine.

A breeze blew in across the common, shaking conkers out of the trees. Maxine opened the door.

'Can we be quick here, Max?' Seb stood on the threshold, tall and sharp in his suit. 'I don't fancy the full tour.'

She put the keys in her pocket and held the door open with her foot. 'I just need a quick word with Alexander. I missed a call from him earlier.'

'His van's not here.' Seb turned and pointed out at the street, the space next to the skip where the van would normally be. 'He'll have knocked off early. It's Friday.'

She pushed the door shut behind Seb and stood at the foot of the stairs breathing disturbed air: brick dust and plaster. Dust sheets were spread out over the tiled floor, covered in boot prints. She called out hello, but she could tell by the quiet that the builders had left. There was a huge saw leaning against the wall and a crowbar blocking the steps down to the kitchen. A black bucket on its side. It looked like they might have downed tools and left in a hurry.

'I hope there wasn't a problem,' she said.

He stood beside her and looked up the stairs. 'Looks like it's still standing, which is all I need to know.'

'Did you hear from Alexander today?'

'Possibly. My phone hasn't stopped.' He smiled weakly, pushing his glasses up his nose. 'Listen, Max. I was going to wait until we got home.'

She heard something in his tone. Something new. She turned to him and held him by the sleeve.

'Things aren't good at work,' he said.

'What do you mean?'

'I think you were right. The rumour you heard about Barclays.'

She stared at him. A lorry passed the house, shaking the ground-floor windows.

'I mean, it's just a rumour,' he said. 'But people are saying Barclays have pulled the plug.'

Maxine looked down at her feet, because she didn't want to hear this, or to see Seb looking at her with that expression on his face. She wanted to walk through the rooms measuring progress, checking jobs off her list.

'Let's not worry about it now,' she said. 'My source wasn't sure it was true. I probably shouldn't have mentioned it.'

'Jason's rattled.'

'Doesn't mean we need to worry.'

'No. But Jason thinks—'

'I don't care what Jason thinks.' She ran her hand down the smooth oak of the bannister and felt the height and depth of the building, the weight of the abandoned rooms above her. 'You'd get another job,' she said, 'if the bank went under. You'd be all right?'

'I'm pretty tied to Lehman's, money-wise.'

She nodded, taking this in. She wished he didn't look so scared. 'How much of your money's tied to Lehman's?'

'All of it,' he said.

'I didn't know that.'

'None of it's vested yet.'

'What does that mean?'

'It means I can't sell the stock. There's nothing I can do, Maxine.'

She tried to think of something to say that wasn't what she was thinking. 'It won't happen,' was the best she could do. 'There'll be some kind of deal.'

He dropped his head, took off his glasses. She thought for a second he might be about to cry. In the year they'd been together she had never seen him cry. He was a few years younger than she was, and he had told her on their third date that he didn't want anything serious. He'd tried to break it off when she'd said she was getting to the age – nearly thirty – where she couldn't really mess around. But he'd called her a week later and asked if he could take her biological clock to the cinema. They'd met up for drinks first, got talking and missed the film. They'd spent every weekend together after that and he'd told her that he'd known from the first date he was going to fall in love with her. He was scared, he'd said, but he couldn't stay away.

'We'll be all right,' she said.

He wasn't crying, but she ran her thumb sideways across his face as he stood beside her at the foot of the stairs. He wasn't vain enough for contact lenses and he was blind enough that his glasses were part of his face, his eyes big and blurred without them. He looked familiar but strange, vulnerable. She tried not to worry. The house was in her name, bought outright with the money her dad had left her; Seb was funding all the work Alexander was doing. This was the deal they had struck. The

7

whole renovation project was dependent on Seb, his inflated banker's salary, his bonus.

'Come on,' she said, fitting his glasses back onto his face.

They went up to the top floor, and Seb stood at the garret window looking out across the common. The loft room was dark and cluttered and it smelled bad, like something was off; like the decaying underside of a root vegetable. Maxine kicked gently at an abandoned sleeping bag in the corner of the room, and it wheezed spores of mould over her shoe.

'What are you looking at?'

'That's Canary Wharf through the trees,' he said, pointing. 'You could see our trading floor with a decent telescope.'

She stepped around the filthy old sofa, which was probably where the smell was coming from. There was a blanket beside it on the floor, and underneath that she could just see the back pocket of a pair of jeans, one grubby trainer.

'Show me,' she said, coming to stand beside him.

He held her by the shoulders and guided her so she could see it from where she stood: the pyramid roof of Canada Tower with its red light on top, and the cluster of skyscrapers around it. 'So it is,' she said. 'Look at that.'

A plane flew low overhead. The common was an expanse of brown, pocked earth, fringed with rush hour traffic. 'It's been common land since forever. Never been built on,' she said, nodding out at the boggy grass. 'The Rye, they call it, locally. I think it's Old English.' She didn't look at him. She knew he loved this kind of thing. He was the only person she'd met who could stand in front of a burial mound on a windy Sunday afternoon in a state of rapture. Stone ruins and monuments blew his mind. 'Some historians believe Boudicca's last battle was fought on Peckham Rye.'

He turned to her. 'Did you make that up?'

'Why would I do that?'

'To distract me.'

She smiled, and he pulled her close against him. He was warm, and his shirt smelled of the dry cleaners. She wished she hadn't told him about that rumour at work.

'I'm sure this will all blow over,' she said.

'I hope you're right.'

'I mean, too many people have too much to lose.'

'True,' he said, looking down at the roof of a bus. 'Way too much.'

Maxine stayed there with her arms around him, trying not to stress. The money was one thing. The other thing – in some ways more scary – was whether she could keep loving him through this. She didn't want to fall out of love again: her old, bad habit. She had moved down to London from the remote part of Scotland where she grew up because she had needed a fresh start, away from her romantic track record. She had bought a house and found a good man who loved her. She had a career and an expensive trouser suit. She was brand new.

The sun came out and the grass brightened, the trees stood out rich green against the traffic.

'Did you see this?' Seb ran his fingers over a row of small holes in the woodwork of the window, in the horizontal strip where the panes were divided. The paint was peeling away, and he scratched at it with his thumb. 'Someone hammered nails into it. Tried to keep it shut.'

'D'you think?'

'It's old,' he said, examining the timber. 'Might be the original window.' He pulled his hand back and looked around at the open door leading to the staircase. 'Do you ever find it creepy? The house, I mean.'

She laughed. 'It's been empty for years. It just needs a good airing.'

'But there's something. Isn't there?'

'Can't say I've noticed.'

'Maybe it's just me.' His phone beeped in his pocket and he jumped. They both laughed, jittery laughter that sounded too loud, too bright in the dark room.

Maxine led the way down the stairs, past the big, sad rooms where she managed not to notice the change in the light, the watchful walls. She locked the front door and they shut the gate behind them, stood together on the street looking up at the house. It was tall and old and dignified, despite the dirty brick and the cracks in the mortar, the heavy growth of ivy and the crumbling steps leading to the front door. The curtains were pulled shut on the second floor, except for an opening at the left-hand window, the one with the crack in the pane.

'Should we mention that window to Alexander?' she asked Seb, but he had turned from her, walking away with his hands in the pockets of his coat, his head down. She chased after him and pushed his shoulders back until he stood up straight, all

10

six foot two of him, handsome with his thick hair cut short and his good skin. Heavy glasses and soft eyes. She'd told him, slightly drunk one night, that he was the perfect combination of metrosexual and geek. Too hot to be a banker, she'd said, and he'd laughed and said he wouldn't argue with that.

'Do you mind if we stay in tonight? We can watch TV,' he said. 'I'll cook.'

'Fine by me.'

'Sorry I'm not the best company. I can't put it out of my head.'

'I'll distract you,' she said, and there it was: his wolf grin. She took his hand.

It was warm for September, that Friday before the crash. Maxine kissed Seb at the junction as the lights changed from red to green and back again. A motorbike cut through the pedestrians at the crossing. A bus nudged forward from the other direction. A woman with a shopping trolley broke into a run and made it to the kerb by a whisker.

'Come on, it won't happen,' Maxine said, although she wasn't really surprised when Lehman Brothers went bankrupt a few days later, bringing the world's economy crashing down around it, sending house prices into freefall, wiping out businesses across the globe. It was a bigger surprise, in many ways, when Alexander called to say he'd told his men to leave early that Friday afternoon because they hadn't been paid. Not a single penny. She'd had to send him what he was owed out of the remains of her inheritance money, plus a bit extra by way of apology. That had been the first alarm bell, but she didn't hear it at the time.

3

19 October 1994

Cookie Delaney sat down on the stairs and took a textbook out of his bag. He held it open on his knees. Traffic passed by outside: tyres against the wet street and the regular, dull clank as wheels hit a drain. It was almost two months before the murder. Almost six weeks since the Delaneys had moved into the loft room at the top of this house. It was a cold, creepy hellhole on a road near a four-way junction, and they were living on top of each other like rats.

From upstairs he heard his mum raise her voice, then his dad replying; he didn't catch their words, and he didn't need to. They had the same argument every time his dad showed his face. He turned to the page he needed in his book.

A force is a push or pull.

Friction is a force that stops two objects sliding past each other.

From the loft his dad raised his voice, which meant things were coming to a head. He would walk out before long. Cookie was glad when a siren passed along Rye Lane, slow and loud, stuck in traffic at the lights. For a minute it was all he could hear. When it passed he heard his mum, shouting because of the recent noise: 'Are you gambling again?'

'Will you keep your voice down?'

'Will you answer the question?'

Their voices faded and Cookie stared at his book. The word in his head, that he was still hearing, was *gambling*. It went from making no sense to making perfect sense in one nauseating moment. He looked down the stairs at the thin carpet and the dark wood of the bannister. He had not wanted to know this. He tried to push it away, to find his place in the world again, the person he had been. But that person had known something was wrong, anyway.

Tension is a pulling force.

The faster an object is moving, the greater the air resistance.

He'd never heard his parents argue when they lived in Rotherhithe. He'd had his own room in their old house, and they'd had their own front door, their own bathroom and a separate living room. His dad had been working, most of the time. Things had been good. It seemed to Cookie that his life had been sliced in half by the move to Peckham: his childhood on one side and on the other, this person he was now, who was not the same.

At some point over the summer, while they'd been packing their things for the move, Cookie had grown almost three inches. His school uniform was already tight and his toes were closing in on the leather of his shoes. He was taller than most of his classmates, taller than some of the teachers. When he was alone in the bathroom he found coarse black hairs growing out of pale skin, shocking in their ugliness. He hated the thought of them. Worse still was the thought that people might know this about him; they might look at him and somehow know this hideous private thing. He twisted inside with the shame of it, sitting on the stairs with his textbook. He wanted to stop it, to be eleven again, or ten, or seven. He often dreamed he was becoming a monster.

Up in the loft, his mum was using a lot of bad language and his dad was trying to calm her down. Cookie read the same two sentences three times.

Magnitude is the size of a physical quality.

Vector quantities have a magnitude and a direction.

The door to the loft room opened then, and his mum's voice was loud at the top of the house: 'When did you last stop here for more than an hour?' she said. 'When did you last spend a night in my bed?'

His dad bounced down the stairs towards him, followed by his mum's voice: 'This is no way to live, Lee!'

Cookie bent his neck low over his textbook. He didn't want to look at his dad, with this new knowledge in him. But when he reached the first-floor landing Cookie looked up from his book and smiled at him, and his dad smiled back, same as always.

'What you doing there, son?'

He brought his knees together and held his book against his chest. 'Reading,' he said. 'Physics. We've got a test tomorrow.'

'What are you learning about?'

'Forces.'

'Forces.' He held the newel post at the top of the stairs and frowned as he remembered. 'Friction and resistance. Right?'

Cookie nodded.

'Velocity?'

'We haven't done that yet.'

Lee passed his hand over his forehead, up over his crown then down again. His hair was receding, forming two bald peaks with a lick of still-dark hair in the centre. Flecks of grey at his temples. 'Velocity is the speed at which an object travels in a particular direction,' he said.

'OK.' He smiled. *Velocity.*

'All good, is it? With the new school?'

Cookie held the book tight against his chest. He thought of the strange classrooms and the grey Formica desks, the plastic chairs which were sometimes hurled across the room. The shoving in the corridors and the fights in the lunch queue. The breaktimes walking around on his own.

'It's fine,' he said.

'That's good.' Lee glanced up the stairs. 'Your mum's had a rough day. Bit tired, I think. We had words.'

'I know.'

'Right.' He gave a long exhale. 'Sorry you had to hear that.'

Cookie mirrored his dad's expression: *What can you do?* They smiled at each other. 'That's OK,' he said.

His dad gripped the top of the post with his big hand. 'I'd best be off, then.' He put one foot down on the step below.

'Dad?'

15

Lee Delaney stood with his legs straddling the stairs, half up half down. Jeans that could have been cleaner, and a sweater with a zip at the neck that hung loosely on him. He looked to Cookie like he might not have shaved for a day or two, and he might not have slept in that time. He looked like he wanted to leave.

'What is it, son?'

'Where are you going?'

This was the wrong thing to say. He knew it as soon as it was out. His dad was already turning from him, his eye contact lost. He sounded like his mum, like he was trying to keep him here in the house, when in fact what Cookie wanted was to go with him, wherever he was going. He wanted to follow him down the stairs and out into the street, to hold his hand and talk to him as they walked. But he was too big for all that.

'There's a bit of work going, over in Nunhead. I said I'd go and meet a bloke to see if I can help him out.'

'A job?'

'Kind of.' He looked away.

'That's good,' Cookie said, and a quietly treacherous part of his brain wondered if it was true. He waited for his dad to look at him. 'Good luck,' he said.

'Thanks.' He took a few steps further down the staircase, turned and looked again at Cookie, their eyes level. 'Look after your mum, would you? She's having a hard time.'

'Dad,' he said.

His dad raised his eyebrows in reply. Cookie wanted to ask, What kind of work is it, that you go out to meet a bloke without changing your jeans? Have you been gambling? Do I have to turn thirteen? But he didn't want the answers to these questions. So he said, 'Do we have to live here a long time?'

'I don't know, son.'

'Nothing's the same, since we came here.'

From one of the rooms along the landing, they heard movement behind a closed door. A stifled cough and the squeak of upholstery. Mrs Lloyd, the landlady, lived in these rooms on the first floor. It was her house, and she had a huge bedroom, with her own bathroom beside it, which the Delaneys were not to use. They shared the big kitchen on the ground floor. On the second floor there were three more rooms which were out of bounds.

Lee registered the noise, and he rolled his eyes at Cookie. It was a family agreement, a sort of pact, that they couldn't stand Diana Lloyd. It seemed to be the only thing his parents agreed on these days; the only thing holding the three of them together. It was them against her. Cookie rolled his eyes back at his dad, and they both smiled.

'I'll get going, son,' Lee said. 'Good luck with your test.'

Cookie stayed where he was. He watched his dad spring down the stairs and take his coat from the hook by the door. Cold air and rain entered the house as Lee let himself out, then he stood for a short time at the top of the steps leading to the concreted space out the front where they kept the bins. He looked up and down the street, hands pushed deep into the pockets of his coat, then he pulled the door shut behind him.

From the bedroom down the hall, another cough. Cookie stood, pushing his textbook back inside his bag. He was at the turn of the stairs leading up to the second floor when Mrs Lloyd opened her bedroom door. He turned and she smiled at him, pulling her woollen cardigan down over her hips. Her white hair was bright in the gloom of the house, and she was small and soft-looking, with a face that folded into a fleshy smile. She winked at him.

He smiled back at her, before he could help himself, and she carried on down the stairs towards the kitchen. Cookie stood where he was for a second or two, his bag pulling heavy on his shoulder, and he thought that he had a hard time disliking Mrs Lloyd. He knew she was charging them rent to live in a small room at the top of her big creepy house. But she liked him, and sometimes when his parents were out she brought him down to the kitchen and gave him a slice of Victoria sponge. He looked forward to the cake. He'd considered mentioning it to his mum, but lately she seemed angry a lot of the time and so the weeks had passed and the secret had grown bigger than he'd intended. He pushed it out of his head as he climbed up through the house. The stairwell darkened and he held the handrail, shut his eyes, and thought of magnitude and friction and velocity.

4

25 May 1843

Horatio stared across the room at the window. It stood wide open, the curtains parted, the stench of the river dense in the air. It was incredible that nobody listened to him, when he had been perfectly clear that every window in the house must be shut. Without exception. He put his papers down on the desk and lowered the sash, managing as he did so to trap a fly on the inside: a small, quick thing that threw itself against the pane, then became lost in the folds of the curtain. The river was attracting these flies. It had burst its banks again in the recent rain and the view across the Rye was of an expanse of filthy water reaching almost to the track at the front of the house. Human waste, with its deadly stink. But still the servants left the windows open, even here in his own study. They did not respect him, he knew this. The fly settled on his arm and he slapped at it, sending it into wild circles around his head.

Isobel had known how to handle the servants.

From the landing he heard the light tread of footsteps, the rattle of crockery on a tray. He had asked that all his meals be left outside his door. Under no circumstances was he to be disturbed. He stood at the window and listened as the girl put the tray down. He felt her nervous hesitation. She was young, only seventeen, and had not been with them long. She knocked, and when he didn't respond she knocked again.

'What is it?' He didn't turn from the window. Behind him the door opened, and he bristled at the intrusion.

'Pardon me, sir.' A rattle as she picked the tray back up.

He did not turn. He could picture her standing there with the tray, her body stooped with the weight of it. She had something about her that brought Isobel to mind. He hadn't made this connection before now, but he knew that if he turned to look at her he would see thick, healthy hair, lifted from the neck with a series of pins. If she were to let it loose, it would fall heavily down her back.

'What is it?' he said, louder than before.

'Where might I set down your tray?'

'You can leave it outside,' he said. 'There is no need to come in. Simply leave it outside and knock to alert me.'

'Sorry, sir,' she said. 'Only I wanted to ask—'

'I have a great deal of paperwork. I must not be disturbed. I thought I had been clear about that.'

He heard her behind him, setting the tray down on his desk. He smelled fried meat and onions. Still he could not look at her, and her proximity was unsettling. Her name was Alice, this girl, and he could not put aside the thought of her dark-blonde hair, which in his mind's eye was long, with a wave through it like Isobel's; lighter at the tips than at the crown. He turned his face so that she could not catch his expression.

'Will you be wanting me to clean, sir?'

'Of course,' he said. 'My living quarters will need to be cleaned today.'

She did not reply, or move. Horatio felt foolish, standing with his back to her, and he disliked her for this. He frowned out at the view across the Rye. A new property was going up on the far side of the river, separated from this one by the wide stretch of low-lying grass and a fringe of newly planted saplings. They had thought it beautiful, he and Isobel, when they had chosen this plot. Isobel had truly loved it. And she had loved him. She had believed in him.

He could no longer see beauty in this aspect. He saw sodden fields and dark skies. Dozens of crows dotted across the grass, motionless, facing east.

The girl coughed.

'Why are you still here?' he said.

'I meant the first floor, sir.'

'The water closet? By all means, yes.'

'Sir, the master bedroom has not been cleaned since—'

He turned then, and the girl stepped backwards. Fear in her face. A thin, fragile girl with none of Isobel's stature. Her hair was darker than he'd remembered. Somehow this stoked his anger and he boomed at her: 'Have I asked you to clean the master bedroom?'

'No, sir,' she said. 'But I don't like to see the dust gathering.'

'I will decide when it is time to clean in there.' The anger in his chest was hot and loose, and he let it fill him, enjoying the lift of it, the distraction from his pain. 'I will decide, and you will follow my instructions, is that clear?'

She nodded. She was afraid of him, and he was glad.

'Do you have the window open, in your room?'

'No,' she said, glancing away.

'I want it shut at all times.'

'Of course, sir.'

'The same throughout the house.'

She looked at her feet. She thought he was unreasonable, that he didn't understand. It was early summer, and the days since the funeral had been warm but not bright. He was hot in his black mourning suit. He was not sleeping well or eating well, and he could not keep his mind on his work. But he did not want or expect this misery to end. The world was wretched, as it should be.

'The same throughout the house,' he repeated. 'To counteract the miasma from the river. Do you see?'

'Yes, sir.'

'The miasma is quite deadly.'

She did not look up. The fly circled the room, enraged. 'Yes, sir,' she said.

When she had gone, he lifted the domed lid away from the dinner plate and considered the fried meat beneath: diced onions swimming in gravy. The food did not smell as it should. His hand shook as he returned the lid; all the energy had leached from him and he was not sure if he felt hot or cold. He pulled out his chair and sat down at his desk. Alice would be down in the scullery by now, telling Archer and Mrs Reeves what he had said; that he had raised his voice in anger. He knew the servants were gossiping, circulating rumours about the way Isobel had died. He knew they thought it was his doing. And when he wasn't careful with his thoughts, he knew they were right.

He pushed the tray aside. The flocked walls closed in on him. The carriage clock on the mantelpiece ticked with loud disapproval. Horatio hung his head low over his desk, his hands spread over his knees. He would insist that his meals were left outside his study from now on. If these rooms on the second floor became insufferable, he would go to the Kings Arms on the corner of the Rye and he would take his meal there. He hoped that he might learn to live this way. He might be able to believe that Isobel was downstairs, that she had asked for privacy in her room, as she so frequently did.

The fly settled on his stack of papers. He watched it, his limbs heavy, his shirt wet against his back. It took off again, returning to the window where it persisted in its furious buzzing. Horatio stood, moved back to the window and pushed the curtain aside. The day had brightened a little, and he thought perhaps a breeze had picked up: the saplings leaned sideways, their leaves shook. Slowly, he lifted the window and held it open until the fly escaped. He despised the small creature for its persistence; for gaining his mercy.

He lowered the sash with more noise than he had intended. He stood at the window and his gaze seemed to darken the scene, sending clouds across the sun, giving flight to the crows out on the Rye.

5

1 October 2008

Seb ran the hot tap in the tiny bathroom on the top floor. The pipes roared, which got his hopes up, but then a rusty plug of grit dropped into the basin, followed by a weak trickle of water which barely made the soap lather. He turned it off again and wiped his gummy hands on the towel. They should have got the plumbing done first. They'd rewired the whole place but they hadn't got round to the plumbing before the economy tanked.

He heard a door swing shut lower down in the house, but when he got back to the second floor it was as he'd left it, with all the doors pushed open to get a bit of light into the place. The house was full of sloping floors and uneven surfaces; loose, irregular floorboards and doors that wouldn't stay shut. The whole building was lopsided, asymmetrical, with rooms that had been divided and rooms that clearly hadn't been used at all in decades. His first impression of it, when he'd come to see it with Maxine, was of an old man leaning on a cane, tall and thin, slumped sideways on wasted muscles. But Maxine had thought it was charming, and he'd agreed, mostly because she was charming.

He wondered if it could have been the front door that he'd heard. Maybe Max had come home early. He leaned over the bannister but all he could see was the turn of the stairs and the black and white tiles on the ground floor.

'Max? You home?'

No reply. He listened, but the house was quiet. A bus passed along the street, slow and heavy. The pipes were still recovering from that short burst of water he'd drawn from the tap. They'd moved in three weeks ago and it had been as bad as he'd known it would be: cold and draughty and damp. Brick dust everywhere. Maxine was working long hours at the paper and he was here all day, kicking around in the debris. Nothing in his life was familiar to him. He woke up every morning in a strange room, to the sound of crows, and asked himself what the hell he'd done.

He went back to the biggest of the rooms on the second floor, where he'd stripped the mouldy flocked paper from the walls. It was criminal, he'd said to Maxine. The paper was almost as old as the house. But it was too damaged to save, and it made the room smaller and darker than they wanted it. The room ought to be beautiful, with its two generous windows overlooking the common and the wide, original fireplace. But the light was flat in here, and it felt stale. He'd tried and failed to open the windows; they were jammed shut and he was scared to force them in case he damaged the glass. One pane was cracked already and Max would kill him if he made it worse. Without the paper the walls were pink and raw, and the room had the offended look of a skinned cat. Standing among the fragments of paper he felt shocked at himself. Guilty, even. But maybe that was nothing to do with the wallpaper.

It was getting late. He was done for today. He saw the room through Maxine's eyes and thought, surely she'll be happy with this. She hadn't been happy with much lately. She seemed to think he was going to renovate the whole place single-handedly, now that he wasn't bringing money in. It wasn't going well. He wasn't the sort of guy who was handy with a screwdriver or who knew how to fix a washer. He could barely hang a picture straight. The more time he had on his hands, the less productive he seemed to be.

He'd found himself thinking, as the long days stretched into long weeks, that his big mistake had been to fall in love with Maxine. That had never been the plan. She'd unhinged him right from the first date, that wine bar near Waterloo where he'd met a few other women, mostly because it was handy for the Tube. Max had drunk water and kept her coat on. She'd been nervous, self-conscious, more beautiful than her profile. He'd wanted to kiss her but hadn't dared, not because he didn't like her enough but because he did. She was funny and natural and unpretentious and complicated.

It turned out she'd borrowed something from her sister that night, a dress that she felt uncomfortable in, that she didn't think was right for the wine bar. Something with small white polka dots, he knew that much because the hem showed under her coat. She never wore dresses usually, she'd said. She was more of a jeans and sweater girl. So on the next date they'd gone for coffee, somewhere quiet and laid-back, and she'd worn jeans and Converse, a grey turtleneck. She'd teased him about his corporate weekend wear and he'd said he wished he'd kept his coat on. He'd been falling for her by then. Couldn't stop thinking about her. It was on the fourth date – the one where they didn't make it to the cinema – that she'd told him about her dad, the way he'd died and the shock of the financial settlement. He'd joked that she shouldn't tell strange men she was moneyed up, and she'd said she didn't think he was *that* strange. And besides, he was moneyed up too, she'd said. So that made it OK.

He squatted down by the fireplace and worked his fingers along the edge of a narrow strip of paper that still clung to the wall. He pulled hard at it, ripped it too quickly and it came free in a cloud of crumbled plaster, leaving a hole in the wall two inches deep, from the top of the fireplace to the floor. He stood and looked at it in disbelief. He kicked the wall and another chunk of plaster fell at his feet, like some kind of tit-for-tat game, like the house was trying to wind him up. He threw his head back and shouted at the stained, flaking ceiling. His voice was strange in the dark house. He didn't like the quality of the quiet afterwards.

On the far side of the room his phone rang. He let it ring out. Then he picked it up and sat down on the floor with his legs stretched out, the bare wall cold against his back. The call was from Jason, as he'd thought it would be. A siren began its long wail on the far side of the common and he followed it in

27

his head, turning onto the East Dulwich Road, weaving through traffic at the junction, heading north towards the hospital. It faded out after a minute or two. He brought his phone to his ear and listened to Jason saying that he needed Seb to call him back. He didn't say why, but Seb already knew why, and Jason knew that. He shut his eyes and felt the dust, sharp in his cornea. He ran the tips of his fingers over the smooth contours of his phone. Then he turned it off.

He stood, picked his hoodie up off the floor and decided to bag up the wallpaper later. He was thirsty and starving. He didn't know how he hadn't noticed that earlier. Hours must have passed while he was working up here, but he didn't remember much about the day. He was halfway down the stairs when he heard the groan of the pipes. He stood still, looked up the stairs and listened. There was the usual tap and clank, the silty hum, then a loud rush of water from the bathroom in the loft. He ran back up.

The taps were both turned on fully in there, water rushing into the basin and splashing onto the floor. He turned them off and stood looking at the water draining into the plughole. His T-shirt was wet and the cold fabric clung to his skin. He didn't understand how this had happened. He pulled his hoodie on and figured he must have left the taps on earlier, after he tried to wash his hands. Either that or there was some fault in the plumbing, something to do with ancient pipes and water pressure that would make perfect sense if he knew anything about it. He used the hand towel to mop the water from the floor and double-checked the taps were turned tightly off. He put the lid down on the toilet seat. It was a horrible room, windowless, filthy with mould. The shower was dripping into the tray, where a grey circle of corrosion surrounded the plughole. The grouting around the tiles was black.

He shut the door and walked down the stairs to the ground floor. Moments passed, and he found himself crouched down in front of the fridge, full of inexplicable fear. He wasn't sure why he was looking in the fridge, which was empty apart from some suspect-looking leftovers in Tupperware pots, and a can of beer on its side on the top shelf. He cracked the can open and drank half of it down. It made him even colder, but after half a minute his brain fogged and the fear softened. He sat down at the table. The pipes were still not entirely quiet: a steady tap from the top of the house, which sounded almost like a hammer, but couldn't be, of course. On the far side of the room, at the sink under the window, the tap dripped.

When Maxine got home he was still sitting at the end of the table, legs stretched out, with the empty can at his side. He looked up and smiled at her. She took her hat off and her hair fell around her face, longer than she used to wear it; she hadn't said so, but he knew she was cutting back on the things she'd usually spend money on, the little extras; haircuts being one of those things. He preferred it shorter, the way she'd worn it when he first met her. She was forever pushing it out of her eyes these days, or behind her ears.

She pulled her headphones out, left them dangling against her coat. 'What's wrong?' Her face was bright from the cold. 'Seb?'

'Nothing.'

She crouched down beside him. 'You're freezing. You look terrible.'

'I'll be fine.'

'Did something happen?'

She gripped his hand and he heard the tinny pulse of music from her headphones. The whole thing with the taps was absurd. She would laugh in his face if he told her, and rightly so. He didn't even want to talk about it.

'The house has been getting to me,' he said. 'I'm not dealing with it. Being out of work, on my own all day.'

'I thought that might be it.'

'I'm not cut out for renovating, Max.'

'No. I know.' She looked so disappointed. 'I've been thinking, maybe we should get someone in to help with the house. It's too much for us on our own.'

'We don't have the money for that.'

'We can't live like this, can we? They're forecasting a cold snap.' She smiled. 'I'd give anything for a hot bath.'

'I know. Me too.'

'Let's get a quote for the plumbing, then. Just a quote.'

'There's no point, Maxine.'

She reached into her pocket and turned her music off. 'Any news on the work front?'

He groaned inwardly at the question. She did try not to ask every day, he knew that, and she had every right to ask. He couldn't look at her.

'I got a call earlier,' he said. 'Merrill Lynch. They're recruiting. I've said I'm interested.'

'Oh my God! That's great!'

He felt bad about the lie as soon as it was out. He didn't like lying, but he also disliked the way she looked at him these days, like an encouraging primary school teacher. Exasperation smothered in kindness. He couldn't bear it.

'Come here.' He took her coat off her shoulders and she pulled her arms out so it dropped to the floor. She stood, and he looked up at her from the chair, held her by the hips. 'Don't you want to change out of this office wear?' he said.

It was insanely cold but she took her tights off, hitched up her skirt and guided his hand as he pushed two fingers inside her. She rocked her head back and pulled at his hair. He loved the smell of her. The way she looked at him. He undid his belt and dropped his jeans down around his knees, pulled her down onto him with her legs straddling the chair. She went slowly; she was good at it and he liked that about her; she enjoyed it and she took what she needed. She put his hand inside her shirt, undid a few buttons for him. After a while she sped up a bit, then a bit more. He didn't look at her when he came, tried to think of someone else but there was no one else in his head, she was the only one. He said her name, because he loved her. He loved her.

'Jesus,' she said, and he looked up at her then, watched her lose herself. The chair creaked and he held onto the table to steady it until she stopped moving.

'That was worth the wait,' he said. They both laughed. 'Jesus Christ.'

He kissed her shoulder, her neck. It was a while before he could speak again. He felt exposed, powerless. He knew, each time they did this, that he had never felt this way about anyone before and that he was out of his depth, trying to hold on to her for as long as he could, knowing he should let her go.

She kissed the top of his head, then his mouth, made him look at her. 'Still got it,' she said.

'Yeah. Sorry it's been a while.'

'It's OK.'

She stood, and he pulled his jeans up. The house was still, watchful, colder than was normal for October. He looked at her to see if she felt it too, but she smiled and pushed her hair out of her eyes. She used her tights to wipe the insides of her thighs.

'Would this be a good moment to say we really need a plumber?'

He laughed, and shook his head at her. 'I'll find a plumber,' he said. 'If that's what you want. I'll call around and we'll get a quote.'

Her phone beeped, and she hunted around for it in her bag, pulling out her book, her purse, her travel pass, a box of paracetamol. It beeped again. After a minute he stood and picked her coat up off the floor, reached inside the pocket and handed her the phone.

'Thank you,' she said, sincere and beautiful. He thought she was going to say that she loved him; it seemed to be on her lips. But she was distracted by her phone, so she didn't say it. He couldn't remember the last time she had. Before the crash, he thought. Back when she'd thought he had money.

6

3 December 1994

Cookie left the house early and walked along Rye Lane, opposite the common. It was a fortnight before the murder and he
was sleeping badly, waking in the night with the cold and lying
there for hours. He couldn't get his brain to stop thinking. This
had never happened in the old house in Rotherhithe. He'd
never even thought about whether he liked his life, his school,
where they lived; whether he was all right or whether he was
strange. Not once had he woken in the night with his brain
alert and waiting for him.

The sun was only just up and a low mist hung over the
common. Cookie zipped up his coat. The mist had a pale glow
to it, stretched out over the wide expanse of grass. A fox crossed
the pavement ahead of him and ran over the road, out onto
the common and into the mist where it disappeared, the tip
of its tail streaking through the white. Cookie followed. The
grass was wet but he kept walking, hoping the mist would

envelop him, that he would become invisible even to himself. It didn't work; the mist disappeared once he was within it, but he didn't. He walked further out onto the common, towards the big London plane in the middle, where the grass beneath his feet was sodden. He stepped back from the tree but it was wetter there. Wherever he trod it was the same: grass gave way to mud, and in places to dark, cold water. He stood where he was and saw brown, wet earth all around him, dotted with crows. Beyond that, only mist.

He kept walking through water that reached his ankles, following the sound of the road. His jeans were cold against his legs. Crows eyed him from clods of mud and he stared back at them, plunging forward through the bog until the road came into view, busy and ugly and normal. Two buses waited at the junction as a woman crossed with a child, both of them blank-faced, wrapped up against the cold. Cookie stayed on the grass and watched as the lights changed and the buses moved on. He felt better, since he'd spent those few minutes lost in the mist. He'd woken up. The thoughts that tracked through his head all night had gone.

The bus pulled out at the lights and behind it, emerging from the Kings Arms, Cookie saw his dad. He stopped on the dryer grass to look at him. The receding line of his hair and the hunch of his shoulders in his donkey jacket. For a second Cookie was overjoyed to see him. He almost ran towards him, like he would have before they lived here. He lifted one wet foot and put it down again. He was too big for that. And he knew that leaving a pub at this hour on a Saturday morning was probably not a good thing. His dad stood at the traffic lights with his collar up, his head hung low, hands deep in his pockets, and Cookie heard his mother saying, *When did you last sleep a night in my bed?*

The lights changed as he reached the far corner of the common, where the grass met concrete, and his dad looked up. Cookie saw him arrange his face: the transition to a smile from something else. He crossed the road with his head down, and when he met Cookie on the pavement he smelled of the pub, wet and stale.

'What you doing out here?' his dad said.

'Just walking.'

'Why?'

'I just wanted to.' He looked across the road at the pub, where another man was leaving from the same door his dad had come out of, with the same bowed head. 'I like it on the common.'

His dad smiled. His eyes were dull. 'Been swimming?'

'What?'

'Your jeans are soaked.'

'I know.' Cookie turned and looked behind him at the bare trees and the chopped-up grass. 'It's like a lake in the middle.'

'That's the Peck,' his dad said.

'The what?'

'The River Peck. You must have waded right through it.' He pointed out to the far side of the common and drew a line with his finger, south to north, past the line of horse chestnuts and across the East Dulwich Road. 'The river rises back to the surface when it rains. There's a time when it was there in all weathers, when it was a proper stream running right across the common. It ran along Rye Lane and then it turned where the Nags Head is now. From there it went north to Bermondsey, then north-east until it met the Thames at Rotherhithe.'

Cookie pictured it: a river with reeds along its banks; shallow, clear water with a rocky bed, running all the way through the common and over the road.

'It was the route of the Kentish drovers,' his dad said. 'Taking their cattle to market in town.'

'Peckham must be named after the river then.'

'That's right. And Rye means waterway,' his dad continued. 'Old English. That's why this area's called the Rye.'

A police car overtook a bus on the far side of the common, siren on. Cookie's dad put his hand on his shoulder and took him further out across the grass, into the mist. 'D'you see?' He pointed back towards the far end of the common where railings separated the park from the open land. 'Do you see the low ground it runs through? Do you see its course?'

Cookie nodded, although what he saw through the mist was sodden grass and mud. His socks were wet.

'You can't stop a river running through a valley,' his dad said. 'There's always been a river here.'

Cookie turned to watch the police car. The siren was loud, pushing through traffic at the junction by the Kings Arms. His dad stood rigid, his back straight, gripping Cookie by the shoulder. The car parked in front of the pub and three policemen jumped out.

'Don't,' his dad said. 'Best you don't look that way.'

'Why not?'

'I said don't. That's why.' Behind them, car doors slammed. A second police car screamed down Rye Lane and stopped at the pub. His dad turned him around, holding him by the shoulders, so they were facing the long street of tall houses. 'These houses were built to look out over the Rye. Nice view, with the river running across here. Would've been very grand to live in Peckham, back then.'

'That's mad,' Cookie said.

'Peckham was one of the first commuter suburbs in London. Rich people lived here and went to work in the City.' He lifted his voice over the noise behind them. 'Only one problem. These are lowlands, Cooks. This is a valley, and all the muck washes into it. Nowhere else for it to go.' He lifted his feet out of the mud. 'All the water and fog settles here. Gets on your chest.'

Cookie looked down at the wet grass, where his dad was pointing, and tried to listen. At the edge of his vision, police sirens flashed blue through the mist.

'The bathrooms were put in later, in these houses. Very basic plumbing. Clay soil-pipes, most likely. Drains that weren't made for that volume of water.' He shouted it, and Cookie nodded, his eyes on his feet. 'You'd have all sorts of disease. Typhoid, cholera. All sorts of problems.'

'Would you?' He was so cold. He didn't know that he wanted to stand here any more, with his dad going on and on, and the police talking into radios behind them.

'The bricks were made by mixing clay with ash and cinders. London brick, it's called. Laid in lime mortar. Did you know that?'

'No.' Cookie sniffed.

'It's porous.' He pulled Cookie closer. 'Breathes everything in.'

'Right.'

'It would have stunk after a while.' His dad seemed to be talking to himself now.

'What did?'

'The river. The waste from these houses would've found its way into the Peck. Would have been a proper pong coming off it.' The lights changed at the junction and a bus rolled past, tall and red, its windows misted up. 'Don't suppose the filthy rich were too happy, looking out the window at their own excrement.'

Cookie laughed, though his teeth were chattering. 'How do you know all that?'

'This is where I'm from,' his dad replied. 'The Delaneys were here before these houses, back when this was all fields and marshes and there was woodland from Deptford to Croydon. The river ran clear back then.'

Cookie looked again at the tall houses, the dirty-looking brick and the black windows. He could see the loft window of the room they were renting; the thin green curtains. He felt his dad's attention slipping away.

'What happened?' he said. 'What did they do about the stink?'

His dad clapped him on the back. 'They buried it,' he said.

Someone shouted behind them. Car doors slammed shut; there was some kind of scuffle. Cookie leaned in against the rough wool of his dad's coat. A crow took off from a park bench and disappeared into the mist.

'You should go in,' his dad said, when the police cars had driven away. 'You must be cold.'

Cookie reached for his dad's hand out of habit as they crossed the road. His dad returned his grip for just a few seconds, more of a squeeze than a hold, and he pushed his hands back into the pockets of his coat before they'd reached the kerb. Cookie did the same. He stared down at the pavement and felt the coarse warmth of his dad's skin fade from his hand.

'Are you coming in?' Cookie asked as they stood together at the gate.

'Not today.'

'Are you avoiding Mum?'

'No, son. It's the filthy rich I'm avoiding.' He smiled, nodding up at the house.

'Mrs Lloyd?'

'That's right.'

'OK.' Cookie smiled back, tried to share the joke, but his dad was looking down the street now, leaning away.

'You go in and get dried off.'

Cookie stood at the door and watched his dad stride off towards the junction. Then he used his key to let himself in. His mum worked Saturdays and she would be leaving soon, rushing to get dressed and ready. He shut the door behind him and looked down at his trainers, caked in mud. He was wiping them on the mat when he heard footsteps from the kitchen, too slow and heavy to be his mum.

'Morning!' Mrs Lloyd walked up the steps into the hallway, carrying a lunch box and a flask, a teacup dangling from her thumb.

'Morning, Mrs Lloyd.'

'Call me Diana,' she said, smiling at him. 'I'm not even married.' She always said this, and he always called her Mrs Lloyd. 'You been out on the common?'

'Yes,' Cookie said. 'It's misty out there.'

'Boggy?'

'Yes.' He looked down at his shoes. 'I'll take them off.'

'Good lad. I mopped these tiles yesterday.' She nodded down at the black and white tiled floor that ran from the front door down to the kitchen. 'Don't want muddy footprints.'

Cookie kicked off his trainers and stood by the door in his wet socks. The house was dark and cold, and he wanted to go upstairs to see his mum before she left, but Mrs Lloyd was sitting on the bottom step, her bag next to her, so he couldn't pass. She took her teacup and set it down on the shoe rack at her side while she packed her lunch box and flask into her bag. The shoe rack was made of wrought iron, with three shelves for shoes to stand on. Mrs Lloyd had balanced the teacup on the top shelf between her fleece slippers and the tapered point of the iron leg on the corner of the rack. Cookie looked at the teacup: a deep china bowl with a red and gold pattern. He thought of how it would shatter on impact with the tiled floor. It was almost irresistible, the thought

40

of the china cracked open, the sound it would make. He pushed his hands deep into his coat pockets so he wouldn't reach out and tip it; he clenched his fists until Mrs Lloyd picked it up again, wrapped it in a scarf and put it into her bag.

'Can't stand tea from a plastic cup.' She pushed against the stair to stand up. 'So I always take a decent teacup with me when I go out for the day. People look at me strangely some-times, and do you know what?'

'What?' Cookie said.

'I don't care.' She laughed. 'I really couldn't care less. It's the best thing about being my age.'

Cookie stood aside to let her get to her coat and hat, which hung by the door. 'Where are you going?'

'I'm going to get the number 12,' she said. 'Top deck. It crosses the Thames at Westminster and then it goes through Piccadilly Circus and along Regent Street. I'm hoping to see the Christmas lights.'

'That sounds good,' Cookie said. He knew the number 12 was a Routemaster bus, with an opening at the back where you could step on or off from the street. He'd never ridden it all the way into town.

'Want to come?' She looked excited. 'You'd be very welcome.'

He did want to go with her. He would be on his own all day otherwise, and he'd spent enough time alone in this house to know that he was never really alone. Those forbidden rooms on the second floor felt dense with presence; someone wanted him to push those doors open and he would do it one day, he knew he would. He balled his fists in his pockets.

'I was thinking I'd go to the Portrait Gallery. They have a fabulous collection. Have you ever been?'

'No.'

'I think you'd love it.' She winked. 'All those dead people on the walls, looking out at you.'

He smiled at this. Mrs Lloyd buttoned up her coat, arranging her bag so the strap crossed her chest. He went to reply, and then from upstairs he heard the groan of the pipes, and the soft sound of footfall. His mum was coming out of the shower in their small, windowless bathroom on the top floor. He thought of his dad, who was avoiding Mrs Lloyd. His dad had smiled, but there was hate in what he'd said about her.

'I've got homework,' he said. 'Sorry.'

'Another time, maybe?' Mrs Lloyd said, and he nodded. He waited in the hallway a while after she'd gone, listening to the noises in the house, the give of the floorboards, the knock of the plumbing.

7

9 October 2008

Seb was the only person in Peckham Rye Park wearing a suit. He was also the only person without a dog or a child, apart from a guy in a baseball cap who was sitting on a bench and managing to occupy the whole thing, his arms reaching across the back, his ankle resting on his knee. Seb had done four circuits of the park and the guy in the baseball cap was there each time he passed, on the bench at the turn of the duck pond where small children in wellington boots stood at the railings to throw bread. He appeared to be watching Seb as he passed, but that might have been because Seb was walking up and down in a suit, feeling self-conscious and jumpy. He'd dry-cleaned the suit, using the only credit card that wasn't yet maxed out, for his fictional interview this afternoon. Maxine would be home from work soon and he needed to get back after her, to appear to have been to the City and back. He needn't have left the house quite so early but once he was dressed he'd been too aware of his lie, alone in the house with his shoes polished and his collar tight at his neck.

On his fifth circuit his phone rang and he stared at the screen until it stopped. He stood on a small wooden bridge where a stream passed underneath, carrying leaves and twigs and the occasional blue plastic. His phone beeped. Voicemail. He listened and then deleted it.

He leaned on the wooden bridge and considered dropping his phone into the water. He held it loosely between thumb and forefinger. Even if it only gave him a few days of peace before they tracked him down, it would be worth it. He was about to let it drop when a dog ran out of the stream and shook itself off, splashing muddy water over Seb's expensively dry-cleaned trousers. For God's sake, he was soaked. He walked away from the bridge, fuming, shaking his wet trousers away from his shins. The owner of the dog called after him, apologising, but he couldn't bring himself to turn around and act like it was OK. He held up a hand, to show he'd heard the apology, and kept walking. He kicked the sawn-off trunk of a tree. Children stared and he stared back. He was being a prick, and he didn't know how to snap out of it.

His phone rang. This time he recognised the number.

'Jason,' he said.

'I was starting to think you were avoiding me.'

Seb kept walking until he was back at the duck pond, where he stood under the branches of a weeping willow.

'Look,' Jason said. 'I want to be reasonable. I can give you a bit of time on what you owe me.'

'Can you?'

'Sure.'

Seb examined his trouser legs. The mud was silty against the surface of the fabric. He tried wiping it away with the hem of his coat but it didn't help. 'I'll pay you back when I'm on my feet,' he said.

'Sure. I mean, I expect we can come to an arrangement.'

He leaned against the railings that circled the pond and watched the ducks fighting over stale bread, honking at each other. He thought, *arrangement*. What did that mean? A child in a yellow raincoat dropped her bag of breadcrumbs and screamed as a duck swooped in from the far side of the pond, wings broad and wide, head low.

'Where are you?' Jason said.

'In the park. Taking a walk.' He moved away from the railings, ducking further under the willow. The screaming died down. A few of the children were being strapped into buggies and wheeled away.

'They're onto us, you know that don't you?'

'Yeah.' Seb cupped his hand around his phone. 'I'm getting calls from someone who wants me to call her back urgently.'

'What have you said?'

'I've been letting them go to voicemail. But she's being persistent.'

'Don't say anything. Don't answer.'

'I'm not going to say anything. I don't want to go to fucking prison.'

'You won't go to prison.'

45

'You don't know that.' He checked over his shoulder to see if anyone was near enough to hear him. Two women were deep in conversation, and the only other people in earshot were still in nappies. 'Maxine knows something's up. I hate lying to her.'

'Make sure you hang on to her.'

'I'm trying.' He turned the other way, and the guy in the baseball cap moved back; he'd been just out of sight the whole time. 'Fuck,' he said. 'Fuck it.'

'What?'

Seb watched him walk towards the gate leading onto the common. 'Nothing. I think some guy was about to mug me.'

Jason laughed. 'Are you serious?'

'He's been watching me for a while. He was right behind me just now.' Seb walked to a bench and sat down. He tried to picture the guy's face, but he'd moved away too quickly.

'You all right?'

'I guess so.' A fine rain was falling. He lifted his face and shut his eyes. He probably looked like he had money, what with the suit and the smartphone. Which was hilarious, when you thought about it.

'I should go, Jason. It's raining here.'

'All right. Leave this with me. Don't take any of those calls.'

He sat with the phone in his lap, holding it face down against his coat. He wondered if he could persuade Maxine to leave London, to start again somewhere new. It seemed unlikely. She was attached to the house, determined to get the work done somehow, whatever it took. Whereas he was starting to wish they'd never set eyes on the place. There was something wrong with it. Twice now he'd woken in the night to the sound of the shower running at full pelt in the bathroom next door. Sometimes he heard the flush running in the ancient disused loo. Maxine said she'd never heard it. She'd pointed out that the shower had almost no pressure: it dribbled pathetically, barely enough water to wash under. And that toilet was an antique; it wasn't even plumbed in. He knew she was right. There was no evidence of it in the mornings, and the whole thing seemed impossible when he tried to explain. But in the middle of the night he knew, without question, that the house was on to him. That he needed to cut his losses and go.

Where to go, was the question.

The thing about Maxine, the thing he envied, was that she had grown up in the same place her parents had grown up, and her grandparents, going back generations. The McKenzie clan. What must it be like to have those sorts of roots in a place, to push off from it knowing it would always be there if you went back? To have people around you who knew who you were, and had always known you. When he asked Maxine about it she said it was claustrophobic and she was glad to be free of it; she was endlessly happy to walk down the street without meeting someone who knew her or her mother or her great aunt. She thought he was the lucky one, but that was because he'd given her a story about his dad being a diplomat stationed overseas, a childhood spent at an international school in Brussels. His parents didn't keep in touch, he'd told her. They expected him to make his own way in the world. So at least there was a bit of truth in there.

He loosened his tie. It was getting cold out here. He would be out of the interview by now, had there been an interview.

He called Maxine.

'Seb! How did it go?'

'Good,' he said. 'I'm pretty sure they liked me.'

'I bet you were brilliant. I bet you get a call soon to say you got it.'

At the edge of the pond a small child sat forward in his buggy, his mouth wide, the silent inhale before the howl. His little face was seized with incredulous rage. Seb's blood pulsed as the child screamed. His mother pushed through a puddle, tight-lipped, and half ran through the opened gate out onto the common.

'What time will you be back?'

'Not sure,' Maxine said. 'There's an exhibition at the Tate I wouldn't mind catching.'

He sat back on the bench. The rain was a mist against his face.

'You don't mind, do you?'

'No,' he said. 'Of course not.'

'When do you think you'll hear?'

'Hear what?'

'About the job.'

He looked up at the sky. 'They said they'd get back to me in a couple of days.'

'Where are you?'

'Peckham. Nearly home.'

'Did you get that broken heater down to the skip?'

He couldn't bring himself to reply. It was getting dark, and the pond was dotted with rain.

'Seb? Are you there?'

He sat forward again. 'Sorry. I'm here.'

'What's wrong?'

'I'm just sick of the way we're living. I don't even want to go back to the house.'

'Seb—'

'I know you love it. But I just—'

'Seb, I have to go. Sorry.' She sounded distracted. 'I'm going underground. I won't be late.'

He heard voices: she was with a crowd of people. Of course she was. 'See you later then,' he said, but she had already gone.

It had been a total waste of money, dry-cleaning the suit.

The sky was dark and the children had left. He stood and walked around the pond, out through the wrought-iron gates and onto the common. A homeless guy was going through a bin and he looked Seb up and down as he passed. Seb checked the man's face for his dad's features, as he always did. He didn't recognise him but he quickened his pace, because if he didn't keep walking he would sit down beside him in the wet grass where he belonged. It was a fine line in this city, between everything and nothing.

He bolted across the road and ran up the steps to the house.

8

8 December 1994

Mrs Lloyd cut the cake open and put a generous slice on a plate for Cookie. She gave him a fork and smiled at him as he sank it deep into the sponge. It was early December, one week before the murder, and Cookie had come home from school ravenous. His maths teacher had held the whole class back over lunch break (she had looked close to tears when a blackboard rubber sailed past her head) and by the time he'd made it to the serving hatch the only food left was a scoop of grey mashed potato.

'Tea?' Mrs Lloyd said.

'Yes, please.' He'd eaten half of his slice before she returned to the table with the teapot.

'There's plenty more,' she said as she sat down.

He took another forkful of cake, barely tasting it. He felt his strength returning. He added milk to the tea she'd poured for him and a spoonful of sugar from a bowl, which was patterned with red and gold leaves, like the teacups. They were from the same set as the one she'd taken with her on the bus.

'Thanks,' he said as she cut him a second slice.

He sipped his tea and tried to slow down, to breathe and swallow between mouthfuls. It was warm in the kitchen and it smelled of the recently baked cake. He had never been in a kitchen as big as this before they'd moved here, but the thing that always surprised him was how shabby it was, for a posh person like Mrs Lloyd. The oven looked ancient, and the fridge was small, the same one his grandpa had, with the tiny freezer compartment at the top where you could fit an ice tray or a pack of fish fingers but not both. The floor was tiled, a deep red colour with black grouting in between. The cupboard doors didn't all have handles, and didn't fully close. The curtains were old-looking, with a faded yellow flowered pattern, strung across the top of the windowpane with cord.

'I've told your mum she ought to make more use of the kitchen,' Mrs Lloyd said. 'We agreed when she took the room that the kitchen would be a shared space.'

Cookie nodded, the fork halfway to his mouth. Mrs Lloyd had mentioned this before, and he'd managed to change the subject. This time he couldn't think of anything to divert her, so he said nothing and hoped she would drop it.

'I've told her, there are empty cupboards she can use. Better than taking everything up to your room.' She looked at him expectantly as he chewed. 'She could keep milk in the fridge, at least. For tea and coffee.'

'I'll tell her. If you like.'

'But I've told her already.'

'We've got our own kettle and fridge. And a gas hob.'

'I know. But this is a bigger space.' She looked around her at the room. 'It's silly to cook up there when—'

'She likes to be private,' Cookie said. 'That's what she's like.'

Mrs Lloyd put her cup in its saucer and sat back in her chair. 'I see.'

'But I like coming down here.'

Mrs Lloyd smiled at him across the table. 'I've never let the room out before,' she said. 'I'm not used to people in the house. I hope you feel welcome.'

Cookie had a distracted, nervous feeling, even though he knew his mum was still at work. She would flip out if she caught him here with Mrs Lloyd, eating her food.

'Are you all right?' Mrs Lloyd asked.

'I'm fine.' He cleared his throat, tried to relax. 'Why did you start letting the room out?'

'I need the money. A house like this is expensive to maintain.'

'Is it?'

'Very. Can't afford to heat the place. It's too much for me, really.'

Cookie looked again at the tired kitchen. 'I thought you were rich,' he said.

'Did you?' She laughed. 'I can see how you thought that. I live in a big house so I ought to be rich. But it doesn't always work that way.' She looked up at the ceiling, then back at him. 'An ancestor of mine had this house built for his family, I think around 1830. A chap called Horatio Lloyd.' She said his name nervously. 'And now it belongs to me.'

Cookie stared at Mrs Lloyd as she tipped her cup back and drank her tea, extending her neck, which sagged with loose skin when she lowered her head.

'He was my great-great-grandfather,' she said. 'The house has always been in my family. One of the first houses to be built on Rye Lane.'

'He must have been rich,' Cookie said.

'I think he lost a lot of money. I forget how.' She frowned into her tea. 'My father had a theory that this house turns good money bad. Same story going down the generations, apparently, over and over.'

Cookie thought of his dad, talking about London brick, the way it breathed.

'Peckham would have been nice back then,' he said. 'When the house was built. Only the wealthy could afford it.'

She looked at him in surprise. 'I heard that.'

'It was one of the first commuter suburbs.'

She blinked. 'Was it?'

'I think so.' He felt too warm now, and slightly sick.

'I didn't know that,' Mrs Lloyd said. 'How interesting.'

'These big houses were built to look out over the river.'

'What river?'

'The Peck.'

Mrs Lloyd's smile became strained. 'The house doesn't look out over a river.'

'It does. You have to wade through it after heavy rain.'

'I don't think that's—'

'You can't stop a river running through a valley.' He said it firmly, with a certainty he didn't feel. 'It was the route of the Kentish drovers, taking their cattle to market in town.'

The kitchen was quiet, and Mrs Lloyd put her cup down in its saucer with a delicacy that sounded apologetic.

'That's interesting,' she said.

Cookie shrugged, and wished he hadn't mentioned it. The river had been beautiful in his mind's eye when his dad had described it. But now, with Mrs Lloyd looking at him like that, it seemed stupid, and unlikely.

'Who told you that, about the Peck?'

'My dad.'

She widened her eyes and brought her cup back to her mouth. Cookie looked at his plate and tried to find the words to defend his dad. He was clever; he knew things that most people didn't know. Cookie was like him in that way, according to his Grandpa Delaney. But he had lost his job, and Cookie could see that to someone who didn't know him he looked like some kind of loser. He pictured him then, coming out of the pub on a Saturday morning, his head bent low, his skin grey.

'It's true.' He ran his finger around the edge of his plate, which had a red and gold design to match the teacups. Fine bone china. It would break cleanly in half if he dropped it, and the inside would be white and chalky; the edge would be sharp along the break. 'My dad knows that sort of thing,' he said, and he pressed his hands together between his knees.

Mrs Lloyd cut herself a thin slice of cake and flipped it

sideways onto a plate. Then she broke off a small piece with her fingers and put it into her mouth. 'You love him?' she said. 'Your dad?'

Cookie nodded.

'That's . . .' She paused, and broke off another piece of cake. 'That's something I never had, myself. Not for my father or anyone else. I come from a long line of shitheads, that's probably why.'

She looked up at him then, and laughed.

'Shitheads?' Cookie said.

'That's the politest word I can think of for them.' She pointed at the ceiling. 'Horatio was a nasty piece of work, apparently.'

'Really?'

She nodded, her mouth full. She held her fingers over her lips as she swallowed. 'Total bastard, actually.'

Cookie laughed, and she laughed with him, cleaning her fingers on her napkin. She stopped laughing, sighed, then started again. She wiped her eye with the tip of her thumb, running it under the lashes.

'We don't have to like our families, do we?' she said.

'Don't we?'

'Of course not.' She became serious, and cleared her throat. 'Of course not,' she said, more softly than before.

Cookie drained his tea, which was cold, and pushed his hands into the pockets of his blazer, where he felt the long, thin wrapper from a stick of chewing gum, and the ridged edge of a pencil sharpener. From the garden he heard the dry scrape of foxes, that cry they made that always sounded like pain.

'Why was he a . . . ?'

'A bastard?'

'Yes.'

'If I tell you, I don't want you to take it too seriously. It's one of those family rumours that may well not be true.'

Cookie swallowed. The house felt very still around him. 'OK.'

'He killed his wife. My great-great-grandmother.' She tipped her head sideways and the loose flesh of her neck sank into the wool of her roll-neck jumper. 'Like I say, it's probably nonsense.'

'Right.' He saw in her face that she did not think it was nonsense. 'Did he go to prison?'

'Apparently not. Nobody knows how he got away with it.'

Cookie thought of the closed doors up on the second floor. The rooms behind them which were empty but occupied. He felt the thrill of fear.

'I shouldn't have told you,' she said.

'Is that why we're not allowed in those second-floor rooms?'

She flinched, and he knew he was right. 'Don't be silly,' she said.

'Is he in there? Is that where he's waiting?'

'No!' She stood, taking his plate. 'It's just a daft family story. My big brothers used to scare me with it as a child. Daring me to go up there.'

'Up where? Up to his room?'

She turned her back on him and put his plate in the sink. Rain hit the window beside her. She ran the tap, put her own cup into the water and wiped the palms of her hands on her trousers.

'Have you ever been in there?'

She shook her head. 'No.'

'Never?'

'I live downstairs, Cookie. The house is too big for me, like I said.' She turned then, and her face was grey. She didn't look at him as she took the teapot over to the sink. 'I shouldn't have mentioned it,' she said. 'Put it out of your mind.'

9

5 June 1843

Horatio looked out from the window of his study as the horse and carriage pulled away from the house. He could see Archer by the gate, looking down the track with an expression of calm concentration. Archer had dealt with it all. He had known what to do, who to call for. He had kept a cool head, taking charge when Horatio was too shocked and afraid to do so. The man's capacity in a crisis was remarkable. He sat down at his desk when he heard Archer come back inside. There was a moment of quiet and then Archer's footsteps came up the stairs, steady and measured, as was his way. The day was growing dark but it was too warm for a fire in the grate, and too early to light the lamps. The candles he had lit were eerie in the half-light. Horatio sat up straight and arranged his papers, took out his handkerchief and ran it over his face.

'Come in,' he said, when the knock came.

Archer closed the door behind him and stood by the fireplace, where the candle gave some light to his features. He stood with his hands behind his back, facing Horatio but not meeting his eye. 'It is dealt with,' he said.

'Thank you, Archer.'

'Mrs Reeves is inconsolable,' he said. 'She was very fond of Alice.'

'I gathered.'

'I wondered what you would have me say to her.'

Horatio sat back in his chair. He crossed his legs and caged his hands around his knee. 'You must tell her that I share her sadness,' he said. 'That Alice will be a great loss to our household.'

Archer did not reply. He stood very still and straight, his eyes directed into the darkness of the room.

'I hope she will soon recover from the loss,' Horatio said, casting about for the right thing to say. His skin was damp under his heavy jacket, the collar of his shirt tight at his neck. He had hoped to speak more openly to Archer, to ask his advice. He had no idea how to calm Mrs Reeves. He had no idea how to contain the problem, how to step back from this and carry on. He did not know how he was going to get out of his bed in the mornings for the rest of his life.

'Mrs Reeves has asked me outright.' Archer cleared his throat. 'She has asked if Alice's passing was the same cause as Mrs Lloyd's.'

'And what did you say?'

'I said I did not know.'

Horatio gestured at the window beside him. 'It is the miasma,' he said. 'From the Peck. The miasma that killed Mrs Lloyd has now killed the girl.'

'Alice.'

'Yes. Alice.' He stared at Archer across the dark room. 'Is that clear, Archer?'

Archer looked at him for the first time. There was a challenge in the set of his face, Horatio thought, a small note of defiance. He wondered – not for the first time – if Archer knew that he did not come from money. If he could tell that Horatio's family had known poverty, and that his maternal grandfather had been in service, a groom and manservant like Archer himself. Isobel had married him despite this, against her own father's wishes. She had married him for love, and he had done his utmost to be deserving of it. Everything in this house had been for her: wallpaper, carpets, clocks, curtains, tiles, fire guards, silk; the finest china. She had wanted for nothing. She had been delighted by the indoor plumbing, the flushing water closet on the first floor which he'd installed at huge expense, setting them apart from the neighbouring houses. She had loved to bathe, and he had provided a tub for her next to the master bedroom, an entirely separate room for bathing, with water piped through taps. She had found it delightful; she had said so, many times.

But always he had feared that it was not enough. And he had extended himself financially, in his effort to please her. It had become insupportable, although he had not shared this with Isobel; he had done his utmost to make sure that she did not know. But her father knew the truth of it. He had provided loans, and he liked to remind Horatio of his debt. He occasionally reminded Horatio that he had given him work when he'd had nothing and no one: he'd made Horatio his apprentice and helped him establish his trade. Implicit in his remarks was his disappointment, his regret.

And it was true that all of this had frayed his temper.

'Miasma,' Archer said.

'From the Peck.'

Archer nodded, looked away.

'I suspect that Alice cracked her window open in the loft, despite my warnings. The Peck is quite unwholesome, Archer. The smell is absorbed into the house and becomes deadly.'

Archer inhaled as if to speak, but did not. Horatio hoped that he would leave. He took his handkerchief from his pocket and pressed it against his face.

'Mrs Reeves is sceptical,' Archer said, in a low voice. 'She has drawn her own conclusions, you see.'

Horatio kept his handkerchief over his mouth. He thought of the girl, Alice, whose hair had come loose from its pins when she had fallen to the floor.

'I shall need a carriage in the morning, Archer. Eight o'clock sharp, to take me to the warehouse at Rotherhithe.' He pulled his chair up close to his desk, rocking the candlestick beside him. 'Could you see to it, please?'

'Of course, sir.'

'I'm expecting a shipment any day. There have been delays, which must be made good when we unload.' His voice was loud, smothering the words Archer had spoken previously. He would need to be more careful with Archer. He knew too much, and it had led to a lack of respect, an erosion of boundaries.

'Very good,' Archer said. 'Will there be anything else?'

'You might tell Mrs Reeves that I will take my meal in the Kings Arms. She can take the evening off.' Horatio pushed his handkerchief back into his pocket and took an interest in the papers on his desk. When he looked up Archer had gone, and the room had darkened. The clock was the only sound; the house was warm and airless. Ordinarily at this time he would have asked Alice to light the lamps.

10

18 October 2008

'Who keeps calling you?' Maxine stood at the front door, holding a cardboard box that she'd filled with things to take out to the skip. She had on one of Seb's old jumpers, navy blue and crew-necked, a survivor of the cull on his wardrobe after he met her. All the corporate weekend wear had gone in that cull. But he looked good in navy, she'd told him; it made him look like marriage material. It was the first and only time she'd used that word in his presence. He wondered whether to remind her, but thought better of it. She was irritable, and he was on the back foot. It was only ten thirty on Saturday morning but it looked like this was how the weekend would go.

'It was a cold-caller,' Seb said. 'Trying to persuade me to take out a loan.'

She put the box down. 'That's a persistent loan shark. He must have called you four times already today.'

'I guess I'm his target market.'

She cracked the knuckles on her left hand. 'I wrote a piece about loan sharks for tomorrow's paper.'

'Did you?'

'They're basically vermin. You should block the caller.'

He nodded and smiled, picturing a rat, huge and muscular, with a rigid tail. 'You're right. Will do.'

She opened the front door. It was a clear day, the sky blue, the trees on the common yellow and brown.

'I started up in the loft,' she said, when he stood beside her. She nudged the box with her foot. 'All that can go in the skip.'

Seb looked down into the box she'd filled. There were a few coffee mugs with stained rings around the insides, one with the handle missing. A small plastic alarm clock with rust in the opening where the battery had been. A pair of trainers. All of it was wrapped in a filthy old sleeping bag, khaki-green on the outside, the orange lining speckled with mould. He'd noticed it up in the loft, on the far side of the room, under a pile of clothing and shoes and blankets, all of it soiled and damp. He'd resisted bringing it down to the skip himself. He tried to think what he'd been doing all week, when really he could have been boxing up some of this junk, so Max didn't end up doing it on her day off. The days were shapeless. He remembered a trip to the launderette, and going to the shop for bread and milk, counting out the change like a student. And he'd spent that afternoon in the park, of course, although he couldn't have said if that was this week or the week before.

He carried the box out to the skip and tipped the contents over the edge. He watched it fall into the rubble: a pair of jeans, a man-sized sweater with a zip at the neck. The last thing to fall from the box was a necktie, black and red, with the knot fixed in place and a band of elastic at the neck.

'How are things?' A woman with a dog on a lead passed Seb on the pavement and smiled. She was small, barely reaching his chest, and her hair was tucked into the elasticated hood of her coat.

'Pretty good.' Seb smiled back, unsure if they'd met. Her dog was caked in fresh mud.

'Have you put your building work on hold?'

'We have, for now.'

'Thought so.' She looked up and waved at Maxine, who stood at the front door, balancing a box on her knee. 'Morning, Maxine.'

'Morning!' Maxine lifted the box down the steps and out onto the street.

'Sorry to hear you've had to stop all the work on the house.' She pulled the dog closer to her heel. 'Must be so frustrating for you.'

'You could say that,' Maxine said. 'Have you met Seb?'

'Very briefly, the other day,' she said, smiling up at Seb. 'I don't think he remembers.'

'I'm so sorry.' Seb laughed. 'I don't think I do.'

'I'm Clare, I live next door. I've been wanting to say hello.' She held her hand out. 'I saw you in the park the other day, when Vinnie soaked you.'

'Vinnie?' He shook his head. 'Sorry. I don't think—'

'Don't apologise! I think Vinnie ruined your suit.' She let go of his hand. 'I was mortified when I saw how wet you were. I said to Howard, Vinnie soaked the chap next door!' She looked down at the dog. 'Didn't you?'

Seb laughed, and he remembered standing on the wooden bridge in the park in his suit. The woman who'd called out to apologise when her dog shook itself off and splashed him. He knelt down, his head rushing, and smiled like a lunatic at the dog. 'This is Vinnie, is it?'

'That's right,' Clare said. 'I tried to apologise, but you—'

'Don't mention it,' Seb said.

'I think you were on your mobile phone.'

Seb laughed painfully, his knees cold against the pavement. The dog was filthy, wet and panting. 'It's nice to meet you properly,' he said to the dog. He wasn't sure how much Maxine had heard. 'Sorry we got off to a bad start.' He didn't know why he'd said that. Maxine was feet away, her trainers visible at the edge of the kerb.

'We're delighted to have neighbours again,' Clare said. 'Awful how long the house was boarded up for. We spoke to the estate agents and they said they just couldn't shift it. It ended up being passed from one agent to the next. Then all the rumours started.'

'Rumours?'

Clare nodded down at him and pushed her loose hair back into her hood. 'I'm so glad you didn't let all that nonsense bother you.'

He stood up. 'What nonsense is that?'

'With the house. Utter nonsense.' She looked up at the

house and back at him, smiling uncertainly. 'We never took it seriously.'

'Took what seriously?'

At the edge of his vision, over by the gate, he saw Maxine lift her chin. Clare twitched Vinnie's lead and the dog went to her.

'There was a silly rumour that some chap had a breakdown after he went in there on his own to value the place. Talk of ghosts and whatnot.'

'I didn't know that,' Seb said.

'Sorry.' She glanced over at Maxine. There was an exchange of information as they locked eyes. 'Anyway. We'll invite you for drinks some time. Howard wants to meet you both.'

'Did you know the previous owners?' Seb asked as Clare turned into her gate.

'We knew Diana.' Clare addressed this to Vinnie. 'Didn't we? She was our neighbour for a long time.'

'Diana . . . ?'

'Diana Lloyd. She lived there all her life. Never married.'

'Did she die in the house?'

'She did, yes.' Clare looked up at the house, the place where their filthy brick met her pale, jet-washed brick in a sharp vertical line. 'I believe her family owned the house from the time it was built. That's what she told me anyway.'

'Really? How incredible.'

'Isn't it?' She looked apologetically at Maxine, who was standing beside Seb now, holding the empty box.

'Did she die of old age?'

Clare smiled widely, and very gently shook her head. 'I think she was in her seventies.' She stopped on the path, the dog straining against its lead. 'No surviving relatives.'

'So she had no children, then?'

'No,' Clare said. 'Why?'

'There was a kid's school tie up in the loft. And an old pair of jeans and some trainers. Things I wouldn't have thought would belong to an older woman.'

Clare let the dog drag her through the gate. 'Diana had lodgers living up in the loft for a while. They might have left some of their things behind.'

'Lodgers?'

'Dreadful people,' she said. 'But Diana took them in, felt sorry for them, I think. She wouldn't listen.' She turned and raised her hand in a wave. 'I wouldn't spend too much time on your own in the house, if I were you,' she said cheerfully, before she shut her door.

Maxine followed Seb back into the house and dropped the empty box on the floor. It was colder inside than on the street.

'Why didn't you tell me all that?' He stood beside her on the tiles by the door. 'About how they couldn't sell the house because of these rumours?'

'Because it's nonsense, like she said. The house needed a lot of work. That's why it didn't sell.'

'Some estate agent had a breakdown, she said.'

'I'm sure that's not true.' She pushed her hair behind her ears. 'Don't dwell on it.'

'She told me not to spend too much time here on my own. You heard her say that, Maxine.'

'I expect she's concerned about your mental health.'

'She doesn't want me to have a breakdown, like the estate agent?'

'She knows you're not working.'

'Does she?'

'She thinks you should get out of the house more, which is a good point.'

'Is there anything she doesn't know?'

'Possibly not.'

Somewhere on the upper floors, a door swung on its hinge.

'I think she said no, when I asked if the last owner died of old age.' He turned to her, and found himself lowering his voice. 'Do you think that means . . . ?'

'She didn't say no.'

'I think she did. She shook her head.'

'Why do you want to know that, anyway?'

'Something happened here, Max.'

She groaned. 'It's an old house. All sorts of things have happened here.'

'You know what I mean.'

'For God's sake.' She pointed towards Clare's house. 'She told me that story about the estate agent the first time I met her. She had all sorts of stories, actually. I got the feeling she was enjoying it, trying to spook me. I didn't tell you because I thought it was rubbish and I wanted to put it out of my mind. I didn't see what good it would do.'

'Right.' He tapped the empty box with his shoe. 'I didn't know that about you.'

'What's that?'

'That you put things out of your mind like that. Compartmentalise.'

She cracked her knuckles again and he held her hand to stop her doing it. It was a nervous tic, a new thing, a sign of stress, he supposed. He missed the way things were before. The nights out and the lazy mornings in bed. These days she was always up early, always working.

'Don't we all compartmentalise?' she said.

He kept her hand in his. He drew breath to say that he thought she should try not to; it was better to be honest with yourself, to face things. But then, that might not work in his favour.

'I guess so,' he said.

She looked up at him. 'What was that about the dog messing up your suit in the park?'

'No idea.' He shook his head, as if confounded.

'Why were you wearing your suit?'

'I think she had me mixed up with someone else. I didn't want to be rude. But that wasn't me.'

'She seemed pretty sure.'

'I'd never seen her before today, Max.'

She ran her eyes over his face. 'Is there something going on with you?'

'No.' The sun shone through the stained glass in the door, throwing red light onto the tiles. He thought he heard a quiet rush of water from the bathroom. 'I wish we hadn't ever seen this place, Maxine. I wish I was working and life was normal. That's all.'

'That's all?'

'That's enough, isn't it?'

She picked up the empty box and led the way up the stairs, touching the bannister with one outstretched finger. He followed her, picturing a rat with a long tail, its nose close to the ground.

11

14 December 1994

Ruth Delaney dressed quickly on the morning of the murder. She put her coat on before her tights, it was that cold. She zipped her coat to the chin. It was dark in the loft bedroom of the house on Rye Lane, but she knew Lee wasn't there. She'd have heard him, for one thing, if he'd got into bed beside her in the night. She'd have felt his warmth. She pulled her tights on and tried to remember the last time she'd been in the same room as her husband, awake or otherwise. Might be a full month ago now. He'd come home one afternoon and they'd argued, said some awful things. She suspected Cookie had heard them, which made it worse. She pulled her tights up and her skirt down, felt around with her feet for her shoes. She didn't know how to make things up with Lee, now they were living like this. No time to themselves; no privacy. How do you live as man and wife when you share a room with a twelve-year-old?

She would try harder, she thought, next time Lee came home. He did come home; she knew from the clothes in the laundry basket and the used teabags in the bin. But he was avoiding her. And that hurt. She pulled the covers over the bed and decided she would leave work early today. She would get back here before Cookie got home from school and she would wait for Lee to come in and change his clothes. She would kiss her husband slowly, like the old days, like they were nineteen. She wouldn't ask him where he'd been at night, when he should have been beside her. She would kiss him and leave it at that. The thought of it softened her and she smiled to herself in the dark. It was almost Christmas. Must be twenty-seven years since she first kissed Lee Delaney and they hadn't left it at that, not for long. She'd remind him of that when she saw him: she'd say it was their anniversary. He'd know what she meant. That first time had been quick and quiet but good; better than she'd expected, anyway. The next time had been better (not so quiet), and it had got steadily better ever since. They were a match, the two of them. It was their magic ingredient. Even when he didn't come home, she never suspected him of going with another woman. He just wouldn't, she knew that. And she could forgive pretty much anything else, it seemed.

That was how it went with her and Lee. They fought, they made up, they carried on.

From the fold-out bed she heard Cookie turn onto his side, then turn back. He flung himself around that bed all night. Never lay still for more than ten minutes, it felt like. And he was tired in the mornings. Lethargic. He was growing so fast she had to crick her neck a bit further each day to get a look at him. Every day he'd changed. His hair was darker and his face was leaner. Long, skinny legs and arms. But he still held her hand at the traffic lights as if he was six years old. He still had that innocence in him. It wouldn't last long, she supposed, at the school they'd had to send him to. You can't mollycoddle him, Lee always said, it'll make it harder on him if you do. He'll get his head kicked in.

She patted the surface of the table – which they ate at, but which couldn't be called a kitchen table, since they didn't strictly have a kitchen – until she found her hairbrush. She gripped the handle. A bus stopped across the street and its doors opened, its lights changed the shade of the green curtains. She thought of the child (nameless, faceless) who might kick her son's head in. She pictured this child pushing Cookie at the bus stop, pulling on his tie, kicking his shins. Cookie bowed his head and took the blows. She stepped in. Grabbed the other boy by his collar and threw him into the road, into the path of a bus as it accelerated. His body crushed under the wheels before the driver had a chance to brake. The screams of passers-by, the sirens; blood on the tarmac.

The bus pulled out and carried on down the street. The room darkened. Ruth dragged the brush through her hair and waited for her heart to slow. She had never hurt anyone in her life. She rescued spiders from plugholes and took in birds with broken wings. She was a pushover, everyone said so. But she could kill if she had to, to keep her child safe. She had known this about herself since Cookie was born. It was a cellular thing, a protective instinct strong enough to overcome her. Lately this urge in her was stronger than ever. Her boy was changing, growing away from her, and she couldn't protect him the way she did when he was small. She saw danger everywhere. She tied her hair back with the band she kept on her wrist. She listened to her boy breathing.

Her knees clicked as she squatted beside Cookie and kissed him lightly on the head. She held the base of the bed for support, balancing on the balls of her feet, delaying the moment when she had to go out into the cold. She'd be fine once she was on her way, but this bit was hard. Poor Cooks, left on his own up here. It wasn't the way she wanted it. This time last year they'd discussed her giving up work, cutting back her hours at least, so she could be at home more. But then Lee had lost all that money. She didn't dwell on it. But their savings were gone and here they were.

A plane flew low overhead, bound for Heathrow. She stood and wrapped her scarf around her neck. It was the fight of her life, trying to keep her faith in Lee; to keep believing in him. Holding them all together. She took her bag from the back of the chair and mouthed a goodbye to Cookie. She would have noticed, if not for the plane, that his breathing had changed; he was awake, listening to her, waiting for her to leave.

On the dark landing at the top of the house, Ruth Delaney checked in her bag for her keys and her purse. She listened out for the usual sounds from the lower floors. The house was wonky, always shaking and rattling; doors swinging on their hinges. And the plumbing was useless, banging and tapping at all hours. She waited, listened, but for once the house was quiet. She carried on to the next landing, holding the bannister in the dark, judging the drop of the stairs from memory.

On the first floor she paused again. She stepped away from the staircase, trod very quietly over to the door next to Mrs Lloyd's bedroom: her fancy private bathroom. Ruth had a fascination with this room. It was huge, with a mottled-glass window, and the same black and white tiles as the ones on the ground-floor hallway. Sometimes, when she knew Mrs Lloyd was out, Ruth climbed into the bathtub with her clothes on and she lay back, looked up at the high ceiling and rubbed her feet against the copper taps. Sometimes she used the loo, helping herself to reams of paper. Often she walked up and down and thought how nice it would be to have this sort of space to move around in while you waited for your bath to run. How nice to have a full floor of spare rooms, come to that, when your lodgers were cramped up together in the loft.

She ought to go. She stood on the landing and pictured Mrs Lloyd curled in her bed, just feet away behind the door.

The room on the other side of the bathroom was a narrow cubicle, full of boxes and dark old paintings in gilt frames. Ruth had had a poke around in there and found nothing much of interest. But behind the boxes, against the exterior wall, there was an ancient-looking toilet with wooden casing around its base, an ornate metal lever to one side that she supposed was a flush. There was something creepy about that old toilet, squatting at the back of the room like an intruder. That morning, in the dark, she couldn't see it. But she pushed on the door anyway and had a look, stared into the black space and imagined her stare was returned. She stood there with her back to the door, her heart pounding.

She'd forgotten this part of herself, the naughty kid who liked danger, who would do the thing she'd been told not to. Always in trouble. She'd stopped being brave when Cookie was born and fear had taken its place. She'd looked at her baby and hoped to God he didn't have this bad streak in him.

But he did have it. She knew this because she knew him. He would look down at the ground when they reached the top of the Ferris wheel. He stood too close to the edge as the train pulled in to the platform. And then a year ago he had broken an ornament at her dad's house, a jug, made of fine bone china. He had looked at her, the pieces in his hand, and she'd seen his fascination and his shock.

Footsteps crossed the floor at the top of the house. He was awake, then.

She went back to the staircase, reached for the handrail, and thought of the day she'd come to see the loft room for the first time. Mrs Lloyd had told her she was sorry but she couldn't let it to a family, the room wasn't big enough; she'd had it in mind for someone living alone. She'd stood here on the landing of her big house and she had made Ruth beg. She had listened with pity in her face as Ruth explained that she couldn't afford anything bigger, that she was desperate. Ruth had been tearful by the time Mrs Lloyd gave in. She'd been mortified. Mrs Lloyd had said she could probably drop the rent a bit if that would help. She'd said she was welcome to share the kitchen. And Ruth had had to thank her for her pity, for her charity.

It had been the worst day of Ruth's life, moving her husband and child into this hellhole. Seeing Cookie's face when she'd shown him the room. She felt it all afresh as she walked down the stairs, down the hallway and down again into the kitchen where she took the envelope with the rent inside from her bag. She put it on the kitchen table, as she did on the fourteenth of each month without fail, and she resented it with every bone in her body. She hated Diana Lloyd. She blamed her for the situation they were in: for the cracks in her marriage; for the way her son looked at her, for his disappointment in what she could offer him. She blamed her for the cold and the damp and the misery of it all. She blamed her for the hate-filled person she had become.

Her shoes tapped against the tiled floor in the hallway. The cold was shocking on the ground floor, and she found she wanted to get out of here; even the bus stop felt more inviting than another minute in this house. She turned the latch of the large front door, shut it quietly behind her, and walked down the path to the street.

12

21 October 2008

Seb crossed the road and paused to look into the skip at the front of the house. He couldn't be sure in the fading light, but it looked like the sofa-bed from the loft had been thrown in there. Maybe a few cardboard boxes, emptied and flattened. He'd only been gone a few hours and Maxine had somehow got more work done than he'd managed in a month. He stood and looked at it until the wind changed and the rain pricked the side of his face.

'Max?' He closed the door and stood on the mat.

'Down here!'

He followed her voice down to the kitchen. She was cooking, holding a wooden spoon, a striped apron tied at her waist. The room was softly lit, fragrant with garlic and coriander. She'd brought a few things up from the basement. There was a picture on the wall – the lino-print they'd bought together at Camden market a few months ago. And she'd put a clay plant pot on the windowsill with her recipe books stacked beside it. A row of tea lights on the kitchen table.

'You've been busy,' he said. 'This is amazing.'

'Thanks.' She lifted a glass of wine, an inch of red in a wide-bottomed glass. 'Want one?'

'Sure.' He stood beside her at the stove. He felt uneasy in this house; it was worse when he'd been out for the day and he had to come back into it. Always that feeling like something bad just happened, like you could turn around and see it. But Maxine was fine. She was radiant, in fact, like her old self.

'Who did you meet in town again? Martin?'

Seb nodded. 'He's going to put a good word in for me with his manager.'

She put her glass down and smiled at him. Her teeth were red from the wine. 'Are they recruiting?'

'Sounds hopeful.' He held her against him so he didn't have to look at her. He didn't actually know anyone called Martin. He'd spent the afternoon at the British Museum looking at the Parthenon sculptures. He wanted to tell her about it, to describe the figures: Gods and heroes and animals with something alive in them, despite being carved from marble and despite being thousands of years old. He knew she would have seen it, if she'd been there. She laughed at him for being obsessed with history, his insistence that he could feel it sometimes. But he knew that she also loved that strange side of him. He had never had that before in his life.

'Great news,' she said. 'Any more vacancies coming up?'

'Don't think so. I'll call a few recruiters tomorrow.' He stopped and looked up at the ceiling. The floorboards creaked, followed by heavy footsteps. 'Did you hear that?'

'Of course I heard that.'

He stared at her. 'What the hell is it?'

'It's just the plumber. He's been here all afternoon.' She gestured at the room with the wooden spoon. 'He helped me bring down the sofa from the loft. And he brought up some of the heavy boxes from the cellar.'

Seb felt the blood return to his head. 'Thought I was hearing things.'

'He's going to quote us for the plumbing once he's had a proper look.'

'Right.' He reached for his glass and rolled the wine around, listening to the movement overhead.

'He thinks it's a cracking house,' she said.

'Does he?'

'He sees a lot of old houses like this where the fireplaces and cornices have been ripped out. It's rare to see a house as perfectly intact as this one, he says. I mean, we knew that. But still.'

Seb held his reply in his throat. She was half-cut, by the look of it. Two glasses of wine was her maximum, before she started slurring and getting soppy. He felt sour beside her. He took a mouthful of wine and put the glass down. Footsteps came down the stairs, then a shout from the door: 'I'm off, then.'

Maxine took a step towards the door. 'Do you want to speak to him before he goes?'

He shook his head. 'You go.'

She leaned the spoon on the side of the pot and half ran up

the steps into the hallway to see him out. Seb stood by the stove and listened as she laughed at something the plumber said. Then she replied and he laughed. The odd phrase reached him: 'I can't thank you enough. Total life saver. So good of you.' A pause, then they both laughed again at something Seb didn't catch. Seb went to the kitchen door and caught sight of a tall, lanky white guy in jeans and a bomber jacket, a black woollen hat pulled down over his ears.

He picked up the spoon and stirred the pot, lowered the heat beneath it a bit. Maxine shut the front door and ran upstairs. He wondered if she was dipping into her inheritance to pay for the odd jobs that Seb hadn't got around to. If that was their private joke, the quiet exchange at the door: that Seb couldn't seem to get anything done, no matter how much she nagged him. If he did make a start, he didn't finish. Or he made things worse, as he had in that room on the second floor where he'd stripped the wallpaper and brought a chunk of plaster down with it. He still hadn't bagged up the paper in there. He hadn't gone back up to the second floor, come to think of it.

Overhead, the toilet flushed and the tap ran. He took a mouthful of wine. He didn't want to fall out with her over it, but he was offended that she'd gone ahead and found a plumber, when he'd agreed to sort that out.

'Did he give you a quote?' he said, when she returned to the kitchen.

'What? No.' She looked into the saucepan and turned off the heat. 'Not yet. He's coming back tomorrow.'

'Did he give you any idea on the cost?'

'No.' She picked up her wine glass and drained it. 'He thinks the pipes are corroded. That's why the water pressure's so bad.'

'Sounds pricey.'

'I guess we'll know tomorrow.'

'If it's going to cost a fortune—'

'It's just a quote.' She took two plates from the cupboard by the window. 'If I do a good job of this feature, maybe I'll get a bit more money. If there's a chance for promotion, I mean.'

He'd forgotten about the piece she was writing. It was the first time she'd written anything feature-length for the paper, although she'd pitched ideas before. 'Sorry, Max.' She had her back to him, and he put his hands on her hips to turn her around. 'How's the feature going?'

'Good, I think.'

'Remind me what it's about?'

She smiled, and kissed him. She tasted of wine and her mouth was warm, slightly open against his. It would be easy to undo her apron, then to unbutton her jeans. She was thinking the same. And it would blow away the bad feeling, which he hadn't quite pinned down. The plumber, he thought, as he kissed her back. The way she'd laughed at whatever he'd said at the door.

'It's about gambling,' she said.

'Is it?' He half heard her.

'People who get in above their heads and lose everything, turn to crime, all that.'

'Right.' He heard her that time. 'I don't think you did tell me that.'

'I thought I did.'

'I would have remembered.' He kissed the top of her head. He thought of Jason, telling him to hold on to her. He felt sick.

'You OK?'

'Yeah. Sounds interesting. Is it nearly done?'

'What?'

'The feature. Is it nearly done?' He went to the stove and looked down into the pot, then back at her in time to see her expression change: disappointment, surprise. He pretended not to notice.

'I'm probably going to finish it tomorrow,' she said.

'That's great.'

'I'll go in early again. I won't wake you.'

Seb sat down at the table and found he had no appetite. Maxine put a bowl of curry down in front of him. She took off her apron and draped it over the chair beside her.

'He reminds me of my ex,' Maxine said, sitting down.

'Who?'

'The plumber.'

Seb looked at her through the steam rising from their plates. She had mentioned early on that she'd had a string of no-hoper boyfriends before she met him, but he hadn't asked her to expand.

'Does he?' he said now. 'In what way?'

'Just something about him.' She frowned, trying to place whatever it was. 'Kind of a misfit I suppose. Bit lost in the world.'

'Did he leave you? Your ex?'

'Not exactly.' She shook her head, avoiding his eye, and started eating. 'I shouldn't have brought it up. Sorry.'

'How serious was it?'

'Seb, I don't know why I mentioned it.'

'I just wondered what happened.' He half-laughed as he spoke. 'How bad can it be?'

She took an age to finish chewing. She looked at him and said, 'He proposed. I said yes and then I regretted it.'

'Right.' He put his fork down. He felt like she'd punched him. 'Did you jilt him at the altar?'

'It didn't get that far.'

'No?'

'I finished it and broke his heart. I'm not proud about that, which is why I didn't tell you before.'

They ate in silence, and Maxine stared at the wall beside his head. She was trying to think of something to say, to change the subject, he thought. She looked like she might cry.

'Not marriage material, then?' It came out more accusatory than he'd meant it.

'Sorry?'

'The ex. He wasn't marriage material?'

'No.'

'What does marriage material mean, for you?'

She smiled tightly. 'Looks good in navy.'

'Seriously, Max.'

'I don't know.'

'But you knew he wasn't.'

'Yes. I knew he wasn't.'

85

'How?'

She sat back in her chair, blew her hair out of her eyes. 'He wasn't going anywhere. I would have ended up supporting him while he signed on the dole.'

'Right.' The room seemed very dark. 'How am I different to him?'

She took a big breath in. 'Seb, you're entirely different to him.'

'In what way?'

'You're brilliant. You worked your way up in the financial sector, found yourself earning a fortune by the time you were twenty-five. You're self-made. Not many people in this city can say that.'

'Maxine, I'm out of work.'

'For now.' She reached her hand out across the table. 'You'll find something soon. I believe in you.'

He gave her hand a quick squeeze. 'Thanks.'

'I mean it.'

'I know you do.' He managed a forkful of food. 'Sorry. It's not an easy thing to hear, that's all. That you were engaged.'

'I've never regretted breaking it off. He was a sweet guy, but he had no ambition.'

He let go of her hand, and gave her the smile she was waiting for. 'Better try to resist him then.'

'Who?'

'The plumber.'

They both laughed. The food was delicious, he told her, and he meant it. They started a second bottle of wine and then they went upstairs and had drunken, wordless sex, leaving the dishes unwashed in the kitchen and the wine glasses empty at the side of the bed. He fell asleep as soon as it was over, avoiding those raw moments afterwards, when she was impossibly lovely and his guard was down. When he woke in the morning she was gone.

13

14 December 1994

Cookie stirred in the early hours to the sound of someone moving through the room. He listened, more asleep than awake, as the sound moved to the far corner. He heard his mum's breathing in the double bed next to the wall. In the corner, the brush of fabric against fabric: someone trying to be quiet. Cookie lay still. He wondered if he ought to be afraid, and why he wasn't. His mum turned in the bed, and in the same moment a night bus passed along Rye Lane, giving a pale light to the room. Enough light for Cookie to see his dad standing on a chair, his back to him, reaching into a space above the broom cupboard. The unmistakable shape of him; the way his jeans hung from his belt, the flat oblong of his wallet in his back pocket. The bus passed and Cookie's eyes closed. That was why he wasn't afraid. It was just his dad, doing whatever he was doing. He'd probably just got home.

The chair creaked and Cookie thought of the Saturday

morning with his dad when they'd stood together in the mist, talking about the river that ran across the common, through Peckham and beyond. He thought of it when he wanted to sleep, like one of those bedtime stories that made no sense, chilling and soothing at once. He imagined the river: shallow and clear, moving quickly over stones and branches. Rugged, muddy banks. He was almost asleep when the door to the loft room clicked shut. The sound altered the scene: he saw mist hanging over the river and heard police sirens at the edge of the common, car doors slamming. He turned in the bed, tried to get back to where he was, but the blue lights coloured the mist and his dad was holding him by the shoulders, telling him not to turn around.

Cookie sat up in the fold-out bed. He pulled the sleeping bag up to cover his shoulders. It was the morning of the murder, and his head was full of the questions he'd been too scared to ask. Had his dad steered him into the mist that Saturday morning so the police wouldn't see them? Had he stood beside him like that, his hands on Cookie's shoulders, so he'd look less suspicious if he was seen? Did that mean it was all bullshit: the stuff about the river, the way it crossed the common? Mrs Lloyd had thought so. Mrs Lloyd's face came back to him, the way she'd widened her eyes behind her teacup. He lay back down, rigidly awake, and thought, My dad's some sort of criminal. The truth of it flared hot in his limbs. He lay in the dark and tried to reconcile everything he'd known with everything he was starting to know. He was long and skinny in the sleeping bag, his pyjamas too short in the leg. He didn't want to get older. He didn't want it all to be bullshit. After a while the planes started flying low overhead and he slept again until his mum got up.

It was still dark. He heard Ruth pull the brush through her hair. She worked as a waitress in the café near the station and she brought food home with her – sandwiches and slices of quiche – if there was any left after the lunchtime rush. She loved him in a fierce way, and he loved her back. She worried about him; he knew this without her needing to say so. She was always looking at him, trying to see if he was all right. She knew he was not all right, not really, and she didn't know what to do.

She crouched down beside him and he heard her tights rub together, the crunch of her knees. She would watch him now. She did this in the mornings, since they moved here. She watched him but she didn't speak, and he waited for her to leave. He felt the lining of the sleeping bag, soft against his nose; the cold metal prongs of the zip.

A plane passed overhead. Eventually his mum stood, took her bag, opened the door and shut it behind her. He listened as she made her way downstairs. Then he sat up, reached across to the lamp and turned it on. It coloured the dark a bit, made it yellow. The room seemed small with all their things crammed into it; there were not enough surfaces for all their stuff and so they had become untidy, putting things on top of things, lifting one thing up to look for something else, losing another thing in the process. They had drawers but no wardrobe, so there were clothes over the chairs, clothes on the floor; dirty clothes piled next to the laundry basket, which was always full;

clean clothes – never quite dry – draped over the clothes airer. His mum had given up on it. She said she couldn't face the launderette more than once a week. She'd stopped picking up after them, stopped trying to keep it nice.

He knelt, and the sleeping bag fell to his waist. He could see his parents' bed, the two pillows side by side. The covers flat against the mattress. He'd had this idea that maybe his dad would be there in the bed, that he might have come back in while they slept. Cookie wasn't surprised, he hadn't honestly believed it, but still he felt the hope go out of him. He stood and kicked the sleeping bag away. He was supposed to fold the bed back into a sofa and roll up the sleeping bag, fold the blankets and push them into the gap between the sofa and the wall. Instead he crossed the room and turned on the overhead light. It was a bare bulb, its light unforgiving. He saw his mum's hairbrush on the table beside his physics textbook. A coffee mug with the teaspoon still in there, gritty with sugar.

It was early. The digital alarm clock next to the lamp showed just gone six thirty. Cookie was tired but not sleepy, an edgy sort of tired that he knew would make the day feel long; his eyes would hurt by lunchtime. He stood by the table and looked at the chair that had been dragged over to the cupboard in the early hours: his dad had left it at an angle, near the table but not back in its place. For some reason the sight of the chair made his throat ache. His dad had come in and left again; he'd been quiet and quick, because he didn't want to see them.

He dragged the chair to the far corner of the room, in front of the broom cupboard, and found he could reach on top more easily than he'd expected. He could see something, a box or a tin, pushed in under a pipe that ran across the ceiling. He stood on his toes to get a grip on it. The pipe was holding it in place, but when he pulled at it with both hands it sprang towards him. He stood on the chair holding it: a Quality Street tin, scratched and dented, octagonal. At their old house, this had been the tin his mum used to keep money aside for bills and rent. It had held rolled-up notes, coupons and receipts, a few loose coins. But it was empty, he could tell by the weight of it. He took the lid off anyway and looked inside. Nothing, just the shiny interior; grit and crumbs in its joins. He sat down with it in his lap, the base of it cold through his pyjamas.

There must have been money in the tin, he supposed. And his dad must have known that. He sat for a while with this new information, thinking of what it meant. He was cold. The window pane was icy on the inside. The birds were calling to each other out on the Rye.

Cookie stood on the chair again and wedged the tin back under the pipe. It was still dark. From two floors down he heard Mrs Lloyd in her bathroom, the clank of the cistern and the roar of the pipes. She was an early riser, and by the time she'd had her morning bath there was rarely any hot water left. His mum didn't have a shower on weekday mornings; she left the water for him so he could get washed before school. She made sure there was always soap in the tiny bathroom on their floor, and a bottle of washing-up liquid which was the same as shampoo (she said) for a fraction of the price. It was a scandal what they charged for shampoo, she said. He thought about her, standing in the cold room with the towel around her, getting dressed on the edge of the bed. *We might not have much, but we are clean, Cookie.* She was proud and sad and she hated this place, and that made her angry a lot of the time.

She was going to flip out when she found out about the tin.

14

22 October 2008

Maxine put her coffee down on her desk and checked her watch: quarter to eight. She hadn't turned the lights on as she came in. She liked the quiet of the office in the mornings before everyone else turned up, the blank monitors and the chairs swivelled away from desks. The colourless carpets, walls, windows. This morning she'd noticed Stella arrive not long after her, walking straight through to her office holding coffee, heavy bags on both shoulders, a woollen scarf wound around her neck. She hadn't put the lights on either. Maxine could just see the glow from Stella's monitor through her glass office door, and the occasional cloud from her e-cigarette. She liked to think that Stella knew she was here, and that maybe she had noted their shared early bird tendency. She pushed the plastic lid off her coffee and allowed herself to imagine the moment that her email arrived in Stella's inbox with the feature attached. Stella's surprise, and her growing interest as she read what Maxine had written. She might want to go for a drink, to talk about the piece, maybe get to know each other better.

It was almost finished. Maxine stared at the document on the screen, put in a paragraph break and deleted an adverb. It was good. Emotionally charged but restrained enough to let the reader feel it for themselves. She had worked hard to get it done ahead of the deadline, putting in long hours, staying in the office past midnight on one occasion. She was still expected to do her day job, after all. She had explained this to Seb and he'd said it was OK, he was proud of her, he knew how much this meant. But then last night she'd had to remind him what the feature was about.

She remembered then, the strained conversation about her broken engagement. She'd upset him. The subject of marriage had reared its head and she'd managed to steer it away.

Her phone beeped beside her. From Seb, just one line: *Plumber's here already.*

She checked her watch: just gone eight. Seb would have been asleep. She pictured him in his boxers and the hoodie he'd been wearing for weeks, stumbling downstairs with his glasses on the end of his nose. He was sleeping badly, since they'd moved into the house. He hated being woken. She replied: *Sorry! Told him to come at nine.*

On the far side of the office, Stella opened her door and walked over to Maxine, holding a croissant. She wore wide-leg trousers with trainers and a cropped denim jacket, buttoned to the neck. She looked fierce. Maxine smiled at her and thought, she's going to tell me she checked my CV and found a few discrepancies. She squeezed her coffee cup and hot liquid ran down her wrist.

'Thought I saw you,' Stella said.

'Hi.' She put her coffee down, still smiling, dabbing her wrist with a paper napkin. She felt foolish, with her grown-out hair and her too-smart clothing, bought before she'd started the job, when she'd thought she would have to dress up for work, not down. Stella did not smile back at her.

'How's the feature going?'

'OK, I think.'

She pulled out a chair and sat down at a desk facing Maxine. 'Tell me more.'

Maxine cleared her throat and tried to match Stella's tone: knowing, jaded, intimate. 'I found a couple of good case studies. One woman who lost a fortune gambling in an online casino. She won a bit of money at the start, then one day in the space of an hour she lost fifty grand.'

Stella peeled a strip of pastry away from her croissant. 'Fifty grand?'

'She had her house repossessed in the end. Her husband left her.'

'Shit.'

'She's even happy for us to use her name.'

'Photos?'

'Yep.'

Stella nodded. 'Great stuff,' she said.

Maxine gulped her coffee and did her best not to smile. 'Thanks,' she said, with a small shrug.

'You write very well. You have a real talent for a story.'

'Do I?'

'Your work so far has been great. And I appreciate the hours you're putting in.'

'Thank you.' Maxine winced at the burn of coffee down her throat. Her whole body burned and she had never been so happy. 'Thank you.'

'You'll need another case study I think, to give a bit of contrast.'

'I found a guy who was homeless for a while. He lived in his car.'

'What type of gambling was he into?'

'Mostly online,' Maxine said. 'But—'

'Might be too similar.' Stella considered her croissant and bit off the tapered end, baring her teeth to spare her lipstick. 'Have you got anyone who didn't gamble online? A different angle?'

Maxine stared at her screen, clicking the mouse furiously. She'd thought the second case study was perfect. She'd spent a day with the guy and he'd shown her the house he'd lived in before he lost everything. His story was so moving, she'd thought it was the best part of the piece, the knockout punch.

'He's expecting to be in the feature,' she said, staring at her copy, the paragraphs she'd honed. 'It took me a while to persuade him.'

'Never promise anything, Maxine. You can never guarantee it'll make it into the paper.'

'I know, but—'

'How did you find those two case studies?'

97

'An internet chat room.'

'Both of them?'

She nodded.

'There you go, then. You won't get different angles if you only look in one place.'

'Right.'

'You were going to focus on gambling as an entry point into crime.' Stella stood and brushed crumbs from her trousers onto the office carpet. 'That's how you pitched the idea to me.'

This was true. She had lost sight of the crime angle. She minimised her screen and nodded. 'OK.'

'Good start though.' Stella made as if to turn, then turned back. 'Did you join a gym?'

'No. Why?'

'Every day you come in early with your hair wet.'

Maxine touched her hair, which was still damp. 'We don't have hot water at home. I've been using the showers in the basement before work.'

'Really? Have you called the landlord?'

'I own the house. Bought it just before the economy tanked.'

'And you've got no hot water? That's a nightmare.'

'It is.'

'God, poor you. You need to get that fixed.'

'Yes, we do.' Her phone beeped as she said it, and she glanced down at the screen. From Seb: *The noise is driving me crazy.* She turned the phone over and said, 'Sorry. My other half.'

'Seb, is it? The banker chap?'

'That's it. I think you met him that night at the Eagle. Back in the summer.'

'I did.' She looked concerned. 'Yes.'

'He's not a banker these days. He worked for Lehman's. So—'

'Ah. Right.'

'It's been tough,' Maxine said. 'Especially as he was meant to fund the renovations.'

'Are you tied to him, money-wise?'

'No. The house is in my name.'

'That's good.' Stella smiled for the first time, red lips framing clenched white teeth. 'Got to watch those slippery banker types, eh?'

'Ha! I know,' Maxine said, turning hot, hearing the word *slippery* as she sat back in her chair.

'Where is it? The house?'

'Peckham.'

'Really?'

'Really,' Maxine said. 'It's a three-storey Georgian town house overlooking the common. It was empty for a long time, boarded up. So we've got our work cut out.'

'Right. A fixer-upper, as they say. You clearly like a project.'

Maxine laughed again without knowing why. Her face hurt.

'I remember when you couldn't get a cab to take you to Peckham.'

'It's changed,' Maxine said. 'It's a great spot. We love it.'

Stella nodded, staring down at the carpet, rubbing the back of her neck. 'Have you thought that you might find what you're looking for on your doorstep? For the feature, I mean.'

'Not really.'

'It might be worth a shot. Ask around locally. Talk to people in shops and cafés. Get out of here for a bit.' A phone rang on the far side of the office and Stella stepped towards it. 'Wait till your hair's dry, obviously.'

Maxine massaged her jaw. She felt unclean, like she had casually trashed everything she loved for Stella's approval. She had defended the house, the location, but not Seb. She picked up her phone, considered calling him, but she didn't know what to say; she was scared she would hear his voice and find that she didn't love him, that it had gone.

On the far side of the office, Stella pulled her office door shut and sat down behind her desk. At least she hadn't sacked her over the lies on her CV. They were white lies, anyway. She would have got her First, if her dad hadn't died when he did.

She scrolled through her contacts and paused over her dad's number, which she couldn't delete, although she had rarely called him when he was alive. She found, lately, that she wanted to talk to him; that no one else would do. She wanted to tell him that she was trying to take his advice. He'd told her to let herself fall for someone, to really fall hard; to take that risk for once in her life. She was trying, and she wished he knew that. She was also trying to forgive him for his betrayal: for leaving her mum for another woman, for following his own advice and making himself happy, even though it made other people sad. For dying while Maxine was busy hating him. She was sorry for hating him, for taking her mum's side over the break-up, for the things she'd said to him before he died. She was truly sorry, and she knew that if she could have told him he would have understood. He had always understood her. She was his girl, his mirror image, and all his mistakes were hardwired into her whether she liked it or not.

It was only just light outside. She heard the mechanics of the lift, the door opening, voices by the photocopier. Another phone rang. She drained her coffee and put on her coat.

15

9 June 1843

Horatio sat at his desk, head low over his writing paper, and composed his thoughts. He had woken in the night with a new idea of how to phrase his argument, and it had seemed so much stronger to him that he had risen at first light to set it down. It had taken two attempts to find the words he needed, once he was at his desk. And on his third attempt the ink had smudged over the exact word he had wanted to emphasise. He had started again, and although he had not changed his wording, he felt that the fire had gone out of his argument. Now his shoulder ached and he was growing hungry. He had asked Mrs Reeves to bring his breakfast tray to his study for eight o'clock: one soft-boiled egg with bread and butter, and a pot of tea. He was not confident that she would follow his orders. She had been openly unsympathetic in recent weeks; she had objected to cleaning the house.

He found he had lost focus. The clock said ten after seven,

and the day was beginning around him: he heard movement from the lower floors, which was promising. Crows cawing out on the Rye. At the window, the grass was parched and the Peck was contained within its banks, more a stream than a river. Sheep grazed on the pasture beside Homestall Farm. This was the aspect that had charmed Isobel and her father, the day they had joined him to consider the plot. They had followed the Peck upstream for a mile or so, walking through farmland to the edge of the Great Wood in the south, and on the return journey they had seen the dome of St Paul's through the trees. Isobel's father had thought it delightful, to be so deep in countryside yet within reach of London. It had put him in a generous mood. Within a week it had been agreed: the house would face the morning sun, looking out over the river. The boys would play on its banks, leaping over it perhaps, when they were big enough.

Horatio rotated his right shoulder, back and then forth. A pain was developing there, from the hours he had spent at his desk composing his letters. He had not left his quarters in almost a week. Archer had taken his letters from him and had agreed to let him know the minute word came of his shipment. He had never known of a delay as long as this one. The pain travelled from his shoulder blade to the base of his skull and he shut his eyes against it. The insides of his eyelids swarmed red. Perhaps this would be the day that his shipment arrived; perhaps they had encountered bad weather and had waited for it to pass. He had assured Isobel's father of this, when he'd met him at Rotherhithe.

But in his gut he knew that the shipment was lost. He knew it when he woke in the night, when he was defenceless against the thoughts that lay waiting. He also knew that Isobel's father held views as to the cause of her death. He grew cold at the thought of it, and his eyes opened to the sight of crows lined up on the grass, facing the house. On the far side of the Rye, the farmer at Homestall Farm stood at the riverbank in his nightgown, holding a chamber pot. The farmer squatted down and tipped the pot into the river, held it there a moment to rinse it clean, then stood again to observe the contents travelling downstream. Horatio watched the man return to his dwelling. He focused his mind on this incident, while rotating his shoulder. Then he went back to his desk.

His thoughts met the page more easily than before, and he finished his letter with words that surprised him in their strength and clarity. All of his loss and regret seemed channelled into his arm. When he finished, he read it through once, allowed the ink to dry and then sealed it. He would give it to Archer this morning. The clock said twenty before eight.

He took a fresh sheet of paper from the drawer. This time he did not feel certain of which phrase to employ, or which words to emphasise. He began haltingly:

Sir, I write in consideration of our conversation at Rotherhithe.

Horatio pictured his father-in-law opening this letter and glancing at it before throwing it into the fire. He tried not to let this thought fill his mind.

Once again, I ask that you might extend your generosity until my shipment arrives, whereupon my debt will be paid in full. The delay is most unfortunate but I am sure there will be word of its arrival within days.

He paused to read over his words. The tone was pleading, earnest, lacking conviction. He felt the pain again, reaching across his back this time. He listened to the tick of the clock. From the ground floor he heard Mrs Reeves talking to Archer, her feet against the tiled floor.

I know that our beloved Isobel would have wanted what was best for her sons. I do not ask this on my account, but on theirs.

He read this last line again and decided it would do. It was true, at least. The rest of the letter did not ring with honesty, but Isobel would have wanted the best for their boys. She would have wanted them to continue their schooling, to stay in their home.

They were to come home for two months in the summer. Every day he longed to see them.

It was eight o'clock. He sealed the letter, and from the staircase he heard footsteps, the rattle of crockery on the tray. He stood, crossed the room and waited at the door for Mrs Reeves to knock. He thought that he might ask her again to clean the house. He would speak assertively: he was her employer and he required her to do as he asked.

As she drew closer he brought his shoulders back and arranged his features, raked his moustache with his fingers. He heard her wheeze on the other side of the door. The clatter as she set the tray down heavily on the boards in the hallway. He waited, and on the far side of the door he knew that Mrs Reeves was waiting also.

No knock came. She did not speak. It seemed that in her silence she was challenging him. He tensed at the audacity of it.

'Mrs Reeves?' he said. His voice was low and cracked, which surprised him.

'I do not clean,' she said, from the other side of the door. 'I cook but I do not clean.'

Horatio stared at the crack between door and frame, where she had spoken. His blood rose up. She had no respect for him, for his authority. He flung the door open, expecting to confront her, but she had gone. The tray was there on the landing with his egg, his tea. Still he wanted to shout at her, to make her fear him as the girl had. He heard her laboured breath at the turn of the stairs, her slow descent to the floor below.

16

14 December 1994

Cookie stood at the window in the loft room, cold and damp from the shower, and looked out across the common. He'd got in the habit of standing here while he dressed in the mornings, to see the beginnings of the sunrise. That morning, in the hours before the murder, the sky was black.

He pulled on his school trousers, buttoned his shirt and pulled his tie over his head. His mum had sewn a short piece of elastic into the tie at the back and had stitched the knot into place. The elastic was hidden by his collar when he pulled it down. He suspected it was a childish thing, to have your tie stitched in place like this. Anything that was done for you by your mum was potentially embarrassing. Packed lunches and name tags and botched haircuts. He had been slow to cotton on to this and it had left him open to ridicule. He pushed the elastic into the fold of his collar to make sure it wasn't showing. Then he pulled on his jumper. Cold water dripped from his hair and ran down his back.

The electric heater wouldn't switch on. It was a huge thing with wire mesh over the filaments, wedged into a gap between the bed and the chest of drawers. But it didn't work. Useless, his mum said. He put his coat on and zipped it up, then he went to the cupboard and considered opening a can of beans, but he couldn't find the tin opener, so he left them. There was a bit of cereal in the box, but no milk, so he ate a handful of dry flakes which stuck to his teeth and made him more hungry than before. He went back to the window. He found the red tip of Canada Tower – the new skyscraper at Canary Wharf – just visible through the bare trees. His dad had told him that the skyscraper was the reason they'd had to move. They'd been priced out of their house because of the City types moving into the area. He was always raging about it, the way they'd put the rent up and forced them to move away. His mum was quiet when his dad said this. She liked to stand here and look at Canada Tower sometimes. It was a torment to see it, she said, but she still looked.

Cookie lost sight of the red light behind the trees. All he could see was his own reflection: his shoulders hunched and his neck jutting out. His face set in astonishment, like a just-hatched bird. He knew from photographs that he always looked like this, that he was weird and gawky, that his confusion at the world was always there in his face. He smoothed his hair down at the sides, although he knew once it was dry it would get that wave through it again, the stubborn bounce that made his head look huge and misshapen. He might be less ugly without his hair, he thought, flattening it with his hands. When he was older he would shave it all off.

He put his foot up on the seat of the chair and pulled on a sock. He tried to push out the thought of his dad, the Quality Street tin, the police cars behind them as they'd stood together on the common. His dad was a loser, a gambler, he had lost everything they had. It wasn't true that they'd moved because of the skyscraper at Canary Wharf. He blamed the rich people and the skyscraper, but really it was him.

Cookie could not tell if this was what he really thought. The shock of the thoughts made them feel true. He stood in the middle of the room with one bare foot, and did his best not to think any more.

'Fuck you,' he said, in the quiet room. He had never said this before. It was surprising how potent the words were, how quickly they shut out the noise in his head. He tried it again, raising his voice as much as he dared, forcing the words out the way he'd heard the kids in the lunch queue do it, with the emphasis on the *F.* 'Fuck you. Fuck you!'

He repeated it to himself as he pulled on the second sock and put his books into his bag. He imagined saying it to the kids who pushed him in the corridors, shouting it into their faces. In his brain he saw them explode into nothing.

The door to the loft room locked behind him with a click. He trod down the stairs in the dark, balling his fists as he passed the second floor, where the killer had lived, where he still waited. He went down again to the first floor and stopped there a second. It was the smell that held him at the turn of the stairs. A citrus smell of bubble bath carried on steamy hot water. He breathed it in. He heard the toilet flush, a tap running, then a door opened and steam crept out onto the landing, lit up by the bathroom light. He found himself frozen there as Mrs Lloyd walked out of her bathroom in a white, floor-length dressing gown, a clear plastic shower cap on her head.

'Oh God!' She jumped, and held the lapels of her dressing gown together.

'Sorry,' Cookie said.

'Cookie?'

'Yes. It's just me.'

'You nearly scared me to death.' Her face was pink and bare. Steam billowed from the bathroom behind her. Cookie stayed where he was, holding the handrail. 'Where are you going at this hour?'

'School,' Cookie said.

She tightened the belt of her dressing gown, which loosened again when she let go. 'Won't you be early?'

'A bit.'

'What time do they open the gates?'

He thought. 'Half eight.'

'It's only just gone seven. It's dark out.'

'I know,' he said.

'Cold out there too.'

'Not once I get moving. Warmer than sitting in that room.'

She looked past him up the stairs, then back at him. 'Is it cold up there?'

'It's freezing. The heater doesn't work.'

'Why didn't you tell me?' Behind her, the last of the bath

water drained noisily down the plughole. 'All right. Don't move,' she said. 'Wait there.'

Cookie stood on the stairs while she moved around behind the closed bedroom door. He looked into the bathroom and saw the black and white tiles, the deep bath with its copper taps.

'Come on then.' Mrs Lloyd's bedroom door opened and she stood on the landing in a velvet tracksuit, dark red, with a gold zip that curved out then in and then out again over her top half. She wore slippers on her feet, the kind with a fleece lining. He smiled at her. He thought of his dad, standing on a chair in the dark.

Mrs Lloyd switched on the hall light and they blinked at each other. She did a sideways nod down the stairs. 'Let's have a cup of tea and a bit of toast. Can't have you going out there on an empty stomach.'

He hesitated. He knew his mum didn't like him leaving for school without breakfast, but he didn't think she would like him eating breakfast with Mrs Lloyd. He was pretty sure, when he thought about it, that if she found out she would kill him.

Mrs Lloyd was already walking down the stairs. 'I've got jam or honey,' she said. 'And butter.'

He was weak with hunger, now she'd said that. He looked down at her from the top of the stairs and saw the sparse hair at her crown; the shape of her skull, the rounded bulb of it. She turned when she reached the ground floor and he saw her smiling to herself.

In the kitchen, Cookie sat down with his coat on. Mrs Lloyd

put a jar of honey out on the big, wooden table, then a butter dish and two flavours of jam. She sliced bread and put it under the grill. While she waited for the toast she plugged the heater into the wall and stretched it as far as the flex would allow so that it was directed at Cookie. He stared at the orange bars as they brightened.

'Thanks,' he said, when she put the toast rack down.

'Tuck in.'

She pushed the butter dish towards him and he took two slices of toast from the rack. Cookie buttered both slices, clumsy with hunger, salivating. He let a thread of honey trail between the pot and the plate. He bit into the toast and gulped it, taking a second bite before he'd swallowed the first.

'You should have told me sooner about the heater.' Mrs Lloyd brought the teapot over and put it down next to the toast rack. 'When did it break?' She held the edge of the table as she sat down.

'I don't think it ever worked.'

'No?'

'Don't think so.'

'Why on earth didn't you say?'

He swallowed a mouthful without chewing. 'Sorry,' he said.

She tutted. 'It's not your fault. What are you, fourteen?'

'Twelve.' He said it quietly, staring at his toast as she drew breath in surprise.

'Twelve?'

He nodded. Adults always did this. They found it amusing that he was freakishly tall. They liked to draw attention to it, as if he didn't already know. For a second he considered standing up from the table and leaving.

'You're mature for your age,' she said. 'That's a good thing.'

'No, it isn't.'

'You don't think so?'

'Not if I have to be a teenager.'

She poured tea into one of her patterned china cups. 'We didn't have teenagers in my day, you know. You were a child or an adult. That was it.'

'Sounds better.'

'You don't have to be a teenager if you don't fancy it,' she said.

'I'm nearly thirteen.'

'Doesn't matter.' She sipped her tea. 'You know, I'm not a big fan of old people. I live in fear of getting stuck with one on the bus.'

He laughed, and she winked at him as she put her cup down. He had an ache in his throat where he'd swallowed his toast too quickly. He pulled his feet away from the heater and felt the scorch as his trousers touched his shins.

'It's important to know who you are,' she said. 'When you know who you are, your age doesn't matter. And it doesn't matter what anyone else thinks of you either. Do you see that?'

Cookie lifted one shoulder and let it drop.

'Don't be a teenager if that's not what you want,' she said. 'Don't let anyone tell you who you are. Just be you.'

He picked up the honeyed toast, took a bite and put it down again. His throat contracted as he swallowed. He wished she would stop talking.

'Just be you,' she said again.

'I don't want to be me.' He said it quietly, but he knew she'd heard him. Her chair scraped and she stood up.

'You're going to come through this.' She was standing beside his chair, leaning forward, her hand on his back. 'This is a difficult time, but it's difficult times that make us, Cookie. You'll look back on this and you'll see I'm right.'

'I don't think so.'

'You will. Mark my words.'

He knew he was going to cry. 'I should get to school,' he said, lifting his school bag from the floor and standing up. He felt the honey in his throat, and the butter, too rich on his empty stomach. He couldn't look at her.

'Thanks for the breakfast,' he said.

'You're very welcome.'

He put his bag onto his shoulder and tried to step past her, but she was in his way, holding him by the sleeve of his coat.

'I know you'd rather not be here,' she said. 'I'm sorry about that.'

He cried then, and when she moved closer he sobbed over her shoulder, his body pressed against the cushion of her velvet tracksuit. She had the citrus smell of bubble bath in her hair. She hugged him as if it was normal that he was crying in her kitchen, as if she had expected it the whole time.

'Do you want to tell me what's wrong?'

He shook his head. But then he said, 'My dad doesn't come home any more,' through the ache in his throat, and he cried again.

'Why do you think that is?' She passed him a napkin to blow his nose on.

'He goes to the Kings Arms.'

Mrs Lloyd nodded, unsurprised. 'It's a bad crowd in there.'

'I know. Criminals,' he said.

'Yes. I think so.'

'He's a criminal. My dad. It's his fault we're here. He's been gambling; I think he's still doing it. He can't stop.'

'I see.' She looked sorry for him, like she was shocked but didn't want to say so. Cookie cried again, because he hadn't meant to say these things, he wished he hadn't spoken. He wanted to leave.

'Poor you,' she said, squeezing his hand.

Cookie's breath shuddered. It took a minute or two to stop crying, to get himself together. Her hand was soft and warm.

They said goodbye at the front door. Her tracksuit was a brighter shade of red than it had seemed in the house, and her hair was a perfect white. 'Have a good day,' she said.

'Thanks, Mrs Lloyd.'

'For God's sake, will you call me Diana?'

He held the handrail at the top of the concrete steps. The rail was cold and damp, rusty in places where the paint had flaked away. 'Thanks, Diana,' he said.

'See you later.' She waited at the door until he reached the gate.

At the bus stop he sat down with his bag next to him. The sky was lightening and a dense mist hung over the common. He felt cracked open, like he had no skin. He thought, as he waited there, that Mrs Lloyd had made him say things he hadn't wanted to say; she had done something to him. When he shut his eyes he saw her walking down the stairs ahead of him, the outline of her skull beneath her thinning hair.

17

22 October 2008

Maxine snatched a bunch of twenties from the cashpoint and declined to see her balance. She shoved the cash into her purse, clumsy with her gloves on, and pushed her purse back into her bag. She had failed to find anyone in Peckham who would talk to her for her feature. People had backed away from her in cafés and pubs. In the bookies, a member of staff had told her to get lost. She'd decided to go home. With any luck she'd catch the plumber before he left. She stepped around a stack of cardboard boxes and nearly collided with the man who was unloading them from the back of his van. Cars and buses were gridlocked behind him and he stopped to shout back at the drivers who lowered their windows to object. Maxine carried on past mobile phone shops, barber shops, nail bars. Open shopfronts with fruit and veg out on display: red and yellow bell peppers, onions and bananas, all bright and neat in plastic bowls. It was a million miles from where she'd grown up. At the junction she nearly missed the green man, thinking about the clean, crisp air at home, the cold lochs and the crashing boredom.

Clare's living room light came on as Maxine looked up at the house. She found her keys in her bag and walked up the steps to the door with her eyes on her feet. She tried to contain the thought at the back of her head. She knew the thought was Clare-shaped and she didn't want it, didn't need it right now. She took a glove off so she could get a grip on her keys and in the fumble of the moment she saw the glow of Clare's living room, the open fire in there and the logs stacked beside it. She thought of the way Seb had reacted that day at the front of the house, the way he'd crouched down next to Clare's dog. He'd been rattled by whatever it was Clare had said, and that was the thought she didn't want to have right now. She pushed her key into the lock. As she stepped onto the mat she thought, love is a gamble. She heard it in her dad's voice: *Love is a gamble, Maxine.*

The house felt loose in its foundations. She felt dust in her eyes and her nose.

'Seb?'

No reply. She called again from the foot of the stairs but the house felt empty. She pushed the door shut and went down to the kitchen, where last night's dishes were drying on the rack beside the sink. Seb's laptop was open on the table next to a mug of cold coffee and the notebook where he kept a record of the recruiters he'd talked to. The notebook was almost full. He had a black pen pushed through the spiral at the top and the pages were softened from use. She cleared the table and wet a cloth to give it a wipe down. Seb's laptop was warm when she picked it up. She hit return and saw his screen saver, the geometric shapes bouncing off the sides of the screen.

There was wine at the bottom of the bottle and she poured a glass, put it down on the counter and noticed the plumber had left a note: a folded piece of lined paper that he must have ripped out of Seb's notebook. He'd written *Maxine* on the outside and underlined it. Inside it said, *Pipes badly corroded. Total replumb: £20k. Call me if you want to go ahead?* He'd written his mobile number underneath.

She took a mouthful of wine, held the taste on her tongue. She shut her eyes with the note in one hand and the glass in the other, and leaned back against the counter in her ugly, old kitchen.

Twenty grand. There was just no way.

She saved his number in her phone and sent a text: *Thanks for today. I took money out to pay you but you'd gone when I got home.*

He replied after a minute: *Don't charge for quotations. Include it in cost of plumbing.*

She was about to reply when he texted again: *Seb explained money tight. Call me when he gets job?*

OK, she replied. *Thanks again.* She almost added that she didn't know when that would be. That she would feel better if she could pay him for his time. But then she thought of the twenties in her purse, and the empty cupboards. It was another week until payday. So she left it at that, folded the note and put it in the pocket of her coat.

It was cold in the kitchen. She'd hoped Seb would be here. They were losing each other; hardly talking, avoiding the difficult subjects. She was trying not to care about the money – the lack of it – but it did matter, and they couldn't get away from it, living in a half-renovated house. And Seb was not the same. He was touchy, over-sensitive, moody. Avoiding sex unless he was drunk.

She sent Seb a text: *Where are you? Got home and you were out.*

He replied: *Won't be long. Stuck at London Bridge.*

She went upstairs. The waistband was too tight on these trousers; she wanted to change into her jeans so she could breathe. She took off the trousers in the bathroom, flushed the loo and listened to the rush of water through the useless old pipes. She stood in her coat and socks, drinking wine. Twenty grand, for God's sake. She could see that the plumber had removed the panel from the side of the bathtub, although he'd done a decent enough job of fitting it back again. Water was dripping into the tub from the shower head. She wondered what time Seb had gone out. If it was a good idea to leave workmen in the house on their own.

In the bedroom she replied: *Hurry home!* She put the wine glass down – almost empty now – then she took off her coat and threw it on the bed. She pulled on her jeans, picked up a jumper from the back of the armchair and pulled it over her head the wrong way at first. She took her arms back out and twisted it around. The too-tight trousers could go in the wardrobe. She had to push Seb's things aside and find a hanger for her trousers in between one of her work shirts and the garment bag where he kept his suit. Most of his suits were stored down in the cellar, but this was the one he'd worn for his interview.

Maxine went to the bedroom door and came back again. She stood in front of the wardrobe. She only half knew why she was doing this: it was some mental itch, a half-formed worry that she'd failed to bury. Her head buzzed from the wine and her fingers were clumsy with the zip. She reached around inside the garment bag and found a trouser leg. Even in the dim overhead light, she knew the fabric was flecked with mud. It came away against her fingernails. She pushed his trousers back into the bag and zipped it up, pushed the wardrobe shut. Heat rushed through her. She shouldn't have looked.

Her phone beeped again: *Don't eat, I'm going to make my famous risotto.*

She lay down on the bed and thought that she would wait here for Seb. She closed her eyes, and when she opened them Seb was downstairs cooking. He'd put the heater on and lit a row of tea lights at the window. She didn't ask him why the suit in the wardrobe was flecked with mud. She didn't mention the note from the plumber, the money they would need to replace the pipes. She meant to, and then she didn't. By the time she'd eaten the risotto she had a headache that she put down to the wine.

18

14 December 1994

In the kitchen at the rear of Marie's Café, Ruth pushed half a quiche Lorraine, cling-wrapped, into her bag. She slid it down to the bottom where it could lie flat. Then she put her purse on top of it, her make-up bag and her gloves. Nobody would miss the quiche. She would claim it had gone off, if anyone asked. But she still felt sick with nerves as she shut the fridge door and walked out of the kitchen, her arm tight against the bag at her side. She shouted bye to Marie and smiled at the man near the window who'd slid a pound coin across the table towards her when she'd brought him his toasted cheese sandwich. There was a tips jar on the counter, next to the till, and the money got shared out once a month. But the pound coin had gone into her shoe when she was on her own behind the counter. Later on, after the lunchtime rush, someone had left her a fiver and she'd gone into the staff room and pushed it down her bra. The pound coin had been crippling her all day.

She would be home ahead of Cookie if she got the bus. She might even catch Lee, although her confidence in that plan had dwindled. She tried to summon the desire she'd felt this morning, but all she felt was tired and grimy. This morning felt like a week ago. All she wanted in this world was to sit down. This was how a marriage went stale, she thought, as she squeezed onto the number 63 outside Woolworths. There was a time she would have given Lee a look, a very small smile, and he would have followed her up the stairs with no question in his mind about what she meant. Today she wasn't sure she could summon that look if she tried. He would probably think she was joking. Standing on the lower deck of the bus, squashed against a man with a patchy grey beard, she thought, This is the closest I've come to sex in months.

The bus edged forward and Ruth grabbed a metal pole near the door. The man with the beard was still pressed up against her, and a woman in a shiny cerise rain mac held the pole just below where she was holding it. The rain mac was buttoned up to her bust, leaving a good bit of cleavage on show, and she had long, painted fingernails and slippers on her feet, pink fluffy ones, worn with glitter tights. At her side she had a double buggy, two toddlers in raincoats, both of them nodding off with their lips parted, each holding a bit of pastry. It made Ruth think of Cookie, so adorable at that age, fascinated by everything. Such a cutie. He'd come along a bit later than expected (all those years trying not to get pregnant, then even more years thinking she'd never conceive) and he'd been a needy baby, always wanting to be held. Always hungry. Her little Cookie Monster.

She checked her watch. Cookie would be on his way home from school. She pictured him crossing the East Dulwich Road at the junction, that lethal set of lights that never gave you enough time to cross before the traffic started revving. It ran through her head: the bus approaching at speed, Cookie stepping out into the road, distracted, his head down. For three or four seconds the whole thing happened and she couldn't make it stop. She saw the impact as the bus hit him, the moment the front wheels crushed his body; the chaos in the street, the blood.

'You all right?' the woman in the mac asked.

Ruth nodded and smiled because it wasn't true, it was in her head and she had to find a way to stop this happening. She'd been a wreck lately, couldn't think about Cookie without imagining some hellish scenario. She gripped the metal pole and thought, It didn't happen, he's OK. She was so tired.

'You sure?' the woman said.

Ruth smiled. 'Honestly, I'm OK.'

She looked up at the man with the patchy beard and saw that he was looking at the woman in the cerise mac, pretending not to but looking nonetheless. She couldn't blame him. She was still smiling, but she wanted to cry because there was a time she could have carried off that coat. There was a time the grey-bearded bloke would have looked at her that way and she'd have thought he was a creep. He *was* a creep, but that wasn't the point.

God, she was going to have to get off this bus; she was hot and crowded, the crush of people unbearable now. She turned to the door, expecting to see the edge of the common, the stretch of muddy grass and the bare trees. But they were stationary, barely twenty yards from Woolworths, and nothing was moving in either direction. Buses and vans gridlocked, pedestrians weaving between them, cyclists mounting the pavement.

The driver climbed from his cab and the engine stopped.

'We ain't moving,' the driver said. 'Burst water main down at the Rye. Everything's on diversion.'

Ruth found herself on the pavement with a pound coin pressing into the ball of her foot; a cold rain falling. She stepped aside, let a stream of people pass her, all of them walking fast with their heads down. Horns blared from the street. A man got out of his car, stood beside it with the door open, hit the roof with his palm in time with the music from his speakers. He gestured at the drivers around him and they honked their horns by way of reply. Ruth stood still, exhausted by the noise and movement, the pinch of her shoes.

Through a gap in the traffic she noticed a man walking along the far side of the street. Someone walked in front of him but she knew it was Lee from the angle of his head, the way he held himself in his black donkey jacket. Car horns sounded long and loud all the way along the high street. It was just gone half past three on the afternoon of the murder and Lee Delaney slowed his pace outside the betting shop, pulled on the door without looking up and disappeared inside.

Ruth had always known of this weakness in him. The gambling, and the deals he did to fund it. She knew he was in trouble, that he owed money to people who would hurt him if he defaulted. But he'd told her, after the last time, that he was making changes. He had cried in her arms and asked her to believe him. He'd sworn on Cookie's life that he would get his act together, that he would get them out of this mess. Don't lose faith in me, he'd said.

She walked on. Past the open shopfronts selling yam and plantain, the barber shops and nail bars; the market stalls selling laundry bags and Santa hats; skinny strands of tinsel getting soaked in the rain. Past the weeping willows on the strip of green separating the traffic on the approach to the common. She didn't look back up the street to see if he was following behind. She wanted to believe that he'd popped into the bookies to see someone, that he wouldn't place a bet. That he was on his way home. She walked at a steady pace and she held her faith in him tenderly, like the fragile thing it was. (He had sworn on Cookie's life. He had sobbed in her arms.) At the junction, where the road was cordoned off, she saw two men leaving the Kings Arms with their hands in their pockets, glancing up and down the street before they turned onto Rye Lane. Ruth stayed behind the tape, leaning against a darkened traffic light. The rain fell.

Lee had lived in this bit of Peckham as a boy. His family was from Peckham, going way back, since before it was built up like this, before it became the place where you lived because you'd hit rock bottom. Lee's mum had worked in the library and his dad had worked down the sewers, as had his granddad before him. Lee had been pleased when she'd told him about the loft room she'd found, looking out over the Rye. He'd been keen to sign the lease, to move in. It's a nice spot, he'd said. You'll hardly know you're in Peckham, with the common opposite. He'd persuaded her. And the day they'd moved in, Lee had gone down the Kings Arms and they hadn't seen him until morning. That was where he was, when he didn't come home. It was a hellhole of a pub, a drug den, a gathering place for criminals. Most people would give the place a wide berth, but not Lee. She'd asked him if he'd wanted to move here because it was so close to that pub and he'd flat-out denied it. It's a lovely old house, he'd said. Would have been grand in its day.

Ruth walked along the edge of the common, past the bare trees and wet grass, past crows lined up on the back of a bench, glossy and formal in the rain. There was a Thames Water van at the side of the road and a group of men in high-vis vests were gathered around a long rupture in the tarmac, where water gushed from beneath its crust. The street had become a river. Water bubbled out of the drains. On the far side of the common a double-decker bus was attempting a three-point turn, cheered on by a group of school kids. The world was skewed today. Nothing had felt right from the minute she woke up.

The men in high-vis vests smiled at Ruth as she hobbled past them and pushed through the gate. From the steps leading to the front door she looked up the street in the hope that Lee might be walking towards her: sheepish but repentant, his head down. But there was no sign. The young woman next door said hello, a quick wave as she walked down her steps to take

127

her bin out. Ruth had forgotten her name – Clare? Karen? – but she waved back and gave her a smile. She had on a nice sweater, cashmere by the look of it, and Ruth was about to tell her she liked the colour, a pale shade of blue. But she ran back up the steps and slammed her door before Ruth had the chance. Which was rude, Ruth thought. It might be raining but you could stop and pass the time of day with a neighbour, surely. She wouldn't have slammed the door like that on Mrs Lloyd, would she? Ruth was tempted to walk up to her house, knock on the door and ask her why she couldn't stop and chat. Did she think they were down and out? Was that it? Had Mrs Lloyd been talking about them? She had half a mind to hammer on her door and see the look on her face, all shocked and surprised in her cashmere. But she didn't. Mostly because she couldn't walk another step in these shoes.

Ruth put her key in the lock. The house was quiet around her. There was no way she could walk up three flights of stairs, so she went down to the kitchen and sat down heavily at the table. She ached all over. She eased off her shoes, wincing, tipped the pound coin out of her left shoe and fished the fiver out of her bra. It was rare to get a fiver as a tip. She unfolded the note and spread it flat across her knee. Once every few months you got a tip like that. She would hold onto the coin, but she would put the fiver in the Quality Street tin on top of the cupboard. She was saving to get Cookie a Game Boy for Christmas. Her dad was going to chip in and between them they should have enough for the new model. He wasn't expecting it. The thought of it was the only thing getting her through the days.

She put the cash into her coat pocket. Then she went to the sink and drank down a glass of water from the tap, rinsed the glass out and stood it upside down on the draining rack. There was a mug left out on the counter, a chunky one with blue and white stripes, with an inch of cold tea left in the bottom. Lee liked to drink tea from a good-sized mug like this one; he liked it strong, with just a splash of milk. Ruth picked up the mug, considered the contents, and put it back down.

She stared into the room. She knew what her husband's tea dregs looked like. She'd been throwing his leftover tea down the sink for nearly three decades. It hurt, that he'd been back here while she was at work, and had left again before she got home. That he was avoiding her. Ruth converted this hurt, neatly, into something else. She thought of how Mrs Lloyd had never acknowledged the rent money, not once. Just took the cash and said nothing. Did she know how hard Ruth worked for that money? Did she have any idea of the hours she put in, how long her days were? It was no wonder her husband was avoiding her, when she was so wrung out, so joyless.

After a while she forced her feet back into her shoes and made her way slowly up the stairs.

19

25 October 2008

Maxine woke to an empty bed and a dry throat. The clock radio said 4 a.m. She drank some water, lay back down and listened to the squeak of the floorboards overhead. Someone was circling the room above her. She listened, and it stopped. She felt her head sinking into the pillow, the bed warm in the cold house. She slept, then woke as the boards moved again, and she reached over to Seb's side. He wasn't there. Her throat hurt.

She finished the glass of water that she kept beside the clock radio. The footsteps were soft, although the rooms on the second floor weren't carpeted. Seb must be walking around barefoot. Sleepwalking? She wanted to sleep. She wondered if she should go upstairs and bring him to bed. And then he was there beside her, his feet cold and his pyjamas soft against her legs. She reached out, expecting his back, but she touched his face in the dark.

'What happened?' he said.

'You were sleepwalking, I think.'

He was quiet and she pulled the covers up over his shoulders. She couldn't tell if he was sleeping or not. A night bus passed along the street outside, diluting the dark.

'Something happened here.' He said it sleepily, under his breath.

She moved closer to him and he threw his arm across her. She listened until his breathing changed and his body fell away from her, the weight of his arm and his warmth gone. He always held her in bed at first, but he slept on his back. When he woke he reached for her again. He was in love with her, she knew it then as she had from the start. She suspected – she hadn't asked – that she was his first love. He'd never mentioned another girlfriend. He'd told her on one of those early dates that the City-boy persona was all a front; he hid behind it, trying to fit in. He didn't know what he was doing in London. She'd found it touching, adorable really, that he was as lost as she was, that he felt an imposter.

He knew that she had fallen for him a bit slower than he had for her. When she'd told him she loved him the first time he'd smiled like she'd saved his life. But it was hard sometimes to love someone who loved you too much. It was hard not to back away, to find fault. Sometimes when she was at work she thought of him and she wondered if he really was looking for work; if he was sitting at the kitchen table in his pyjamas doing nothing. If she was his meal ticket, a roof over his head. But this was the old Maxine surfacing, finding reasons to walk away.

She knew he was looking for work. She had seen his notebook, all those pages and pages of notes he'd taken down. She turned from him and as she slipped back into sleep she thought she heard footsteps upstairs, the creak of the boards.

Seb was gone again when she woke.

She sat up, worried by the light around the curtains and the street sounds that were not rush hour; the complacent sounds of late morning. Then she remembered: Saturday. The clock radio said nine thirty. It was the latest she'd slept in months. She swung her legs over the side of the bed and sat for a moment, rubbed her hands up and down over her face. Her head was clogged. The jumper she'd worn yesterday lay across the back of the chair so she stood and pulled it on, then found a pair of socks from the drawer. She drew the curtains back, looked out across the Rye, where the leaves were falling from the horse chestnuts, the sky a crisp blue. Overhead, footsteps crossed the room, back and forth.

It was cold and dark on the landing and she was reluctant to go up to the second floor. She stood at the bottom of the staircase, her hand on the rail, and wondered what was wrong with her. It was only Seb, walking up and down. She went to call out to him but her throat hurt and she had this fear in her that he wouldn't reply if she called him; that he was downstairs drinking coffee in the kitchen with the heater on. Seb never went up to the second floor. It gave him the creeps.

She climbed the stairs. On the landing the doors were all ajar. Maxine stood and listened to the movement in the largest room. She forced herself to say his name.

He didn't reply. She stepped closer to the door and before she could speak she heard his voice, very quiet but unmistakable. She laughed, relieved, and then she heard him say, *She's not as rich as you think.*

She pushed on the door and he turned quickly to face her. He was a dark shape, the light behind him.

'Max?'

She stared at him. 'Who were you talking to?'

'When?'

'Just now. Were you on the phone?'

'No.'

'I heard you.' The light changed and she saw his face. He seemed confused. Dishevelled. He wasn't holding his phone. 'Were you talking to yourself?'

'I don't think so.'

'I heard you say something.'

He pushed a hand through his hair, shook his head. 'What did I say?'

She couldn't say it. He looked like he needed her to drop it. Like he might not be coping, she thought. His hair was getting long and he needed a shave. When she met him he used to shave twice a day, without fail. Always a fresh shirt, a tie, cufflinks.

'What are you doing up here?'

'I woke up early.' He gestured at the room with his arm outstretched. The floor was clear of wallpaper and three black bin liners stood full beside the window. 'Thought it was about time I bagged up all that paper. I know I've been promising to do it for weeks.'

'Right.' She trod across the floorboards to where he stood. 'Are you OK, Seb?'

'Me? I'm not sleeping so well.'

She remembered then, he'd been sleepwalking. He'd been up half the night, walking around in the dark.

'Are *you* OK?' he said. 'You sound croaky.'

'Sore throat.'

'You feel hot.' He held his hand against her forehead.

'Do I?'

He put his arms around her and she thought that she did feel ropey. She leaned against his chest. 'I thought I heard you say something about me. Like you were talking to someone, about me.'

There was a small pause before he laughed. 'Max, I'm up here on my own. I left my phone charging downstairs.' He ran his hands down her back. 'I'm going to get you a Lemsip. OK?'

She looked up at him. He frowned and smiled, like he was waiting for her to wake up, to see him.

'OK,' she said, and she followed him down to the kitchen, where his phone was charging on the countertop next to the kettle. He made her Lemsip and French toast, and he brought the duvet down to the huge, bare room at the front of the house, so they could watch TV. The walls in there were recently plastered, clay-brown, and Alexander's tools were stacked next to the fireplace: his bucket, his saw, his crowbar; a rolled-up dust sheet and a large hammer. He'd gone bankrupt, despite the money she'd sent him. She'd asked him if he wanted his tools back but he didn't reply to her text.

134

They sat with their knees up on the sofa, warm under the duvet. They watched *The Shining*, because they had both seen it before, but not together. Seb held her hand and said he'd forgotten it was so fucking scary; he felt like the walls were looking at him, he said, and they'd had to watch the snooker until he felt better. When she got a fever later on he went to the chemist for paracetamol, throat sweets and a box of tissues. He stroked her hair as she slept and filled a hot water bottle for her when she shivered.

'Will you read to me?' she asked him, when she woke up out of a dream. He was sitting beside her reading a book.

He looked at her over his glasses. He held up the book: *The History of Disease.*

'Appropriate,' she said.

'Are you sure?'

'Sure.' She moved so her head was in his lap, and he held the book open on her hip. 'Go on.'

He started reading. 'Typhoid, in Victorian times, began as a disease of the poor; associated with poverty, overcrowding, and the unhygienic conditions of the slums, where people lived in filthy conditions, without drainage.'

He paused, shifted his position on the sofa.

'Keep going,' she said.

'The introduction of flushing water closets to middle-class homes led to multiple outbreaks of typhoid, as drains designed for rainwater were unable to cope with large quantities of flushed water from houses. Basements were frequently flooded and local waterways became open sewers.'

135

Maxine loved the sound of his voice. She loved that he was reading a book about disease. She knew that he would read it cover to cover, turning over the corners, checking the references in the appendix. She loved him. She'd been having doubts, but she didn't know why.

'A typhoid diagnosis carried quite a stigma,' he said, and she closed her eyes, felt herself falling into sleep. When she dreamed she saw him standing at the window with his back to her, and when she said his name he would not turn around.

20

13 June 1843

Horatio found Mrs Reeves in the kitchen, kneeling at the range and stoking it with a poker. She had lately stopped answering when he rang for her. He cleared his throat so that she might turn around.

'Mr Jardine is coming this afternoon,' Horatio said, trying to keep his voice level. 'I have only now received word of it.'

Mrs Reeves did not stand. She held the poker upright, and stared up at him from the tiled floor. 'It will have to be pork cheeks, if he wants luncheon,' she said. 'I'd have gone to the butcher's for chops if I'd known Mr Jardine was coming.'

'That will be fine, Mrs Reeves. Thank you.'

A fly circled the room. Mrs Reeves watched it land on the windowsill and then take off again.

'I am sorry to ask this of you.' He waited as she pulled herself upright, resting the poker in its hook. 'But I'm afraid, on account of this unexpected visit, that I—' he lost his nerve in the face of Mrs Reeves' expression. She pushed her sleeves up past her elbows and leaned forward with her hands spread out across the table. It was extremely hot in the kitchen, and Horatio noticed that behind Mrs Reeves the back door stood ajar, contrary to his instructions. Which would explain the fly. He decided in this instance not to mention it.

'I will need the drawing room to be spotless,' he said.

Mrs Reeves looked him long and hard in the eye. 'Mrs Lloyd did not employ me to clean.'

Horatio nodded in agreement. From the back door he thought he smelled Archer's pipe.

'Mrs Lloyd employed me as a cook. I have been Cook in this house since these walls went up. I was never once called upon to clean the rooms in all those years.' She stabbed the table with her finger. 'Not once.'

Horatio nodded again, and smoothed his moustache. 'I am your employer,' he said.

'I work for Mrs Lloyd.'

'Mrs Lloyd is—'

'I carry out her wishes, and hers alone.'

Horatio paused, and thought of Isobel's measured tone, the assured ring in her voice. Her calm authority.

'Are you saying, Mrs Reeves, that you will not have the drawing room prepared for Isobel's father? Would you have him see this house in disarray?'

Mrs Reeves breathed in sharply, and shut her eyes. Her fingers pressed white against the table.

'What time is he expected?' she said.

'He will arrive at noon.'

'Noon?'

'I believe so.'

She made a high-pitched sound at the back of her throat, rushed past Horatio and called out from the hallway. 'Don't let him out of the drawing room,' she said.

'Very well.'

'And he will have to make do with the outdoor privy.'

Horatio stayed where he was. The birds were loud in the garden, and the tobacco smell through the gap in the door was unmistakable. He had asked Archer to sweep the front path, and the steps, in preparation for Mr Jardine's arrival. Archer had said he would do so without delay. He went to the door, pushed on it, expecting to find Archer leaning back against the wall, his face turned to the sun. But there was nothing. The garden looked tidy, the shrubs nicely pruned. The tobacco smell had faded.

He took his newspaper into the parlour and sat down by the window. Mr Brunel's tunnel under the Thames was attracting thousands of visitors, a headline said. He turned the page. The Great Western Railway had been granted approval to extend its line as far as Oxford. The University's chancellor had expressed concerns that the railway would allow the lower orders to move about, threatening the morality of his students. But he had been overruled.

Horatio read the same paragraph several times. He thought of his father-in-law, who would have read and considered his letter. He wished he had phrased his request more elegantly.

He did not know what to make of this impending visit, which seemed designed to catch him unawares. He did not know how he would look the man in the eye.

In the drawing room, Mrs Reeves was moving furniture and ornaments as she dusted. He heard her hasty movements, her resentment. He opened the newspaper back up and cast his eye over the letters to the editor. At the front of the house he heard the beat of horses' hooves, and the creak of wheels. The carriage did not pass the house, as he had expected it to. He let the paper rest in his lap. Surely it was not yet noon.

Mrs Reeves gave a shout: 'He is early!'

A knock came at the front door, then Mr Jardine's voice as Mrs Reeves showed him inside. Horatio put down his paper, folded it and stood. Thomas Jardine was early. He stood by the chair, frozen, his composure gone. When Mrs Reeves opened the parlour door he stared back at her in a sweat of panic.

'He is early,' she said.

He managed to nod, holding the chair. 'Thank you.'

'He will not take a drink. He does not want luncheon. Just to speak with you, he says.'

Horatio swallowed. He knew, in a small glimpse of lucidity, that blood was not reaching his brain. He could not order his thoughts.

'Breathe, sir,' Mrs Reeves said. 'Breathe in, then out. Then again.'

He did as she said, and presently he felt that perhaps he would not fall. He loosened his grip on the back of the chair. 'Thank you,' he said. 'I will speak with him. Thank you, Mrs Reeves.'

The drawing room was flooded with sunlight and Thomas stood by the window in his black mourning suit, facing the far wall where several paintings hung in gilt frames. Flecks of dust swirled around him as he turned and met Horatio's eye without expression. Horatio shut the door. He felt an uncomfortable knot in his bowel.

'I received your letter,' Thomas said.

'I hoped you would have.'

Horatio knew, without needing to look, that Thomas had sought out Isobel's portrait among the paintings. It was positioned centrally on the wall, larger than the others. She was pictured with James, their eldest boy, standing at her side; William seated in her lap, a plump and solemn baby, his face Horatio's own in miniature. Horatio had commissioned the portrait himself, and had always admired its likeness. He felt now that it dominated the room, that it was a larger presence than his own.

He remembered Mrs Reeves' advice: to inhale, to exhale. From the grass outside they heard the bleat of sheep.

'It is timber, this shipment you are expecting? From Quebec?'

'A large shipment.' Horatio nodded. 'Oak. A large quantity of tall oak.'

'Oak does not travel well.'

'It is much sought after.'

'But the risk is high,' Thomas said. 'Is it not?'

Horatio cast his eye around the room, hoping to find a suitable reply. He stood in the full heat of the sun and let his eyes rest on the rug that he had imported from Persia, that he had hung on the wall behind the grand piano. An arrangement of peacock feathers stood in a vase on the mahogany tallboy, a fine piece with brass handles. He wished he had asked that the handles be polished. Dust was visible on the lid of the piano, and on the mantelpiece, where Mrs Reeves had not lifted the porcelain.

'The risk is high,' Horatio said. A sweat rose up his back. 'But the return is a good one.'

Thomas pulled his cuffs down over his wrists. 'Rather like your investment in the railways,' he said.

'My railway shares look very promising.'

'They were a margin purchase. Is that the correct term?'

'It is.'

'Your debt will be considerable, if the shares do not perform as you hope.'

'The railways are a good prospect,' Horatio insisted. 'There is new track proposed that will connect every town in England.'

'How many railways does the country need?' Thomas looked behind him at the view across the Rye, frowning into the sun. 'It pains me to see our countryside butchered by these fire-devils.'

'It is the future, sir.'

'Is it a future worth having, if we have nothing of value left?'

Horatio considered Thomas, his fine profile, and tried to decide if he knew the secret that Horatio was holding inside himself. Archer had told Thomas of the miasma rising from the river Peck. Its deadly vapours. But today in the noon-day sun Horatio felt the reality of Isobel's death standing beside him for all to see.

'I objected to your letter,' Thomas said.

'You objected?'

'I did.'

Horatio stood rigid at the window. Sweat ran down his spine. 'I did not mean to offend,' he said.

'Your letter implied that I might not provide for my grand-sons. You implied that I might leave them wanting.'

Horatio made a small, high noise. He longed to leave this room, to loosen his collar.

'Did you think I would not meet the payments on their home?' Thomas turned at last from the window. 'Did you think I might neglect their needs?'

'No,' Horatio said, although he knew that his letter had of course implied this. 'I had every faith that you—'

'I wish to God that you had never set eyes on my daughter. You have no rightful place in her world.'

Horatio did not object to this. After all, he knew it to be true.

'If it were not for James and William, I would finish you,' Thomas said. His face was damp, his greying hair flat against his head, his eyes watery. He was not going to finish him, Horatio thought peripherally. Whatever he knew, he would keep it to himself. The air cleared somewhat, and the fear ran from his veins.

'That is as I thought,' Horatio said.

'Then we understand each other.'

Thomas reached for his hat, which he had left on a small leather-topped table. He brushed a layer of dust from the underside of its brim. His movements were brisk, energised, and Horatio felt his tightly contained anger, his disgust.

'I expect you to make good your debts, when your ship comes in.' Thomas nodded, and made for the door.

In the hallway, Mrs Reeves showed Thomas out. Horatio watched from the window as he climbed into his carriage. He felt a strange elation, a lightening of his spirit, as Thomas drove away.

21

31 October 2008

Maxine's phone beeped on her way back from the shop. She stopped and took it out of her pocket, expecting it to be Seb, reminding her to get coffee. But it was the plumber: *I can get started on your job next week?*

She leaned against the wall at the front of Clare's house. A woman in black lycra flew past with a speed and ease that left Maxine weakened; she had been sick for a week, and the world felt noisy and fast and brutal. She wasn't sure she had the strength in her legs to climb the steps up to the door. She stayed where she was for a minute, looking up at the house. A crow drank from the guttering that ran under the roof.

Another message came through: *If no budget for plumbing I could make a start on smaller jobs for you. Decorate rooms on second floor?*

He was persuasive, she had to give him that. She had an image of the rooms upstairs finished and clean, full of light.

She replied: *Let me discuss it with Seb. Will let you know ASAP.* She thought, there was no way Seb would OK it while he wasn't working. He hadn't got the job he went for at Merrill Lynch, and she hadn't asked him if anything else was coming up. Anything related to money was pretty much unmentionable.

Her phone rang again as she was putting the shopping away. She caught it just before it rang out. 'Mum.' She sat down at the table and switched the heater on beside her. 'How are you?'

'You sound out of breath,' she said.

'Do I?'

'Are you all right?'

Maxine shut her eyes. She felt weak. 'I've had a bit of flu.'

'Oh, Jesus.'

'I'm on the mend. It's been a week.'

'A week!'

'I feel much better.'

'Are you eating?'

'Yes.' She pulled the heater closer to her feet. 'I mean. Not much.'

There was a pause as Maxine's mother gathered herself.

'Get yourself on a train, Maxine. You could get here by tonight. I'll meet you at Inverness.'

'I can't.'

'Of course you can. Do you want me to book you a ticket?'

'Mum, I'm thirty years old.'

'You won't get well in that house, with no hot water and the whole place falling down around you.'

Maxine leaned back in her chair. Overhead, she heard the taps come on; the squeal of the pipes. 'Seb's been taking care of me. I'm feeling much better.'

'They're forecasting a cold snap over the south. I heard it on the news.'

She moved her phone to the other ear. 'You're breaking up, Mum.' She listened as her mother kept talking, the odd word making it through the noise. The signal was terrible in the remote spot she'd recently moved out to. She had to stand at the back door and lean in the direction of the mast. Even then it dropped out every few minutes.

'I know you think I overreact,' her mum said, when the line cleared. 'But a half-finished house is not good for your health. All that dust, for a start.'

'I know.' She took the pen from the spiral of the notebook Seb used for his conversations with recruiters. She ran the ball of the pen along the edge of the wire, creating a line of waves at the top of a blank page. 'We've found someone who can get going on the renovations.' She thought of the rooms upstairs, all finished and bright. 'He's going to start on the smaller jobs. Plastering and decorating.'

'Really?'

'He's going to start next week.' Maxine drew a tall house in Seb's notebook, with a chimney and a plume of smoke, a garden path and six windows. She could hear in her mum's tone that she was trying not to ask about the money; she knew that Seb was meant to be funding the renovations, and that his money had dried up since the crash. And that Seb hadn't paid for

147

anything so far, not even the work that Alexander did before they moved in. She drew the cracked pane across the window on the second floor, and a figure standing at the window, looking out.

'Is Seb back in work, then?'

'No, not yet.' She stared at the page, the creepy house she'd drawn. She was still sick, she could feel the fever in her veins.

'Then how are you—'

'I just want the work done. It's not healthy, like you say. It's silly to hold off on the smaller jobs when I have the money to pay for it.'

Her mum was quiet, and Maxine drew a row of flowers at the front of the house, with big cheerful petals and oversized leaves. She heard the hinge creak on her mum's back door.

'Your dad would have wanted you to spend your money carefully, Maxine.'

'He would have loved this house.' She pushed the heater away. She was too hot now, and her drawing looked like something from a nightmare. 'He would have loved it,' she said.

'I'm sure you're right.'

'He would have loved Seb.'

A pause. 'Of course.'

'Dad would have understood.'

'What do you mean?'

'He told me to take risks. To be brave enough to fall in love.' Her skin was damp against her layers of clothes. She knew that her dad's advice would sting, that her mother would be standing at her back door processing it. It was the advice of a man who had left his wife for his lover, and did not regret his decision.

'I do like Seb,' her mum said.

'Do you?'

'As far as you can like someone you only met for an hour.'

Maxine wished she hadn't answered the phone. She felt detached from herself. The conversation was happening elsewhere while she sat here at the table, sweating. 'Seb was on his lunch hour. And you were in London for one day. You gave me no notice that you were coming.'

'Why don't you bring him with you? Come and spend a few days here, the pair of you.'

'I can't, Mum. We can't.'

'Why not?'

'I have to go back to work. Seb has interviews.'

'Has he?'

'Yes!' It came out as a shriek. 'He has to be available for interviews, if he gets a call.'

'I see.'

'He won't get a job if he's in Scotland when a recruiter calls, will he?'

'I don't know. I have no idea.'

'He needs to be available at the drop of a hat. There's a lot of competition right now.'

'Well. I imagine it *is* cut-throat, in his line of work.'

'It is.'

'I hope he comes good and pays for the plumbing, at least.'

Maxine allowed a prolonged silence to make itself felt. She

listened as Seb moved from room to room upstairs. It sounded like he was talking to someone. 'I knew you didn't like him,' she said.

'I barely know him.'

'He's been taking care of me, while I've been sick.'

'Maybe you wouldn't be sick, if he'd paid for the renovations.'

'He lost his job, Mum!'

'How convenient.'

Maxine laughed. 'You really have no faith in humanity, do you?'

'That's not true.'

'Not everyone's like Dad, you know. I'm not going to spend my whole life on my own just because of what happened to you.'

Maxine hadn't meant to say that. She'd thought it a hundred times, but she hadn't planned to say it aloud, not to her mother at least. She'd discussed it with Lin, who was two years older, and they'd agreed their mum had changed when their dad died. She'd hated him in quite a healthy way before that. He was a bastard, and Mum was a saint. But then they'd got the news that he'd been killed at work and it had been harder to hate him. Harder to say so, anyway. He'd gained a bit of moral high ground, as dead people do.

'Fair enough,' her mother said, after a pause. 'Bring Seb for Christmas. Come for a week, if you like. Let me have a good look at him.'

Maxine sneezed into the hanky she kept up her sleeve. She wondered if her mum had even heard what she'd said.

'Unless Seb's family want you to go to them?'

'I don't think so. He doesn't see much of them.'

'No?'

'No. Not really.' She sneezed again.

'They live in France, don't they?'

'Belgium. His dad's a diplomat.'

'I see.'

'I'm sure he'd love to come for Christmas.'

'Great! I'll let everyone know you're coming.'

'OK.' Maxine sketched a large crow on the roof of the house she'd drawn. A door swung shut upstairs. She listened, but Seb had gone quiet.

'I'll look forward to that,' her mum said, brightening. 'That will be lovely.'

'Yes, it will.' Maxine felt exhausted. The signal dropped out for a minute and she switched ears. 'Hello?'

'Did you hear me?'

'No. What did you say?'

'I said I'm getting a landline put in. I need to give you the new number.'

Maxine opened Seb's notebook back up. 'Go ahead.'

'I wrote it on an envelope. Hang on.'

She looked down at a page of Seb's handwriting. He'd written a column of dates down one side, starting in 1841. Names and occupations alongside the dates. *Merchant. Housewife. Cook. Groom.* She turned the book over and flicked through the pages. It was definitely Seb's notebook; his handwriting and his favourite pen. But she could see at a glance it was full of obscure historical details, with capitalised headings and underlined sub-headings. He'd gone down a rabbit hole of research on the early Victorian period. For God's sake. He was researching the history of the house.

'Found it!' Her mother came back on the line.

Maxine wrote the new number down on a blank page then looked through the pad again, scanning each page for notes on the jobs he'd applied for, names and numbers of recruiters. But there was nothing. Sometimes he changed the pen he was using; sometimes his writing loosened, as if his arm was tired. Some words were circled for emphasis: *Railway Mania* caught her eye, with pages of dates and figures beneath it. Some words were written in large, square capitals: *DRAINAGE. DISEASE. STIGMA.* It looked obsessive, like some kind of mad diversion tactic. The back of the page she'd just written on was blank apart from a heading at the top, which he'd underlined: *River Peck*.

'Maxie?'

'I'm here, Mum.'

'You went quiet.'

'Sorry.' She felt mentally numb. She slid the pen back into the spiral and closed the notebook. He must have another one somewhere for his job-hunting notes. He probably had a file on his laptop.

'I'll let you go,' her mum said. 'You should go to bed. Take it easy.'

'I will.' She felt awful. She cracked her knuckles against her thigh, one joint at a time.

'Take two paracetamol every four hours,' her mother told her. 'And lots of water.'

Maxine promised. Seb's feet were on the staircase as she ended the call, then in the hallway. She tried to remember when she last took any paracetamol.

'Hi there,' he said as he walked into the room. 'Did you get coffee?'

She nodded. 'Could you make it?'

'Sure. You OK?'

'Don't know. That walk to the shop knocked me out.'

He frowned at her, then he turned to fill the kettle. 'Maybe you should lie down, Max.'

'I will in a bit.' She strummed the pages of his notebook, then she pushed it away. She thought: *drainage, disease, stigma.* 'I was thinking, it might be an idea to get some of the rooms decorated. Get a professional in.'

He plugged in the kettle and flicked the switch. He looked like he might be about to reply, but then he didn't.

'I think it's a good idea,' she said.

'Do you?'

'It's not healthy, living like this, all the dust and—'

'It adds up quickly, you know. Decorating and plastering. It'll eat into—'

'And I'm really fucking sick of living like this.' She stared back at him. 'So I'm going to pay to get those jobs done.'

'Is this a discussion? Or are you just letting me know?'

'I guess I'm letting you know.'

The kettle rumbled, and they waited for it to click off. Her

153

blood was running hot. She thought of all the things she could say that would start a row, that might be bad enough for him to decide to move out. She wanted to tell him that she wouldn't be sick if he'd paid for the renovations. And he hadn't even paid Alexander; he'd run out of money before he could cough up. That was convenient, wasn't it? She couldn't sit here another minute with those thoughts in her head, turning to poison.

'How's your mum?' he said.

'She's all right.' She listened to the tick of the heater as he made coffee. 'How did you know it was her on the phone?'

'You're always in a foul mood after you speak to her.'

'Am I?'

He carefully put her coffee down in front of her. He smiled. 'I heard some of it. Sounded intense.'

'It was.' She smiled back at him, and the poison ebbed back. 'Who were *you* talking to?'

He looked at her like it was a strange question. 'Me? No one.'

'I thought I heard you.'

'When?'

'Just now. I'm sure I heard you.'

He took his glasses off and polished them on his sleeve. His eyes were red-rimmed. 'That wasn't me, Max.'

'Who was it then?'

'I don't know.'

She watched him: he was unfamiliar suddenly, and she wondered if he was coming undone. He kept rubbing at a smudge on his lens. 'Are you OK?'

He didn't reply. He blew on the lens and rubbed it again with his sleeve.

'Are you getting much sleep?'

'Not much. No.' He looked blindly at her. 'Have you found someone to do the decorating?'

'Just your same guy who quoted for the plumbing. He's multi-skilled, it seems. Very keen.'

'He's hardly my guy,' Seb said.

'You know what I mean.'

'I think you mean that you want to sink more money into this house.' He returned his glasses to his face. 'I'm not sure it's a good idea.'

'What are you saying?'

'Maybe we should cut our losses. Get out of here.' He gestured at the front door, the street beyond it. 'We could jump on a train, or a plane.'

'What are you talking about?'

'Why not? Neither of us is from here. We could go anywhere. Start again, just us.' He ran his hand along the counter, which was warped and ugly; they had planned to rip it out before they moved in. 'No amount of money will fix this place, Maxine. Nothing will. Nothing's ever gone right here.'

She reached for her coffee. She was so cold. She looked at Seb and thought that she didn't know him at all, he was a total stranger standing in her house, half mad, talking nonsense. She felt the heat through the mug but it didn't warm her.

'I'm not going anywhere,' she said. 'I still want the things I moved to London for. I'm ambitious, Seb, you know that.'

'How could I forget?' He stood a moment looking down at his feet, the old, cracked kitchen tiles. Then he pushed the box of paracetamol across the table so she could reach it. 'You should take a couple of those. You look like death.'

22

14 December 1994

Cookie walked around the barriers at the junction. There was a Thames Water van outside the house and it looked like the whole street had cracked open, water forcing its way out of the tarmacked surface. It was getting dark, and the streetlights caught the rain in bright shards. He looked up at the house and saw the black windows, the flaking paintwork; thick ivy over the dark brick. The concrete steps leading to the front door were crumbling in places, the steel supports visible through the gaps. If it hadn't been raining he might have turned from the house, walked around the park for a while.

But he was soaked, so he let himself in and stood on the mat, his coat dripping. The murder was close now, just hours away. He kicked his wet shoes off and put them on the rack. Then he carried on up the stairs to the second floor, with its expectant rooms. Its closed doors. He wondered if today would be the day he went in. He said the killer's name quietly to himself: *Horatio Lloyd*. He felt fear jostling with temptation: pushing and pulling.

And then he heard the radio, coming from the loft. Someone was home. He took the last flight of stairs at a run.

'Mum?'

Ruth was sitting at the table with her coat on, leaning back in the wooden chair, watching TV with the sound down. On the far side of the room the radio was on: a newsreader saying that Labour had increased its lead against the Conservatives, according to the latest poll. The room was silvery-dark with the glow from the TV. His mum turned to look at him. 'Hello, love,' she said, sitting up straight. 'You got soaked!'

'It's chucking it down.' He took his bag off his shoulders and put it on the floor. It was cold up here, and the air felt damp.

'There's a burst water main out on the Rye. I had to walk home.' She lifted her arms to show him the rainwater still darkening her coat. 'I got you something to eat if you fancy it.'

She'd put a large slice of quiche on a plate. The pastry around the edge had crumbled and the centre looked sunken and grey. He felt unwell, a bit nauseous.

'You're home early,' he said.

She bent over and rubbed at her toes through her tights. 'I got back a little while ago. My feet are killing me. I sat down in this chair when I got in and I haven't moved.'

They both stared at the TV. People were running around a fake supermarket, throwing things into trolleys without looking at what they were buying. The sofa-bed was still extended with the sleeping bag slumped across it, the way he'd left it that morning. He went to the bed and picked up the sleeping bag, rolled it up and folded the blankets.

'She's been in here,' his mum said.

Cookie turned to face his mum. She was still rubbing at her toes.

'Who?' he said.

'Mrs Lloyd. The room was unlocked when I got home and the heater's gone.' She pointed at the spot where the heater had been, beside the chest of drawers. 'She let herself in while we were out.'

'The heater was broken,' Cookie said.

She looked up at him from the chair. 'Doesn't mean she can come in here without permission.'

Cookie went to explain, but he knew she would overreact, she would go mad. He watched her re-tie the band around her hair. She took a clump of ponytail in each hand and pulled in two directions.

'She let herself in,' Ruth said. 'It's unbelievable.'

'We need the heater fixed.' He said it softly, with a shrug. 'It's cold.'

'I'd rather be cold than have her in here, poking around.'

Cookie said nothing. He thought of Mrs Lloyd standing in his way this morning when he'd wanted to leave; the things he'd told her. He thought of what his mum would say if she knew; if he looked at her now she would see it in his face. He felt – he always felt – that his mum knew all his thoughts, that there was no hiding from her.

'This is our private space,' his mum continued. 'It's bad enough that she makes us live this way, without her snooping around up here, judging us.'

He was so tired, listening to her. His brain ached. He lifted the base of the bed so it folded in on itself, and shunted it back into the cavity. He sat down on the sofa, his wet trousers cold against his legs. 'I don't think she's interested in our things,' he said. 'She probably didn't even look.'

'Of course she looked.'

'You don't know that.'

'I do know that!' She nodded across the room at where his towel was draped over the back of a chair, still damp from this morning. The plastic clothes airer had all their pants and socks hung out to dry; his mum's bras and tights. The laundry basket was full, like always, the lid lifted up by the clothes inside. 'She bloody well looked, I can tell. I can feel it.'

'No, you can't.' He stared at the TV. He had never spoken that way to his mum before. He flinched inside when she sat forward in her chair. An advert for toilet paper came on: the one where a dog drags the entire roll of paper through the house while a little kid sits on the toilet with his feet dangling.

Ruth stood and turned off the set. The newsreader on the radio was talking about Myra Hindley: she would never be released from prison, the newsreader said. The room was dark without the light from the TV. He was shaky with the cold.

'How did she even know about the heater?' Ruth said. 'I didn't tell her it was broken.'

'Don't know.'

'I haven't said a word about it.'

'I know. You said that.'

'Sorry if I'm repeating myself.'

He didn't reply. His mum suspected that he'd told Mrs Lloyd about the heater; he could tell she did, and it made him hold the secret tighter. He listened to her breathing, the wheeze in her chest from when she used to smoke. He wished she didn't breathe like that. He wished she could breathe in a way that didn't annoy him, so he could love her again like he used to before they moved here, when she'd been everything to him. He pushed his hands under his legs and thought, I don't love her. He felt her hurt, and he was glad.

'You hungry?' she said.

'No.'

'Don't you feel well?'

'I'm all right.'

'It's not like you to turn down food.'

He thought of this morning's toast and honey. It had been heavy in his stomach all day. He let his head fall back against the sofa.

'What's wrong with you?' She stepped closer and put the back of her hand against his forehead. 'Are you sure you're not coming down with something?'

'I'm fine.' He moved his head away from her hand.

'You don't seem fine. Did you have lunch?'

'I said, I'm fine.'

She went to the window and stared out. A song came on the radio, the one that had got to number one in the charts. It was

161

playing in every shop and café and pub you walked past. Until today, Cookie had quite liked it.

'No need to be shitty with me,' his mum said.

'I'm not being shitty.'

'Yes you are, Cookie.'

'Don't call me that.'

'What?' She turned her head sharply. 'What was that?'

'I said, don't call me that.' His voice cracked as he said it. He cleared his throat. 'I don't want to be called that any more.'

'Why not?'

'It's not my name, is it?'

She stared at him. The song on the radio reached its chorus, and they both listened. When a new verse started, Ruth turned back to the window. 'You don't look like a Colin,' she said.

'But it's my name.'

'You never minded before.'

'I did,' he said, because he felt mean. And then, 'I'm not a baby any more.'

She pulled her hand down over her face and blinked, leaning closer to the pane. He knew she was looking out at the red light of Canada Tower, over towards where they'd lived before.

'I can't call you Colin,' his mum said. 'It feels wrong.'

'Why did you name me Colin if you don't like it?'

'Your dad chose it. He was set on it, so I let him have his way.'

The wind changed direction, rattling the window. They both listened as the chorus rose up again. This time there were Christmas bells ringing behind the vocals. Ruth swayed slowly side to side, mouthing the words to herself.

'Can I ask you something?'

She turned to him. 'Course you can.'

'Is Dad a criminal?' He dug his fingers into the sofa.

'What?'

'I saw him coming out of the Kings Arms on a Saturday morning.' He felt the release of saying this; his mum was angry and he didn't care. 'It was early. He looked like he'd been there all night.'

'That doesn't mean—'

'The police raided the pub not long after he left.'

'That doesn't mean anything. You can't—'

'Is he gambling?'

She went quiet then. Her shoulders dropped. 'Where did you get that idea?'

'I heard you arguing.'

'Did you.' It wasn't a question. Her eyes darted over his face. 'Look. No one's to know about that.'

'I haven't told anyone.' He stared back at her, hot with the lie inside him. 'I haven't,' he said.

'Because that's our private family business.'

'I know.'

'And other people might judge him. They might think badly of him, if they knew.' She pushed her hands into her coat pockets; he heard loose change rub against her house keys. 'But we know him, the man he is. We need to hold our faith in him. Do you understand that?'

He swallowed. 'No,' he said.

'You don't?'

'I don't know how to have faith in him, when he brought us here.'

She looked like he'd slapped her. Rain hit the window. Another Christmas song started on the radio, an old one this time. She looked down at the radio like it had insulted her; a roll of flesh appeared under her chin. She tutted and switched it off.

'He didn't bring us here.' Her voice was loud in the fresh quiet. 'This isn't his fault.'

'It is.'

'Don't you dare say another word.' She shouted it. Spittle flew from her mouth. 'Not another word. Do you hear me?'

He gave a one-shoulder shrug, and her eyes widened.

'I said, do you hear me?'

'Yes,' he said, because he had pushed her as far as he could. His heart raced.

'Good.'

He sat back again, his limbs heavy. His mum stared out at the rain. It took him a minute to realise she was crying.

'Mum?'

She shook her head. 'Don't talk to me.'

'Are you crying?'

'No.' She cupped her hands around her face. 'I never thought I'd hear you talk that way.'

He got up and went to stand beside her at the window. She really was crying, her face contorted in the effort to stop. He put his hand on her back but it seemed to make her cry harder so he dropped it down to his side. After a while she took a tissue out of her coat pocket, examined it and blew her nose. It was nearly dark outside. A crow lifted from the gate post and took off on wide, slow wings.

'As a family, we have faith in each other. We believe in each other.' She held him by the arm. 'When you stop believing in someone, they're lost, Cookie.' She corrected herself: 'Colin.' She dropped his arm, blew her nose again and returned the tissue to her pocket. 'Lost,' she repeated. 'Do you understand me now?'

'Yes,' he said, because it was the only thing to say.

She held her arm out and he moved closer to her, relieved to find that he loved her again, that he was sorry. He felt the damp fabric of her coat and her bones underneath.

'I don't know what's got into you,' she said. 'Talking that way.'

'Sorry.'

'You need to remember who you are.' She blew air out of her cheeks. They stood together a minute looking out of the window. He felt her lean against him, the rigidity leaving her. 'It's all gone wrong since we moved here,' she said.

'I know.'

'I hate this house.'

'Me too.'

She pulled away from him, reached up and smoothed his hair down. She tipped his head forward and sniffed. 'Did you wash your hair this morning?'

'Yes.'

'With shampoo?'

He didn't reply.

'Did you?' She held his head, covering his ears. 'Don't lie to me.'

'My hair sticks out when I wash it.'

'For God's sake.' She smoothed it again. 'You should be happy to *have* hair. Look at your father.'

The front door slammed shut downstairs and Ruth froze. 'Speak of the devil.'

'Is that Dad?'

'Think so.'

'Are you going to tell him about the heater?'

She looked at the space where the heater had been. 'Best not mention it for now,' she said. 'He'll go spare.' She went to the chair where her shoes lay on their sides and she nudged them upright with her toes, swearing under her breath as she pushed her feet into them. 'Wait up here, would you? I need a minute with your dad, downstairs.'

Cookie sat back down on the sofa and took his coat off, then he pulled his tie over his head and threw it onto the floor. He unbuttoned his collar. His mum ran down the stairs, down and down again. He wondered if it was true, if his dad was lost now, if he had cut him adrift because of the things he'd said. He didn't want that. He listened a while to the rain on the roof. He tried to picture the river, the way it ran across the common, but the image wouldn't come to his mind and all he saw was mist and mud and flashing blue lights.

23

3 November 2008

Seb caught the post as it dropped onto the mat. Three letters, all addressed to him, with *Return to Sender* stamped across each envelope. He pushed them into the pocket of his jeans and carried on down to the kitchen. He filled the kettle, made coffee and tried not to mind too much about the letters, which he'd sent a few weeks ago to the last known addresses of people he'd thought might remember his Aunt Jane. He'd hoped Aunt Jane might know where his mum was living. He'd been wondering if he might tell Max, if he did manage to trace his aunt. Maybe she would coax him to tell her all of it, she would insist that she didn't care where he came from, she loved him regardless.

But in the light of day he knew he was kidding himself. There was no rosy future where he and Maxine were together. As Jason liked to remind him, it was the internet that had brought Max into his orbit. He had no rightful place in her world.

He switched on the heater and moved his chair close to it as the bars turned orange, making his jeans hot but creating no warmth to speak of. The kitchen was always cold. He had two sweaters on and he was still frozen. He finished off his coffee – his second of the morning – and opened his laptop. There was an email at the top of his inbox, something Jason was forwarding on, with no subject heading. He read it quickly, made a mental note of the details and deleted it. Then he went into his deleted items and deleted it from there.

Upstairs, the plumber was walking around, his feet heavy on the bare boards. Seb sat for a minute with his eyes shut. He must have slept two hours last night. He felt the pull of sleep, his head nodding forward.

'Morning.'

Seb sat up as the plumber walked into the room, resting a few lengths of wood on his shoulder. He wore his black woollen hat pulled down over his ears and a grey hoodie, jeans hanging low on his hips. Seb realised he had a blank on the guy's name. He took a mouthful of coffee and thought: Robin? He looked like a Robin. Fine features. Gentle-looking, except that he was easily six foot four and he could probably knock you over if he wanted to.

'Think you were talking in your sleep,' the plumber said.

Seb stared back at him. 'Was I asleep?'

'Think so, yeah.'

'What was I saying?'

'Something about a letter, I think.'

'Must be cracking up.' He laughed, to soften the truth of this.

He thought that this wasn't going to work; things were bad enough without some total stranger watching him go round the bend.

'How's the job hunt going?'

'Badly.' Seb stared at his screen.

'Sorry to hear that.' He threw the back door open, filling the room with cold air, and left it open as he stacked the planks of wood against the wall, taking his time to get them angled right. 'Not easy, is it?' He shut the door and stood there rubbing his hands together.

'What's that?'

'Trying to make ends meet. Not since those bastards fucked the economy.'

Seb wondered if this was some kind of provocation. Maybe Max had told him their situation and he thought it might be funny to wind him up. He studied his face for a sign of challenge but there was none.

'Can I get you a coffee, Robin?'

'Sure.' He rubbed at his neck. 'It's Colin.'

'Colin! Sorry.'

'That's all right.'

'You don't look like a Colin.'

'No. Been hearing that all my life.'

Seb stood and took a mug down from the cupboard for Colin, who seemed distracted, looking around him at the cracks in the tiled flooring, the tired kitchen units, the rotting woodwork at the window.

'Coffee?' Seb repeated.

'Wouldn't say no, if you don't mind. Milk, no sugar.' Colin stood by the back door as Seb filled the kettle.

'How's the work going?' Seb asked.

'Not bad. I should be out of your hair in a few weeks.'

'Right.' A few weeks sounded like a long time.

'You could always move out for a bit, if it's getting to you. Maybe treat yourselves to a stay in a hotel.'

'We don't have the budget for that, unfortunately.'

'Could you move in with your folks for a few nights?'

Seb sniffed the milk and decided it would do. He didn't look at Colin. 'My parents live overseas. In Brussels.'

'You don't sound Belgian,' Colin said.

'We lived in Brussels when I was growing up, for my dad's job. But I was born here.' Seb poured boiling water into each mug and tried to remember what he'd told Maxine. 'My dad's a diplomat,' he said, with the tone of worldly confidence he imagined a person might have, if this were true. 'We're not a close family,' he added. 'I don't think I could just turn up on their doorstep.'

Colin pulled out a chair and sat down at the kitchen table. 'That's a shame,' he said. 'Still, this place will be a home for the two of you, when it's done.'

'That feels a long way off.'

'You'll get there.' He took a mug of coffee from Seb, nodded his thanks. 'My advice would be to start with the rooms you want to spend the most time in and worry about the rest when you've got the budget. You'll be comfortable enough that way, in a house this size. My guess is whoever lived here before didn't use the rooms at the top of the house.'

'No. We thought the same.'

'Didn't have the cash to modernise either. Which is why you've got all your original fixtures and fittings intact. Not often you see that.'

Seb wondered if this guy was going to keep telling him things he already knew about his own house. He wondered if Max had given him the impression that it was *her* house; if she'd told Colin that Seb wouldn't be around for long. He was being paranoid, he thought. Probably. He was too tired and strung out for this. His shoulders ached from tensing against the cold.

'There's an old toilet on the first floor that looks like some sort of antique,' Colin said.

'I know. We found it when we first looked around. The previous owner used it as a box room. It was full of junk.'

'It's a shame.'

'What is?'

'The mahogany casing around the pipes is all ripped open.' Colin pointed up at the floor above, where the disused toilet was situated, next to the current bathroom. 'It was probably very fancy back in the day. A real piece of history.'

'True. That is a shame.' The heater was burning the right side of his body, singeing the stitching of his trainers. He moved away from it and hit a key to refresh the screen on his laptop. 'I've been looking at all the old documents for the house. Census records, things like that. I'm interested in the history of the place.'

'Right.' Colin pointed at the laptop. 'Got a bit of a project going, have you?'

'Kind of.'

'What did you find out?'

'I mean, I'm just getting started with it really.' Seb clicked more fiercely than he needed to on the mouse pad and opened the document he wanted several times. It took forever to load. 'The original owner wrote letters to *The Times*. I found them in the online archive.'

Seb wasn't sure that Colin was interested. He was staring at the laptop, his face inscrutable.

'What was his name?' Colin said.

'Horatio Lloyd.'

'Christ.' He coughed, and put his coffee down on the table.

'I know. What a name.'

Colin coughed into his fist, and banged his chest. 'Right. Don't get many Horatios in Peckham these days.'

'True. Although he was born John Horace Lloyd, if my research is right. He came from nothing, from slum dwellings by the Thames. He did well to end up living in a house like this.'

'Social climber,' Colin said.

'Exactly.'

'What's he say? In his letters?'

'They're letters of complaint. He was kind of obsessed.' Seb felt protective suddenly of Horatio and his letters. He didn't know why he'd brought this up.

'About what?' Colin nodded at the screen. 'Go on.'

Seb leaned forward and read: 'Sirs, I repeat my plea that the tributaries of the Thames be covered over and that drainage from domestic dwellings such as my own be directed into adequate sewers. I am sickened by the river that runs across the grassland at Peckham Rye, in full view of our home. It is well known that the miasma from unwholesome smells is the cause of disease.'

Colin picked up his coffee and drank. He tapped his fingers against his knee.

'I think there was a river once, running across the common.' Seb nodded out at the front of the house. 'Horatio had two letters published in *The Times* in the space of a year, asking for it to be covered over.'

Colin rubbed his jaw. He sat up straighter in his chair. 'You like history?'

'I do.'

'Did you find out anything else?'

'Nothing that explains it.' Seb heard his own words, which he hadn't meant to say out loud, and he put down his coffee before he spilled it. 'Sorry. It's just—' Colin was looking levelly back at him. 'I mean, there's this feeling I get sometimes, like something bad might have happened here. It's like—'

'Like it hasn't gone away?'

Seb swallowed. 'Exactly.'

'You might be right,' Colin said, and he smiled slowly. 'You may well be right.'

'Why do you think that is?'

'An old house like this won't let go of much.' He gestured at the walls, lifting a forefinger from his coffee cup. 'London brick holds on to everything. It's porous, made of clay and ash.'

'Holds on to everything?'

'That's right.'

'Do you believe that?'

'Sure.' Colin nodded at the wall behind Seb. 'There must be things that went on here, that didn't get dealt with.'

'What sort of things, do you think?'

'Lies,' he said, without hesitation. 'Bad ones. That's my guess, anyway. That's my feeling.'

'Right.' Seb felt very cold. 'I hadn't thought of that.'

'What about Maxine? What does she think of all this?'

'She's not really interested,' Seb said, although the truth was he hadn't told her. They avoided the subject of what he did with his days. He didn't feel he could tell her he'd spent weeks researching Horatio Lloyd's family tree, looking at birth certificates and death certificates for the whole household; his professional and personal mistakes. Or that the more he found out about Horatio, the more he felt they had in common.

'It's a big project you've got here,' Colin said. 'Impressive. All that research.'

'It's easy enough, if you know where to look online. The census only goes up to 1901, so it'll be harder to find out about the more recent occupants.' Seb tapped the table. 'Might have to look at the national archives.'

Colin stared fixedly at the open kitchen door. 'You're researching up to the present day then?'

'Up to whoever lived here last, if I can.'

'Sounds time consuming.'

'Just a bit of a hobby, while I wait for the phone to ring.'

Colin put down his coffee and stood, hitching up his jeans. 'Best crack on. Good luck with the job hunt.'

'Thanks.'

'What is it you do?'

'I'm a stock market trader in the City. I worked for Lehman Brothers before the crash.'

'You're a banker?'

'A trader. I'm one of the bastards who fucked the economy.'

Colin ran his eyes over Seb. 'Put my foot in it there, didn't I?' After a pause he said, 'Sorry for saying that.'

'Well. Sorry about the economy.'

'I mean, you did a good job of it. We're looking at a global recession.'

'I'm aware of that, Colin. Thanks.' It came out sharper than he intended. Colin considered him; he turned his body just an inch, and Seb felt Colin's hostility, the switch of it in the room.

'You're looking to go back into that game, are you?' Colin said.

'It's what I do.'

'You like it?'

'Sure. It's fantastic.' He didn't bother to smile at him. 'Do you like what you do?'

'I do on the whole, yeah.'

'That's good.' Seb took a gulp of coffee and put his cup down heavily. He watched the geometric shapes bounce off the edges of his screen. 'How come you took those floorboards up?'

'Sorry?'

He nodded in the direction of the back door. 'Those boards you stored out there. Why did you take them up?'

'Right.' Colin stood in the kitchen doorway and scratched his head through his hat. 'A few of your boards are past saving. I told Max I'd replace them.'

'Did you?'

'She texted me this morning.'

Overhead, the pipes hummed. Seb looked up at the ceiling, then back at Colin, who was leaning with one hand against the door frame, filling the space, like he lived here.

'I imagine you think Maxine's a soft touch,' Seb said. 'You probably think you can let the project grow week by week and she'll keep dipping into her savings.'

'What?' Colin gave a small laugh.

'You start off saying it's just decorating and you end up with the roof off and a new heating system.'

'What are you saying?' He glared at Seb.

'I'm saying, stick to the decorating.'

'I'm just doing what Maxine asked me to do.'

'I'll have a word with her about that.'

'Will you?' Colin looked at Seb with interest: his head tilted, mouth slightly open, as if Seb were an exhibit in a museum. Then he turned his back and loped off, clearing the steps to the hallway in one stride.

'Yes, I will,' Seb shouted after him. 'And don't lift any more boards until I speak to her. OK?'

Colin continued up the stairs, whistling an old song, a Christmas hit from years ago. Seb brought up the website he'd been using to research the house, opened up his notebook, but he was too angry to focus and he sat back in his chair, tapping his pen against the palm of his hand. The guy was a total prick. He picked up his phone, went to call Maxine, but decided against it when he ran over the conversation in his head. She'd only dig her heels in and defend him, and he didn't think he could risk an argument. He stared at the walls and told himself to be careful, to keep his head.

24

21 June 1843

Mrs Reeves put her bags down by the front door, stood up to her full height and fastened a button at her chest. She wore her coat and hat, despite the heat. 'No,' she said. 'I will not reconsider.'

'Listen, I beg of you.' Horatio ran his thumb and forefinger along his moustache. He lowered his voice. 'I understand your misgivings,' he said.

'It is not a decision I have taken lightly.'

'I should be lost without you, Mrs Reeves.'

'I should imagine that you will.'

'I do not know what I would say to the boys, when they arrive home for the summer.'

She adjusted her hat. 'Those boys are the reason I've stayed on until now.' Beyond the door, a horse stamped and snorted. She turned her head in the direction of the noise.

'You have a carriage waiting?'

'I do.' The stained glass in the door caught the sun, casting bright red oblongs across her coat. 'Archer is waiting for me,' she said. 'I have a new appointment across town. I start on Monday.'

Horatio stepped closer to Mrs Reeves, and pressed his hand flat against the door. 'You would leave your post, after twelve years of service?'

'I would.'

'I shall not permit it.' He knew it was pointless, but the words were out before he could stop himself. 'I will not allow this, Mrs Reeves.'

She looked at Horatio's hand where it rested. She picked up her bags. 'I imagine that you have heard a woman scream, Mr Lloyd.' They held eyes. 'I imagine that you have.' She looked again at his hand, the stretch of his arm in his black mourning jacket. 'I can assure you that Archer will hear me should I scream. They will hear me at Homestall Farm across the way. They will likely hear me at Goose Green.'

'There is no need for that.'

'Then kindly open the door.'

Horatio did not move. He thought that he would be glad to see her go, despite the long years of her service, and the boys' attachment to her. She had been present when William took his first steps. She had liked to stand both boys at the kitchen table to roll pastry for her, both of them dusted head to foot in flour. They had wept in her arms at the funeral. Despite this, he was glad to be rid of her. He felt a slamming in his chest, hard and quick as a guillotine.

He shifted his weight and dropped his arm. He held the door open for her. As she passed him, she said, 'I know how they died. Mrs Lloyd and Alice.' She hissed it, and he stepped back from her. 'I will not be next.'

Horatio stood in the doorway with her words in his ears. So, she knew. And she would talk. He reeled with it, hot and afraid, as Archer lifted her bags onto the back of the carriage and helped Mrs Reeves into her seat.

'Good riddance,' he said as the horse walked on.

Crows stood watchful on the Rye, and he looked steadily back at them. Archer had told him once that crows lived in close colonies, their nests a dark woody mass, high up in the trees. The rookeries, where the poor of London lived, were named for the behaviour of these birds: crowded and unwholesome dwellings, filthy and teeming with disease and moral weakness.

Archer knew too much. Horatio had thought so for some time.

The smell of the river reached his nose and he turned from it, pushed the door shut behind him and stood alone in the house. The heat of the sun gathered in the hallway and it struck him that he could remove his mourning jacket, if he so chose. He could do as he pleased and no one would know. He took the jacket off and stood on the tiled floor in his shirtsleeves. Dust had balled in the corner near the door, and lay thickly along the skirting boards. He knew it was worse still in the drawing room and the parlour.

On the first floor the doors were pulled shut. He opened the door to the water closet and stood a while admiring the mahogany casing around the bowl, concealing the pipes beneath: so smart and well made, like all the carpentry in this house.

The water closet was the best money could buy, with its modern flush mechanism. The same model had been installed in Queen Victoria's home on the Isle of Wight. He had told Isobel of this fact and she had laughed; she had called it a folly, to have such a monstrous thing in their home, making a song and dance out of something private. She had said that she would continue to use her bedpan.

She had later apologised. Eventually she had quite taken to the water closet. Horatio wished now that he had not taken her comments to heart. That he had kept his temper.

He stepped forward and pulled on the flush. The rush of water was impressive, he always thought so. Quite something. The prolonged trickle afterwards, as the waste was expelled through the pipe. He had watched over the workmen as it was installed, and later he had imported the floor tiles from Italy: black and white hexagons arranged diagonally, matching those in Isobel's bathroom and the hallway on the ground floor. Another extravagance, Isobel had said.

There was a bad smell in here, despite the lack of a window. Horatio stood in the small room and sniffed. He could not account for it. He lifted his arm and sniffed his sleeve, buried his nose into the crook of his arm. It was his worst fear – he barely let himself think it – that he carried on him the smell of the rookeries. That he had brought this dangerous impurity into the house. It was the fear that woke him in the night, that felt incontestably true in the small hours.

He left the room, pulling the door shut behind him, and stood on the landing with the stench still in his nose. He put his mourning jacket back on, although the heat in the house was intolerable, the air thick and dark. He stood outside the master bedroom, where a bright seam of sunlight traced the outline of the door. He knew that if he turned the handle he would see the large, neat room with the bed centred between the two windows. The silk bedspread that he had bought for Isobel from Paris: peacock blue, embroidered with a green thread. She had loved it. She had adored beautiful things; it was a love they had shared.

There would come a day when he would feel able to go in there. He would see the things she had touched, the way she had left them, the imprint upon the room that was uniquely hers. When that day came he would stand beside her bed, or perhaps by her wardrobe, and he would tell her that he missed her terribly. That he was more sorry than he could bear.

But not today. He took the next flight of stairs up to his study, where the window was shut fast, and sat down at his desk.

25

14 December 1994

Ruth found Lee in the kitchen on the ground floor, his black coat dotted with rain.

'You're home early,' he said.

He'd got thin in the weeks since she last saw him up close. His coat hung loosely on him and the flesh had gone from his face. Maybe it was the weight loss that did it, or the way he looked at her. What she saw that afternoon, in the kitchen of this house that was not their own, was the man she fell for all those years ago. Lee Delaney, eldest of the Delaney brothers; the tall, quiet one who had a thing for her. He'd had a good head of hair in those days and he'd earned a decent wage in the housing office. Clever, was the thing people said about him back then. The clever one. A bit strait-laced, if anything. It threw her, the sight of him, and she couldn't speak for half a minute.

'I saw you,' she said, when she found her voice. 'Going into the bookies.'

He shrugged, and rainwater fell onto the tiles at his feet. 'You should've said hello.'

'You swore on Cookie's life you'd never place another bet.'

'I swore I'd get us out of this hole,' he said. 'I swore I'd fix things.'

She couldn't believe it. He wasn't even sorry. 'I believed you,' she said. 'I really did. And then I saw you just now and I –'

'Don't get yourself in a state, Ruth.'

'You swore on your son's life—'

'Listen.' He raised his voice, held up his hand. 'I need you to listen to me now. I might not have long.'

'What are you talking about?'

'It's all dealt with,' he said. 'You and Cookie are going to be fine.'

'What's dealt with?'

'I don't owe anything to anyone. I've seen to it. Nobody's going to come for you.'

Ruth didn't like the way he was talking. The rage in her bounced clean off him; he wasn't having it, he didn't seem to care. Something chilling in the tone of his voice.

'You'll be able to set up somewhere new,' he said. 'Away from here.'

'Why? What are you saying?' Even as she said this, his meaning reached her. She felt the shock of it in her bones.

'I'm going down, love,' he said. 'They're coming for me.'

'Lee.' She shook her head. 'Prison? You mean prison?'

'It's the best thing.'

'Oh my God.'

'It's the best thing, Ruthie.'

'Don't say that.'

He gave a small, one-shouldered shrug and dropped his eyes. She saw Cookie in him when he did that. It was a thing she'd figured out recently, that Cookie was the boy in Lee, the boy he'd been before she met him. He made more sense to her, now that she knew his son. They were confused and lost and strange, the pair of them, and she loved them both.

'It'll be my first sentence. They might be lenient,' he said. 'If I plead guilty.'

'Plead guilty to what?'

'I'm not going to resist it when they come. I'll go quietly.'

'But what did you do?'

'Nothing. I mean.' He stared at the wall. 'I didn't do the thing I'm going down for.'

'You're making no sense.'

'I'm serving time for someone else,' he said.

'What? Why?'

'All my debts will be written off. I'll come out with a clean slate.'

She went to the kitchen table, pulled out a chair and sat down hard. He stayed where he was, his hands pushed into the pockets of his jeans. She tried to breathe.

'Tell them no,' she said. 'Tell them you can't serve time for something you didn't do. You have a child. You can't do it.'

'It's for the best, Ruth.'

'No, it's not!'

'There's no choice. This is the deal. I wouldn't do it otherwise.'

'The deal?'

'I could be out in five years, if I plead guilty, as it's my first offence.' He sniffed, and rubbed at his nose. 'I've fixed it so the two of you will be all right. You won't need to worry about any of it.'

The tap dripped over at the sink. Ruth slipped her left foot out of her shoe and rubbed at the place where it hurt. The coin had made a hole in her tights and a ladder ran all the way down the sole of her foot and up into her leg. Lee was staring at her, waiting for her to say something.

'Tell me I heard you wrong,' she said.

He didn't reply. The tap dripped.

'Let me see if I've got it straight, then.' She put her shoe back on and stood up. Pain shot up her legs as she walked towards him. 'You've done a deal, so your debts can be written off. A deal which means you won't be here while your son grows into a man. He'll be an adult by the time you get out. He'll be gone.'

Lee mumbled, avoiding her eye. 'He can always visit.'

'*Visit?* Are you serious?'

'I'll make it up to him.'

'No, you won't.' She pushed him hard with her palms against his chest. He took a step backwards. She pushed him again and he tensed against her. 'These are the years he needs you. He's getting big and lanky. He doesn't know himself. He needs you to help him through it.'

'Ruth. Stop that.' He reached for her and she lifted her arms to release his grip, then pushed him again, unbalancing him more easily than she'd expected. He fell back against the sink, stood up and reached for her again. 'Ruth, I need you to listen. Will you listen to me?'

They both looked up at the open kitchen door. There were footsteps further up in the house, which faded as they listened.

'Go ahead then,' she said.

'I lost more money than I let on. A lot more.'

The floor swung close and he pulled her against him, held her tight, his coat damp against her face.

'Did you hear me?' he said.

She nodded. 'How much?'

'It spiralled, Ruth.'

'Thousands?'

'Tens of thousands,' he said. 'Fifty or so.'

She felt acid rising up in her throat. His coat smelled of stale beer and cigarettes. 'I need to sit down, Lee.'

'I had no way of paying it off.'

'Lee, I need to—'

'There are people who want me dead.'

She twisted free of him and made it to the sink before she retched. Lee stood beside her and rubbed her back. She ran the tap and splashed her face, stood upright. The pipes hummed and clanked.

'Jesus, Lee.'

'I'm sorry,' he said.

'How can you lose that sort of money? How can you let that happen?'

'Listen.' He looked up at the door, and lowered his voice.

'I need you to listen now. This is important. I might not have long.'

She found she was crying. He held her upright, his arms tight around her, and she felt something bulky in the lining of his coat.

'I did have one last bet today,' he said.

She tried to push him away but he was holding her too tight.

'I had a win,' he said. 'I'm going to go upstairs now and put the money in the Quality Street tin. It's a lot of money, Ruth. They'll have a warrant, when they come for me, so you might want to bank some of it, hide some of it if you can. Hide it where the police won't look. Because it looks suspicious, that amount of cash. They might use it against me.'

She nodded, to show she was listening, but she was still hearing him say that he'd placed a bet: it was the way he'd said it, without apology. Her head swam.

'Did you hear me?'

'Yes,' she said.

'Tell me what I just said.'

She looked into his face. 'What's the crime you're going down for?'

'It doesn't matter about that.'

'It matters to me!'

'I had no part in it.'

'Nobody's going to believe that, are they?'

He turned from her and stood at the window, hands resting on the edge of the sink. Rain washed down the window pane. She noticed a bit of grey by his ears, and the retreat of his hairline.

'Armed robbery,' he said eventually.

'Armed *robbery*?'

'Will you keep your voice down?'

'The police are going to come here and arrest you for armed robbery?'

'Will you stop saying that?'

'Why? Do you think Cookie won't notice when the police arrive? Do you think you can stop him finding out?'

'I want to be the one who tells him,' he said. 'I don't want him hearing it from anyone else. Do you understand that?'

She did. She heard the shame in his voice and it blunted her anger. 'I'm not going to tell him. OK? I'll leave that to you.'

He exhaled. 'Thank you.'

From the staircase they heard footsteps going back up towards the first floor. Slow, careful footsteps. They stared at each other.

'Was that her?' Ruth looked at the door, then back at Lee. 'Do you think that was Mrs Lloyd?'

'Sounds like it.'

They listened as she made her way along the hallway on the first floor, then into her bedroom. Lee had gone white.

'She was there the whole time,' Ruth said.

'She'd better keep her mouth shut.'

'She won't.'

'Do you think she'd . . . ?'

'She'll tell Cookie if she gets a chance. I'd put money on it.' She caught herself. 'Sorry. I mean—'

'What?'

'She's got her claws into him,' Ruth said. 'She's been talking to him when he's alone here with her. Bad-mouthing us to him.'

'How do you know that?'

'I can tell. Things he's said. She's turning him against us.'

Lee went to the door and swung it open. 'Wait here a minute.'

'What are you going to do?'

'I'm going to tell him myself,' he said.

26

14 November 2008

The cold snap arrived on a Friday. Maxine opened the front door to find the sun rising over a bright frost: the bins, the parked cars and the wide expanse of the common all had a crisp white coating. She stood on the top step at the front of the house and took in the brightening sky and the sting of cold air. She must be over the flu, finally, because it was lovely. Even the low-flying planes were lovely, and the crows, and the queue of buses at the junction. She loved it the way she had never loved the Highlands, which everyone else loved. But then she had always loved the wrong things, and the wrong people.

Colin waved at her from the common, walking towards her in his combat trousers and his green bomber jacket, his woollen hat. The crows parted around him as he cut through the horse chestnuts. It was ten to eight.

'Morning,' he said, pushing the gate open.

She held the front door ajar for him as he walked up the path. Seb could sleep on for a bit. She'd woken in the night to find him shivering and anxious beside her, saying the shower was running on the top floor. She hadn't been sure if he was dreaming.

'Hi,' she said to Colin. He stood beside her on the top step, his breath white. 'Do me a favour and don't do too much hammering for an hour or so. Seb was awake half the night.'

'Sure.' He looked up at the house. 'Is he sick?'

'I don't know. Maybe. There's this flu going around.'

'I'll be quiet then,' he said. 'I'm an early riser, can't help it. I love this time of day.'

'Me too.'

'Best time for getting things done.'

She stamped her feet. It must have been close to freezing overnight. The common shone white, the sun diffused behind the trees.

'Hope the pipes don't freeze,' she said.

'They might. It's only going to get colder now.'

'Maybe you should order in the new pipes then.' She felt in her coat pocket for her gloves. 'Just so you're ready to get started.'

'Really?'

'I think so.'

He exhaled white mist down the steps. 'That's a big outlay, Max.'

'I know. We can cover it.'

'You sure?'

She pushed her fingers into her gloves. A plane crossed the sky. 'Seb's got an interview on Monday. I'm sure he'll get it. So.'

'Maybe we should wait and see, then. Make sure he's happy before I place the order, at least.'

'It's OK. I'll deal with that.'

He looked straight ahead at the common and blew into his hands.

'Is something wrong?' she said.

'I don't want to speak out of turn.'

'What do you mean?'

'Has he said anything to you? About the work I'm doing?'

She shook her head. She'd been getting home late from work, making up for the lost time while she was ill. Leaving the house while he slept.

'Come in,' she said. 'It's freezing. I'll make some coffee.'

'Don't you need to catch your train?'

'I can get a later one.' She pushed the door open and led the way down to the kitchen. She put the heater on and filled the kettle. Colin stood in the middle of the room with his hands in his pockets. When she looked at him, he looked away.

'What's going on?' She took milk from the fridge and mugs from the cupboard.

He sat down and took off his hat. Maxine stood by the kettle and he looked up at her before she could hide her surprise at his shaved head, dark with a growth of stubble. She tried to look away but she failed. He passed his hat from one hand to the other.

'Seb doesn't want me here, Maxine.'

She leaned back against the counter and put her gloves in her pocket. 'What makes you think that?'

'It's obvious.'

'Obvious how?'

'He suggested I was trying to rip you off.'

'What?'

'I'm surprised he hasn't said anything. He said he was going to.'

'Hold on. He said what?'

'He said I was trying to do more than we'd agreed. Letting the project grow and then billing you for more than you expected.' He turned in his chair, looked at the empty hallway, then turned back. 'He said that I must think you were a bit of a soft touch. That I thought maybe you had money and I could take advantage.'

Maxine took her own hat off and smoothed her hair down. 'I'm so sorry,' she said.

'He told me to stick to the decorating.'

'It's hard for Seb. He wants to contribute financially, and he feels bad that I'm paying for things while he's out of work.'

Colin leaned forward, arms on his knees, and held his hands out towards the heater. Maxine let herself look at the back of his head, where the shadow of his hairline met his collar. The jut of his bones.

'Or maybe he wants your money.' He said it quietly, without looking up, but Maxine heard it as if he'd spoken into her ear.

'Don't say that.'

'Sorry.' He glanced at her. 'Sorry. I shouldn't have said that.'

'No. You shouldn't.'

'He probably is just being protective of you. Wanting to be the one who pays for all this.'

'Of course he is.'

'Sure.' He looked back at the heater. 'I'm going to hold off ordering the pipes for now, if that's OK.'

'OK.'

'But I'll start prepping upstairs. I'll lift some of the boards. Maybe you could let Seb know you approved it.'

She made coffee, stirring in the milk. She heard what he'd said belatedly. 'I will,' she said.

'You all right?' He took the mug from her, holding it at the base, then he put it down on the table.

'Honestly, I don't know.' She lowered her voice. 'Things have been hard, since we moved in.' She trailed off. Colin looked at her, and she thought that he was exactly her type, with his long limbs and his dark blue eyes and his way of looking at her, like he recognised something in her, like he knew things she barely knew about herself. She'd thought it the first time he was here, when he'd helped her take that old sofa down from the loft. He'd told her about his background, how his family was from south London going back to when it was all woodland and marshes, too low and wet for houses. People died young back then, he'd said, what with all that water and fog; that's why the lowlands are so haunted. She'd laughed, but he'd been serious.

She held her coffee and blew on it. A shiver went through her, and he smiled.

'Thought you'd be used to this weather,' he said. 'Coming from Scotland.'

'Different sort of cold up there. More bracing.'

'Bracing,' he said. 'I like the sound of that.'

'You wouldn't last five minutes,' she said, and they both laughed, jittery with the cold.

'Do you miss it up there?'

'Not really. Don't tell my mother I said that. She'd disown me.'

'She must be proud of you, buying your own place?'

'I guess so. I still feel guilty though.'

'Why's that?'

'She's on her own since my dad died,' she said. 'She's moved house and I wasn't around to help her.'

He folded his hat on his knee, in half and half again. 'When did your dad die?'

'Eight years ago. Accident at work. He was a crane supervisor. He was killed by the swing of an overloaded crane.'

'Right. I'm sorry.'

'I miss him lately, more than I used to.'

'It goes like that,' he said. 'My dad died too. Ages ago, but I miss him more now I'm older.'

'Really?'

'There are things I want to ask him. Things he said that I didn't understand at the time.'

'Yes. Exactly that.'

'Should've paid more attention.'

She went to reply, but the floorboards creaked overhead and she listened as Seb went into the bathroom, flushed and ran the tap. Then he went back into the bedroom and Maxine pictured him sitting on the bed, reaching around for his glasses, yawning. Lying back down. He still hadn't carried the faulty heater out to the skip. She could have done it herself but it had become a sticking point, and every day when she got home to find it still there in the corner of the bedroom she wondered if he'd really forgotten or if he was just a total shit, if it really was as simple as that.

Colin was looking at her. She thought that he would take that heater out to the skip in two minutes flat if she asked him to. And he would be just as obliging if she took her clothes off. He turned his hat inside out, colour creeping up his neck, like he'd heard her have that thought. Like he knew that she was at the make-or-break moment in a relationship, and that the distraction of another man would help her to wind the thing up. Like he knew that she always did this.

Overhead, the plumbing hissed.

'How did you guys meet?' he said. 'You and Seb.'

'Online. A dating website.'

He nodded. Looked away.

'I didn't know anyone when I first moved to London,' she continued. 'Just my sister, but she's married with a toddler. So I thought I'd give it a go.'

He tapped his knee. He almost said something, then didn't.

'Can you look out for a delivery for me today?' She said it breezily, so that he wouldn't say it, whatever it was. 'I've been expecting a parcel for weeks. A present for my sister's new baby. The company aren't responding when I contact them.'

'Did you buy it online?'

She nodded, gulping her coffee.

'They probably went bust,' he said.

'Oh God. Do you think?'

'It's happening all over. Bankruptcies, redundancies, economies crumbling.' He shrugged a shoulder. 'You probably heard.'

'I did. Of course.'

'But I'll look out for the parcel, anyway.'

She tipped the rest of her coffee down the sink. 'I really should go, I need to get the next train.'

'Thanks for the coffee.'

'Make yourself at home, OK?'

'Will do,' he said as she left the room.

She went back into the hallway, put her gloves on and called out goodbye to Seb at the foot of the stairs. She left the house quickly, before he could come down to see her. She walked out into the cold morning, down the steps and onto Rye Lane, where police sirens met with birdsong, and she thought, *Love is a gamble, Maxine.* Her dad's voice. She wanted to ask him, how do you know if you've backed a loser? When do you stick and when do you twist? She should have asked him at the time. But instead she'd told him to stick his advice, to leave her alone. She'd sworn at him down the phone and hung up. The money from the industrial accident had gone equally to her and Lin, and she'd always felt that it wasn't rightfully hers. She'd tried to give it to her mother, but she had said she would rather starve.

A crow flew along the Rye, straight and steady as a plane.

On platform 3 she checked the departure board: ten minutes till the next train. She paced, her heels loud against the cold concrete. A woman in a long, duvet-like coat sat down on a bench and started applying make-up in a small mirror: mascara, then a dark red lipstick. Maxine stopped pacing and thought of Stella, the feature and the conversation they'd had that morning when they'd both come in early. She heard the word *slippery* and she thought, as the train was announced over the tannoy, that she had never once met Seb from work in all the time she'd known him. He'd never brought her along to the functions he got invited to, the fancy gatherings at the Guild Hall or Ascot. She'd never met any of his colleagues, not even Jason.

The thought was a quiet one, easily buried. It had gone from her head by the time she'd found a seat on the train and checked her emails. The stations flew by, and she stared at her phone. A message from Lin, who was nine months pregnant: *Come and see me before this baby drops!* Maxine thought of her sister's neat terraced house across town, bought because it was near a good school and didn't need any work. She had used their dad's money to pay off the bulk of the mortgage, because Lin never did anything messy or stupid, or self-destructive. Or mean or hurtful. Maxine replied: *Cross your legs! Free on Sunday?*

The train pulled into Blackfriars as an email popped up from Stella, sent to the whole team: Woolworths was about to announce bankruptcy. All its stores would close; there would be 27,000 job losses across the country. She typed a reply before she stepped onto the platform: *I can work late tonight if that helps.*

Waiting for the lift, she remembered the day she'd called Seb to tell him the rumour she'd heard, that Barclays had pulled out of the Lehman's takeover. His initial reaction had been strange. He'd been more shocked than she'd expected. And something else. Just for a second, she'd thought he sounded happy. Not remotely like a man whose career was about to implode. It nagged at her. It was possible, when you looked at it coldly, that he'd never even worked in the City.

She sat down at her desk, glad of the phones ringing, the distraction.

27

14 December 1994

Cookie sat down at the foot of the narrow stairs that led from the loft room to the second floor. From downstairs he heard his dad's voice, raised in urgency, and his mum saying something back. He put his chin on his knees and sat there listening. They were in the kitchen, he thought; he couldn't hear their words, just the rumble of their voices. He heard the rain on the roof. A plane. From the first floor he heard Mrs Lloyd come out of her room, the floorboards giving under her weight. She stood on the landing, listening to his parents, probably. After a while she carried on down the stairs, treading quietly.

He stood, and his dad said something else, louder than before. He stayed where he was, listening. It was dark, and Horatio was waiting behind the door for him, just along the landing. He was getting impatient. Cookie stared at the door and imagined the room behind it, the man in there who had killed his wife. He stepped closer and touched the door handle, felt the smooth, round shape of it in his hand.

Downstairs, his parents were quiet. He pulled his hand back, walked up and down the landing from the top of the stairs to the farthest room and back again. He considered the closed doors, then he touched each door handle in turn. He liked the fear, the shock of it. He felt his heart beat hard.

It sounded like his mum was crying now. He listened. It was the only sound in the house and it sounded like the end of everything.

He went to the farthest room again and repeated his circuit, turning the door handles this time, right then left. He felt the spring inside each one, the stretch as he turned it to the right, the release as he let go. When he got to the top of the stairs he could hear his mum: her voice was a shriek; she was losing it.

Cookie went to the door where the killer stood waiting. He felt sick, a vertigo feeling, because he knew he would do it; the push was stronger than the pull. He turned the handle quickly, expecting a face, a voice, but when the door opened there was no one there. Just a huge, bare room. He almost laughed. He went in, looked around. It was just a room. Green, ugly wall-paper. No pictures on the walls, no shelves or cabinets; no furniture at all, just a big fireplace and two windows, one covered by long curtains and the other letting in a pale light where the curtains were parted. He walked up and down on bare floorboards. It was quiet: no cars or planes or shouting. The door he'd come through was shut.

At the window the rain was heavy, falling hard against the pane. Cookie stood with the curtain at his back and wiped the window with his sleeve. It was dirty and he couldn't see much. He could make out the green of the common, the trees, the white of the sky. He stood closer. The street was deserted; it was like everyone had left. The curtain was heavy behind him and he rubbed again at the window. Through the rain he saw a long, dark line stretching across the common, all the way from the south to the north, crossing the road where it was surrounded by trees. A channel through the grass, he thought. He stood straighter. He was almost sure it was the river. The Peck.

It struck him then that it had been dark outside, before he came in here. The sky had been black.

Fear washed through him. He stepped back from the glass, afraid to turn or look away. The rain slowed, the pane cleared and when he edged closer the common was just an expanse of green under a white sky. No river cut through it; no dark line from south to north. It had gone.

He reached for the cord at the side of the pane. He wanted to see it again, to know if it had been real. He tugged on the cord but the pulley at the top was jammed, painted over and grey with dirt. He tried lifting the window open with his shoulder under the central frame, and when that didn't work he pushed with both hands from underneath. It wouldn't budge. He gave the window another shove, harder than before, and the pane cracked diagonally, a clean fracture that cut the scene in half. He dropped his arms.

When he turned the room was empty but he was not on his own. He stood by the window and he understood that everything had stopped in here a long time ago. It was a different time in this room, and the light came from another day. His heart thumped. The old man was always here and he was sad and sorry, so sorry that Cookie breathed it in, he drew it into his lungs. He was held there a while, the air thick with presence. When he crossed to the door he wasn't sure he had chosen to move.

Cookie stood on the landing, his hands clamped under his arms. His body shook. It was dark out here, and loud: the background roar of London; rain on the roof. He waited for the fear to go out of him, for his eyes to adjust. The shivers subsided. He held the bannister, leaned down into the stairwell, and his dad's voice reached him. It seemed like a year had passed, since he last saw him. He felt a swell of love for him, a big, easy love like the old days.

His dad was home.

He started down the stairs in the dark.

28

16 November 2008

Maxine let herself back into the house, wiped her feet on the mat and shook the worst of the rain off her coat. She'd got as far as the junction before she'd realised her iPod was in the pocket of her work bag, hanging on the bannister in the hallway. She took a minute to find it, and another minute to disentangle her headphones from the mess at the bottom of the bag. She turned for the door, which she'd left very slightly ajar. The traffic was light on Sundays, which is how she could hear Seb, down in the kitchen, talking on the phone. She stood at the door and she thought, He didn't notice me coming back in.

'I've told you,' Seb said. 'I can't get hold of the money. It's not going to happen.'

Maxine stood at the door and looked at the rain and the yellow trees on the common, the pewter sky. She tried not to listen. Everyone knows you shouldn't eavesdrop; you'll hear what you least want to. She lifted the latch, pushed her iPod into her pocket, and his voice reached her again before she could walk away.

'I've told her I've got an interview in the morning,' he said. 'I feel like such a bastard, Jason. It's getting so I can't look her in the eye.'

She left the house before he could say anything else. She slammed the door, ran down the steps and through the gate, pulled her hood up against the rain. She was still waiting for it to make sense, to be nothing, a misunderstanding. She stood a moment at the gate in case he came out of the house and begged her to let him explain. But he didn't.

At the junction she stood sightlessly at the kerb until everyone else crossed. She walked past the huge weeping willows, the open shopfronts, the fruit and veg out on display: yam, aubergines, plantain, onions. She waited at the crossing, where the Nags Head stood at the turn in the road. A bus pulled up and she stared at the driver behind his window; the wipers squeaked against the soft spit of rain. She thought, Seb was talking to Jason, his boss from his Lehman's job. She had taken a dislike to Jason, despite never having met him. Something about the frequency of his phone calls, the way Seb jumped when Jason's number came up on his phone. The way Seb defended him when she suggested Jason was more demanding than a boss ought to be, that the boundaries were blurred. He'd be nothing without Jason, he'd told her.

The bus driver sounded his horn and she realised she didn't need to cross. 'Sorry!' she mouthed at him, and he held both hands up in response.

She kept walking. The pavements were crowded. She stepped onto the kerb, avoiding several sacks of basmati rice stacked on pallets at the side of a shop. A woman holding her child by the hand pushed past, apologising, and Maxine stepped into the gutter, sending a tide of rainwater inside her trouser leg. She felt the cold water against her calf, the creeping damp inside her shoe as she walked on, past a narrow shopfront with mobile phone cases out on display, an electronic sign that said *Bargain Prices Today!* Her trouser leg clung to her shin and she thought of the wardrobe in their bedroom, a garment bag with Seb's suit inside it, the one with the fine pin-stripe that he'd worn to his interview with Merrill Lynch. The trousers had been flecked with mud.

A slow heat passed through her body, emptying her head so she knew nothing at all except for the trousers and the wardrobe, the mud splashed over the fabric, the way it had flaked against her fingers. Seb's notebook, filled with obscure historical facts, pages and pages of obsessive research. She kept walking. She didn't know where she was going or why. She saw sodden cardboard boxes piled high against a disused phone box. A wall of graffiti leading to a car park. A man with a crutch, begging with one outstretched hand. There had been no interview with Merrill Lynch; he'd lied about it, of course he had, she'd halfway known it for weeks. The interview tomorrow was a lie too. He wasn't looking for work.

She burst into tears outside the Halifax. People stopped, looked at her in concern, and she shook her head and motioned them away. A little boy stared at her from his mother's hip and his face crumpled as she tried to smile at him. She wiped her eyes but she was still crying. She had fallen for a liar. The alarm bells had been ringing and she'd silenced them because she had wanted so much to make this work, to get it right this time. She wondered when he'd started lying. If all of it had been a lie.

'You all right?'

Maxine looked up to see a familiar face: an older woman, sixty or so, with short, greying hair and wild eyebrows. She was holding Maxine by the elbow, guiding her out of the rain.

'Come and stand here,' the woman said.

Maxine stood beside her at the front of the bookies, in a narrow space that was protected by the small overhang of the flat above.

'June,' the woman said. 'Remember me? You came in the other day and I sent you packing.'

Maxine nodded, and it came back to her that she'd tried to interview this woman for her gambling feature.

'I remember,' Maxine said.

'What's up then?' June cupped her hand around her cigarette and flicked her lighter. 'One of those days?'

'Guess so.'

'Hope it's not because I wouldn't give you an interview.'

'Would you change your mind if I said it was?'

'Nice try.' June inhaled deeply, then she held her cigarette at her side, out of the rain. 'Why don't you make something up? That's what they normally do, isn't it?'

'I'd rather not,' Maxine said. She was losing faith in the feature being written. The whole thing seemed unlikely, part of the fantasy she'd spun for herself. She'd thought she could be a career woman, with a nice house and a good man who adored her. She was so stupid. Her life was a joke.

'Don't take the hump,' June said. 'I was only kidding.'

'I know.'

'Only you can't walk into the bookies and ask questions like that.'

'I can't ask about gambling in the bookies?'

'No.' June looked at her. 'You need to hedge around it.'

'How would I do that?'

'I don't know. You're the journalist.'

A gust of wind blew down the high street, lifting sheets of newspaper into the air. Rain hit the side of Maxine's face, and she thought of the time that Seb had taken her to Rome for the weekend, an impromptu trip to get away from the British weather. They'd stayed in a tastefully expensive boutique hotel and she had tried not to show her shock at the world he was part of, where a holiday didn't have to be planned or saved for. Seb had insisted on paying for everything. It must have cost a fortune. At the Colosseum, under an ancient archway, he'd said that he loved her; that he hoped one day she would marry him. When she thought of it, she still got the same stomach flip.

He did love her. And there had been money, at the start, anyway.

'I grew up around here,' June said now. 'I'm not going to tell you people's business.'

Maxine put her head down against the rain. 'Maybe you

could tell me about the way things have changed since you've worked here. Some of the things you remember.'

June took her cigarettes back out of her coat pocket and offered one to Maxine. 'Smoke?'

'No, thanks.'

'I'll tell you one thing that's changed around here, and not for the better.' She tapped ash onto the pavement. 'You can put it in your article.'

'What's that?'

'You have to stop work to smoke outside, in all weathers. You could catch your death.'

'That's not really the angle I'm going for.'

'And don't tell me to try vaping.'

'I wasn't going to,' Maxine said.

'Because I'm not interested. Do I look like I want to try vaping?'

'I guess not.'

'Have you tried it?'

'I haven't.'

'My son's into it. I said to him, You don't know what you're inhaling into your lungs. Could be anything in there.'

The door to the shop opened at her side and Maxine looked up to see a man coming out, short and big-bellied, a folded newspaper under his arm. 'See you, June,' he said.

'See you later, Harry,' June replied.

He turned in the direction of the library, overtaking a woman in full-length batik with a child strapped to her back.

'It would be off the record,' Maxine said. 'If you told me anything.'

'Here we go.'

'You obviously know everyone.'

'I do.'

'It doesn't need to be anything scandalous.'

'I know exactly what you're after.' June pointed her cigarette down the street. 'You want stories of people who've got themselves into debt and ruined their lives. People who started out decent and ended up criminals. All that.'

'Sometimes people want to talk about it,' Maxine said.

'The ones who go that route are mostly dead, to be honest.'

'Fair enough.' Maxine stepped out onto the pavement. Her head ached from crying. She wanted to be wrong about all of it, so she could go home and make coffee and watch a black-and-white film with Seb under the duvet.

'Chin up,' June said.

The door to the shop opened again. Maxine stared down the street, bracing herself for a sprint to the sports centre, where at least they had hot showers. She heard June saying hello, and then she heard Colin's voice, unmistakably him, and she turned around to see him looking at her.

'Thought that was you, Maxine,' he said. 'You OK?'

'Just on my way to the sports centre.' June was looking at her with renewed interest. She took a step backwards. Her trainers were full of water. 'Going for a swim.' She knew this was funny, that she was drenched already, but the sight of him did something to her and she started crying again before she could stop herself.

Colin moved closer. 'What's happened?'

211

'Nothing.' She shook her head. 'Sorry.'

'Did you argue with Seb?'

'No. It's not that.'

'What's he done?'

'Nothing. I mean, I don't know.' She wiped her face on her damp sleeve.

'Shall I walk you home?'

'No, don't worry.'

'OK.' He glanced at June, then he said, 'Do you have anywhere else to stay, Max? If you need to?'

She nodded. She realised she couldn't face the sports centre, with its shabby changing rooms; matted hair in the drains. 'I could go to my sister's.'

'I'll walk you to the station, then, shall I? Can you get there on the train?'

She felt a surge of relief. 'OK. If you're going that way.'

'Sure.'

She turned to June, who crushed her cigarette under her shoe. She looked at Maxine in concern. 'Good luck with your article,' June said. 'Take care of yourself.'

'Thanks. You've got my card, in case you think of anything.'

'I have.' She pulled the door to the shop open. Across the street, a man tapped a microphone and shouted louder than he needed to: *The banks have robbed the people!*

Colin stood waiting for her. 'I was at school with her kids,' he said, pointing at the spot where June had stood. 'Her eldest was in my year at school. We were good mates for a while. Both went a bit off the rails in our teens. Then we lost touch.'

212

He walked alongside her, big loping strides that she tried to match. 'Did he move away?'

'No, I did, for a bit. When I came back, everyone my age was married with kids.'

'Most of my friends from home are too.' She stepped around a stack of sodden newspapers, bound in tape and left abandoned in the street. 'I'm the only one who can't seem to find someone.'

He stared down at his feet as they walked. 'I know you probably don't want to tell me what's going on.'

'Not really.'

'But I think you're a good person and I don't like seeing you like this.' The pavement was crowded and he held back to let her pass ahead of him. When he reached her side again he said, 'I don't like the idea that someone would take advantage of you.'

They turned into the entrance to the station, past all the rough sleepers, huddled against the wall in blankets. People running to escape the rain. She walked the long way around a dirty-looking puddle, although her feet couldn't have been more wet. Colin jumped the puddle and she met him in the ticket hall, which was quieter than usual, and dimly lit, the kiosks closed. Sunday, she remembered. A tannoy announced a cancellation on platform 3.

'What makes you think Seb's taking advantage of me?' She said it quietly, and he bent his neck towards her, straining to hear. 'Why do you think that about Seb?'

'I'm there all day, Maxine. I hear him on the phone.'

She looked down at her feet, so she didn't have to see his face. 'What did you hear him saying?'

'He's trying to find money. A lot of money.'

'Right.'

He paused, and she looked up at him. 'Don't be angry with me for asking this,' he said. 'When your dad died, did he leave you money?'

She stared at him. He nodded, so she didn't have to answer.

'I thought so,' he said.

'Seb's never asked me for money.'

'Of course he hasn't.'

'What does that mean?'

'Max, I could be wrong about this. I don't want to—'

'Just say it.'

'I mean, you hear about these scams, don't you? Men who find women online. Women who are lonely, looking for a relationship. They spend money on you and make you feel loved and then the next thing you know the money's run out and—'

'OK. I don't need to hear this.'

'Sorry.'

She felt numb as she patted her coat pockets, looking for her travel pass. She couldn't think. The tannoy announced her train and she took her backpack off her shoulders and checked the pockets, her fingers clumsy.

'Fuck.' She was crying again. 'Can't find it.'

'Try your pocket,' he said softly. 'Your jeans.'

She reached into the back pocket of her jeans and found the travel pass. She didn't look at him as she went through the barriers.

'Will I see you tomorrow?' he said.

214

She turned and faced him. He had his hands in the pockets of his bomber jacket, hunched against the cold. 'Not sure,' she said. 'Do you have enough to do, at the house?'

'I can lift a few more boards. It's fine.' He held up his hand and started walking backwards towards the exit. 'See you,' he said.

She took the steps two at a time all the way up to the platform and made the train as the doors were closing. She found a seat and stared out of the window at Victorian terraced houses, walled gardens, small patches of lawn and patio. People cooking and talking and watching TV behind softly lit windows. She was so cold. Her jeans were wet against her legs. She thought of Seb, the way he'd looked after her when she was sick. Reading to her on the sofa. Nerdy, lovely Seb.

But he had tried to finish with her, early on, and he'd changed his mind after that date when she'd told him about her dad. About the money he'd left her, the financial settlement. He'd come home with her after that date. He'd stayed the whole weekend.

Her hands were stiff with cold as she took her phone out of her bag. She sent him a text.

29

16 November 2008

Seb picked up the faulty heater and looped the flex around his arm so it didn't drag on the floor. He got it to the bottom of the stairs before he had to take a breather. It was a huge, cumbersome thing, with wire mesh over the filaments, covered in grimy dust. He put his coat on. Leaves blew into the house as he opened the door and he had to turn sideways as he walked down the steps, so he didn't get an eyeful of grit. He had a hard time lifting the heater into the skip with the wind in his face. He stood for a minute and watched it settle itself against the rubble and the rolls of carpet, the broken-up strips of plywood.

'Seb!' Clare strode towards him with Vinnie at her heel. She had her hood up, her hair pushed inside it, her jeans tucked into green wellington boots.

'Hi,' he said.

'Are you off for a walk?'

'Maybe.' He zipped up his coat. 'Looks a bit blowy.'

She smiled. 'Don't go out on the common without your wellies on. It's always a lake at this time of year.'

'True,' he said. 'That's the Peck.'

'The what?'

'The River Peck.' He stood beside her and pointed out at the waterlogged grass. 'It was culverted a long time ago. Channelled into a sewer. But it rises back to the surface when it rains.'

She looked at him doubtfully.

'It would have been there when our houses were first built, running right across the common.' He traced the line of it with his finger. 'It would have met the Thames at some point. I haven't figured out its exact course yet.'

'Sounds rather lovely.'

'It probably was at first, but then all these houses were built without proper drainage. The river would have been an open sewer after a while.'

'Gosh.' She pulled a face. 'I didn't know any of this.'

'I've been researching it, over the past few weeks.'

'Have you?' She ran her hand around the inside of her hood, pushing her hair back inside. 'How come?'

'I'm looking into the history of the house. I've got all the records going back to when it was built. Every census, every marriage, birth and death.'

'How marvellous.'

'The census stops at 1901, so I thought I might try the national archives for the most recent records.'

Clare looked down at Vinnie, who was sitting obediently at her side. She scratched at the fur between his ears.

217

'Unless you can help me,' he said.

'What's that?'

'Unless you can help me.' He smiled at her as she straightened back up. 'You mentioned you knew the previous owner. You said her name was Diana.'

'Ah. Yes.' She looked up at the house. 'I possibly shouldn't have mentioned it, actually. Tactless of me.'

'Not at all.'

'I don't know anything really.'

'You mentioned she had lodgers.'

'Did I?'

'Yes.' He nodded, and her face fell. 'You did say that.'

A bus passed, then a white van, both of them slowing at the junction. The lights changed and several pedestrians crossed, parents dragging their children by the hand.

'It was donkeys ago.' She looked down into the skip. 'Early nineties, I think.'

'Did one of the lodgers kill Diana?'

'Yes.' She nodded, staring down at the rubble. 'Yes, he did.'

He stood very still beside her with his hands in his pockets. He felt shock spread through his body, and at the same time he found that he had known this all along. He'd always known something bad had happened in the house.

'I didn't mention it when we talked before,' Clare said. 'People don't always want to know that sort of thing.'

'I wanted to know.'

'Maxine didn't. She shut me down, when I tried to tell her, shortly after you moved in. She changed the subject.'

'She does that,' he said, and he thought of Maxine, holding a cardboard box, asking if there was something going on with him. He'd brushed her off and she hadn't pushed it. Any other woman would have seen through him long ago.

'I thought, fair enough. They don't need to know what happened,' Clare said.

'What did happen?'

Clare shut her eyes a moment as the wind picked up. 'Diana was murdered. He didn't deny it. He told the police he'd shoved her down the stairs.'

'Do you remember his name?'

She shook her head. 'He was always down at the Kings Arms on the corner. It was a meeting place for criminals, that pub. The police must have raided it once a week.'

The heater rocked in the skip and fell onto its side, settling under the old sofa from the loft. Clare didn't move.

'I can picture him. Shifty-looking. Bad posture.' She looked up, raised a finger. 'Delaney. Lee Delaney. That was his name.'

'Delaney. OK.'

'They were a family of three. Parents and a young boy. Awful people. Noisy. Always shouting and slamming doors. Lee Delaney was into gambling, it turns out, and he got so far into debt that he ended up in trouble with the police.'

'Gambling?' His mouth went dry.

'I know. Awful.'

'Is he in prison?'

'Dead. Never got as far as prison, as I recall.'

Seb stared ahead of him at the trees on the common, luminescent against the grey sky: tangerine orange, fizzy lemon yellow. They rocked side to side in the wind.

'Thanks. You've been very helpful.' He took a step back from the skip. 'Where was the pub you mentioned? The Kings Arms?'

'It was on the corner, at the junction.' She turned and pointed. 'They had to pull it down in the end. They built flats on that corner and the criminals went elsewhere.' She laughed. 'Underground, probably.'

Seb looked at the low-rise flats on the corner of the junction. Someone's light came on in a downstairs window. 'It's still happening,' he said.

'What is?'

'The history of the house.' He made a circular movement with his hand. 'It's repeating.'

'I don't understand.'

'This has happened before.'

'What's that?' She squinted at him. 'Are you all right?'

He looked at her, recalibrated. 'Yep.'

'You're being strange.'

'Am I?'

'Are you sleeping?'

'Not really.' A gust of wind blew rain into his face. He took off his glasses and wiped them against his sleeve. 'Money worries. You know.'

'No luck with the job hunt?'

He shook his head. 'I think I need to move on.'

'What do you mean?'

'Nothing. I don't know.'

Clare looked concerned, or confused; he wasn't sure through the rain on his glasses. He stepped away and she waved as Vinnie pulled her up the steps to her front door. 'You'll get soaked,' she said.

'Send a search party if I'm not back in an hour.'

Clare laughed, waved again, and he crossed the road and walked along the edge of the common, where the wet grass gave under his feet. He stopped at the waste bin and emptied his pockets: two more letters, both marked *Return to Sender*. He didn't dare put them into the recycling in case Maxine saw them. It seemed absurd now, that he'd thought he might tell her, that he'd thought he might trace where he came from. If his family were getting his letters, they didn't want to hear from him. He was glad he knew. He could bear it as long as he didn't have to tell anyone, to feel their sympathy or their surprise.

He thought of Horatio, who had come from nothing, who had died in that house, who was still there. Horatio knew him; Seb had felt this for a while. Horatio's mistakes were his own.

It was raining hard. He sat down on a bench in the park and shut his eyes. A wood pigeon called out from the trees. No matter where he was, no matter the distance he put between himself and the house, he always knew where it was in relation to him. He could feel it now: behind the trees and the open stretch of the common, standing tall and vigilant. He knew that it held him in its story, that he would never be free of it.

His phone beeped in his pocket. Then again. He didn't open his eyes. He knew Max had heard him on the phone; he'd heard the door slam shut and he'd sat at the kitchen table for ages, scared and ashamed, trying to decide what to say to her. He thought that he might sit here until she got back from the sports centre, and he would tell her he had loved her from the start; he had lied about a lot of things, but he had never lied about that.

Another beep from his pocket. This time he looked. All three were from Maxine.

Staying at Lin's tonight.

Home tomorrow.

Don't be there unless you want to tell me what's really going on.

30

14 December 1994

Cookie met his dad on the first floor. Lee was in a hurry, taking the stairs two at a time. He stopped when he saw Cookie, and looked up and down the landing. Cookie wasn't sure what to say. He wanted his dad to stop running, to stay here with him.

'I saw the river,' Cookie said.

Lee looked back at him, distracted. 'What's that?'

'The River Peck. I saw it.'

'Right.' He caught his breath. 'Did you?'

'It goes right across the common, like you said.'

Lee smiled, and rubbed his jaw. 'That's good to hear. I wasn't sure you'd remember that.'

'I did.'

'Good lad.' He reached out and held Cookie by the shoulder, then he pulled him closer, his arm strong against Cookie's back. 'It does cross the common, that's right,' Lee said, and Cookie put his arms inside his dad's coat, turned his face into the collar of his shirt. Lee closed his arms around him. 'You can't stop a river running through a valley, Cooks.'

'I know.' He breathed. 'There's always been a river here.'

The house was quiet and dark. Cookie shut his eyes and thought of the river, the way it cut through the grass and continued north, a dark channel across the common. He *had* seen it. He was certain of it. He felt his dad's heartbeat, his wiry body, strong and lean. He smelled of stale beer and second-hand smoke and Cookie loved him.

'They didn't have proper drainage, these old houses,' Lee said. 'Clay soil-pipes and drains made for rainwater. All that waste would have ended up in the river. Would have stunk, after a while.'

Cookie nodded, remembering the next part: 'So they buried it.'

'They did.' Lee turned his body towards a sound from down-stairs: shoes on the tiled floor. 'Listen,' he said. 'There's something I need to tell you, son. It's important.'

'What?'

Lee hesitated as Ruth ran up the stairs, heavy on her feet. He couldn't seem to find the words he needed. 'I'm glad you saw it,' he eventually said. 'That's all.'

Ruth reached the landing and Cookie dropped his arms, stepped away from his dad. 'What did you say to him?' Ruth asked.

'I said, I'm glad he saw it,' Lee said. He looked at Cookie, and Cookie knew his dad wanted it to stay between them; he knew the river was their private thing. Later, he would try to recall the exact words his dad had used as they'd stood together on the landing. He would try to guess at the things his dad seemed about to say. It was the conversation that would sound through his whole life.

'Saw what?' Ruth said. She still had her coat on, and her hair was coming loose from its band. She looked angry, like her fuse had gone, Cookie thought. She looked like she wanted a fight.

'I went into the big room up there,' Cookie said, pointing to the floor above.

'Did you?' Ruth said. 'What's in there?'

'It's just an empty room. No furniture. Just two windows with long curtains.'

'Empty?'

Cookie nodded.

'Sounds very nice.' She raised her voice then, and turned her head in the direction of Mrs Lloyd's bedroom, just a few yards away along the landing. 'Must be nice to have big, empty rooms in your house that you don't need.'

'Don't, Ruth,' Lee said.

'Nice, big rooms with nothing in there,' Ruth continued. 'Must be lovely.'

'Ruth, for God's sake.'

'Shame some of us have to live on top of each other, when there's empty space not being used.'

There was movement then from behind the door: a creak of upholstery. They all turned as the door opened. Cookie looked away when she stepped onto the landing and caught his eye. She had on the same red tracksuit with the gold zip, and her fleece-lined slippers. He stepped backwards, closer to his dad.

'Did you want to say something to me?' Mrs Lloyd said. She switched on the light, and squinted at them all: Cookie in his uniform, his parents in their coats, damp and bulky.

'My son was telling me there's a huge, empty room up there,' Ruth said. 'Nothing in there at all.'

'Those rooms are out of bounds,' Mrs Lloyd said. She pulled down the top of her tracksuit, and she looked at Cookie.

'Out of bounds. Really.' Ruth gestured up the stairs towards their own room. 'I know you've been snooping around up in the loft. The door was unlocked when I got home from work today.'

'I wasn't snooping,' Mrs Lloyd said.

'You came in while we were out. You had no business doing that. That's our private space. It's all we have.'

Mrs Lloyd moved closer to where they stood at the top of the stairs. Cookie and his dad took a step back. 'I wasn't snooping,' she said. 'I went up there because Cookie's alarm clock was going off. He didn't switch it off before he left this morning.'

'That's not true. His alarm goes off early.'

'He was up earlier than usual today,' Mrs Lloyd said. There was a smile in her voice, although Cookie didn't look up. 'He didn't turn his alarm off before he came down. Did you?'

Cookie felt his parents' eyes on him. He hung his head.

'The beep was getting on my nerves. I went in to turn it off, and while I was there I took the heater to get it fixed. I called

Derek at Rye Electrics and he wants me to bring it down to him later in the week. He thinks it's probably the thermostat.'

Cookie looked up at Mrs Lloyd and saw that her smile was uneasy. She was looking at him to back up what she'd said.

'I wish you'd told me sooner,' she said to Cookie, and he looked away.

'Told you what?' Ruth said. She turned to Cookie. 'What does she mean?'

'Ruth,' Lee said. 'Let's leave this here.'

Mrs Lloyd pushed past Ruth, went to the top of the stairs and held onto the newel post. Cookie saw the bones in her hand, the spread of her fingers and the pinch of her rings against her flesh. He made the mistake of looking at her face and she met his gaze, confused and afraid.

'We don't enjoy living like this, you know,' Ruth said. 'It's not good for a marriage. Not good for any of us.'

Mrs Lloyd moved back an inch, still holding the newel post. 'You saw the room before you moved in. I told you I didn't think it would suit a family. I only—'

'I didn't know—' Ruth shouted over her, and all the muscles stood out in her neck.

'—I only said yes to help you out. I even dropped the rent for you.'

'—I didn't know you'd be lording it over us,' Ruth said. 'With your empty rooms and your fancy bathtub.'

'My fancy bathtub?'

'I haven't had a decent shower in months. Do you know that?'

Mrs Lloyd took a step backwards, her foot on the next stair down, her hand on the bannister. 'Well, *I* haven't had a rent payment in months,' she said. 'Do you know that?'

Ruth spluttered. 'That's not true. I leave your rent money on the kitchen table.'

'Do you?' She looked from Ruth to Lee, who was standing behind Cookie now. 'I wonder what could have happened to it?'

'I work hard for that money,' Ruth said, leaning down towards Mrs Lloyd. 'I work long hours. On my feet all day. I have to watch every penny. My son goes to school on an empty stomach. But I always' – she paused to inhale – 'I *always* pay the rent!'

'Ruth.' Lee put his hands on Cookie's shoulders. 'Let's leave this now.'

'You might want to talk to your husband about where the money could have gone. You might find he knows—'

'Don't,' Ruth shouted, close to tears now. 'I know what you're doing. Don't think I haven't figured it out.'

'What's that?' Mrs Lloyd lifted her chin.

'Trying to come between us.'

'What nonsense.'

'I know you've been talking to my son,' Ruth said. 'Trying to turn him against us.'

Mrs Lloyd held on tighter to the handrail. 'That's not really how it went,' she said.

'What do you mean?' Ruth turned to Cookie. 'What does she mean?'

'Mrs Lloyd,' Cookie said. He didn't know what he planned

228

to say. He hoped she might stop talking, but she smiled at him and her smile was a sort of betrayal.

'Haven't I told you,' she said, with a wink. 'Call me Diana.'

'I knew it!' Ruth said, and her voice became shrill. 'What have you said to her?'

Cookie stepped closer to Mrs Lloyd. He tried to signal to her, to show in his face that he wanted her to stop. He was hot with regret for the things he'd told her; he would do anything to take it all back.

'We had a nice talk, that's all,' Mrs Lloyd said. 'We're friends. Aren't we, Cookie?'

'What have you said to her?' Ruth asked him. She was crying.

'Nothing.' Cookie stood at the top of the stairs, looking down at the thinning carpet, the black and white tiles at the bottom. 'I didn't say anything.'

Mrs Lloyd was still for a moment. Cookie could see her at the edge of his vision, hopeful and surprised. He stared down the staircase, willing her to drop it, to go away.

'I'll leave you to it,' Mrs Lloyd said, and finally she turned and took one step down, her slippered feet treading carefully. 'You don't have long, I shouldn't think. Since the police are on their way.'

Cookie felt the air in the house sharpen. Behind him, his dad's body tensed.

'I didn't tell her anything,' Cookie said, but the lie was there in his voice. He said it again and his voice was thin, unconvincing. His dad was at his side, trying to push past him. His mum shouted his dad's name. He saw Mrs Lloyd treading down

229

the stairs, quickening her step; her white hair and the fragile shell of her skull.

She had called the police. He had said too much; he'd told her everything and she had betrayed him.

'Fuck you,' Cookie said to her retreating back. His mum reached out and grabbed him by the arm, but he pulled away from her. His dad was beside him on the second step from the top. Cookie felt his dad's rage, the hard heat of it. 'We're not friends,' Cookie said, but his dad wasn't listening to him. 'We're not friends,' he repeated, 'we're not! It's not true.'

31

16 November 2008

Lin sat beside Maxine on the green corduroy sofa in her small terraced house, with her hands resting on the dome of her stomach. She was three days overdue and she looked tired and huge and beautiful, Maxine thought. Her skin was plush and her hair was shiny, pulled up into an off-centre topknot. Maxine wore Lin's pyjamas and a white towelling dressing gown and she felt cleaner and warmer than she had in months. She felt rescued. The whole mess of her life was neutralised by Lin's oatmeal carpets and the hum of the central heating.

'Tell me exactly what you heard Seb say,' Lin said. 'Use the same words you heard him use.'

Maxine remembered standing at the door, her hand on the latch. 'He said: "I can't get hold of the money. It's not going to happen."'

'Could he be behind with a loan or something?'

'Possibly.'

'What else did he say?'

She didn't want to say the words he'd said next. She couldn't bear to hear them in her own head. She ran her fingernail between the narrow stripes of corduroy in the arm of the sofa, back and forth, and she thought of Colin, sitting with his back to her in the kitchen, saying that maybe Seb wanted her money.

'Max? What else did he say?'

'He said that he'd told me he had an interview in the morning. And that he hated lying to me.'

'Right.' Lin gave a long exhale. 'Do you think he's got an interview then?'

'No, I don't think so.'

'Really?'

'I don't think he's even looking for work.'

Lin stared across the room at the TV, where a kids' TV show was paused in a blur of colour and movement. 'Remind me again why you didn't ask him what he meant?'

'I just panicked. I didn't want to hear any more.'

'But now you're here, imagining all sorts.'

'I should have asked him,' Maxine said. 'I know.'

'If Eliot was acting shifty and I thought he was telling me a pack of lies, I'd ask him what was going on.' She raised her voice, as if imagining this confrontation. 'I wouldn't shut up until he told me.'

'I know that's what you'd do. And Eliot wouldn't lie to you, anyway. You know that.'

'But why didn't you ask him?'

'I just wimped out.'

'Right.' Lin turned, shifting around on the sofa, and squinted at Maxine as if she were a mile away. 'Is there something else here that I'm missing? You were sure about Seb, I thought. You were going in big. Next stop babies and wedding bells.'

'And now I'm not sure.'

'You said he was different. He's like no one else, you said.'

'I know.' She felt her throat tightening. 'I was sure about the house too, but that's turned into a nightmare.'

'Oh, God. OK.'

'My judgement's off. I don't trust myself, Lin. I'm a disaster.'

'I feel like you're waiting for me to disagree.'

'I'm waiting for you to tell me there's nothing to be scared of.'

'You need to figure that out yourself, Maxine. Talk to Seb, give him a chance to explain.'

They heard Eliot upstairs, talking patiently to Rudy, who was three years old, or *free-and-free-corners*, as he'd told Maxine earlier. Rudy was chatty and adorable and he liked to start the day promptly at five. She heard him laughing, the squeak of his body in the bath.

'You know, Dad told me to be brave,' Maxine said.

'Did he?'

'He told me to be brave enough to fall in love. It was his one bit of parental guidance.'

'That's more guidance than he ever gave me.'

'You're already brave, Lin.'

'That's because I don't have any choice.' Lin looked down at herself and ran her hand over the bump, the stretched weave of her sweater. 'I wake up every morning convinced today's the day Rudy's going to swallow a battery or run out in front of a car or fall from a window.'

'Really?'

'Or develop an allergic rash that I won't notice in time. Or pull on the handle of a boiling saucepan.' She nodded in the direction of the bathroom upstairs. 'Or drown.'

'God.'

'There's more, obviously. Fire hazards and choking hazards and child sex traffickers. I don't know what the hell I'm going to do when I've got two of them. I really don't.'

Maxine reached out a hand and Lin took it. 'It'll be OK,' she said, uselessly. 'I don't think I could do it. But you can.'

'You could do it.'

'You must be kidding.'

'I'm not. If it came to it, you would cope. Your judgement would kick in and you would cope.'

Maxine stretched out her legs and ran her toes through the rug. Rain hit the window behind them. She thought of Colin walking beside her, on the way to the station. He hated Seb. It was unnerving, that he saw something bad in him, something she had failed to see.

'Fear is helpful,' Lin said.

'Maybe I should be more afraid, then.'

Lin squeezed her hand. They sat quietly side by side for a while, each with their own thoughts.

'That's not what I mean,' Lin said. 'I mean, don't push fear away. Let it help you.'

'I don't know how to do that.'

'You need to let your guard down.'

'Do I?'

'I think so. You're a bit . . .' She searched for the word, tutting at herself. 'Guarded,' she said. 'You're a bit guarded.'

'Am I?'

'You are.' Lin's eyes started to close. They listened to Rudy in the bath, asking endless questions, Eliot's gentle replies.

'I bought a present for the baby but it hasn't arrived,' Maxine said. 'I think the company went bust.'

'Doesn't matter.'

'It was the cutest thing on the internet.'

'Did it have small parts?'

'I don't know. Maybe.'

'I would have had to hide it then. Choking hazard. I've hidden pretty much everything Mum's bought for Rudy,' Lin said, under her breath. 'Don't tell her.'

'OK.'

Upstairs, Eliot said something quietly to Rudy, and Rudy said, *Why?*

'He's in his *Why?* phase,' Lin said, without opening her eyes. 'It's helped me to realise that I don't know anything at all. Literally nothing. All those years in education, completely pointless.'

Maxine wondered if Lin was going to fall asleep there and then, sitting upright on the sofa. Her head tilted back very slightly and her lips parted. From the landing, Rudy's *Why?* became tearful, high-pitched. Eliot's voice rose, and Rudy's cries rose accordingly. Lin pushed herself upright with her eyes shut, stumbled across the room and climbed the stairs.

32

5 July 1843

Horatio knew he was sick when Archer showed his sons into the drawing room. They filed in, eyes down, and stood either side of the window. They greeted him, one by one. James met his eye only briefly but William stared, his face soft and afraid. Horatio knew it must be warm at the window with the sun at their backs. It was mid-summer and the grass out on the Rye was a parched yellow-green. But he was not warm. He rested his hands palm-down on the blanket that covered his knees and wondered if they had been told he would die.

'Thank you for coming to see me.' He sounded like a dying man. 'Sit down,' he said, nodding at the chairs arranged around the fireplace.

William went to sit but James stood still with his eyes fixed on the wall before him, where their mother's portrait hung. William looked at James, then at Horatio. He did not sit.

'I was not expecting you,' Horatio said. 'Not for a week or more.'

'Archer came for us in a carriage,' William said.

'Did he?' He coughed, and was seized with the dry pull of it, the painful rasp on the inhale. When it passed he looked again at William and did his best to smile. His muscles ached. 'Archer fetched you, did he?'

William nodded. He might cry, Horatio thought. He saw himself in the boy: his softness, his need of reassurance. William still had the boyish want to climb into his father's lap; he could see it from here, he recognised it in his face. He wished he knew how to take this softness from him, how to help him become a man. He would be thirteen on his next birthday. Horatio wished that he would sit down beside him, where he could see him properly, without the glare of the sun at the window.

'Are you unwell, Papa?' William asked.

'I believe so.' Horatio wiped his damp palms against the blanket. 'It is the miasma from the river. It has penetrated the house, and found its way into my blood.'

Both boys were quiet at this. William's brow was damp, his eyes glassy.

'I trust your studies are coming along well?' Horatio said.

The boys nodded that they were. He felt exhausted by this encounter, by his sons with their pale, blank faces. From the top of the house, the sound reached them of a hammer against a nail. Again and again, the noise came. Horatio had asked that the windows through the house be nailed shut, and Archer had said that he would see to it himself.

William cleared his throat, and spoke over the sound of the hammer. 'Might *I* catch the miasma, Papa?'

'I will see to it that you don't,' Horatio said. 'I have asked Archer to seal the windows with paint, as an extra precaution. The rooms will be secure when you come home for the summer.'

'Did Mother die of it, Papa?' William asked.

'I am sorry to say that she did.'

William went to reply, but thought better of it. Horatio was glad. He would sleep, when they had gone. He longed to close his eyes.

'There are people who say otherwise,' James said, in a moment of quiet.

'What's that?'

'There are people who say that Mother did not die of this miasma. Nor Alice.'

Overhead, the hammering stopped. Horatio felt that he might be ready to die here, in this room, with his eldest son staring past him. He felt a new heat in his veins, the blanket hot and heavy across his lap.

'Which people?' He directed this at James. 'Who has said this to you?'

'It is spoken of at school,' James said, his voice tight. 'People whisper when we pass.'

'And what do they say?'

Horatio waited. James was silhouetted at the window but he could make out the line of his features. He took after his mother, he always had, but today he saw Thomas Jardine in his son's stature, his height.

Above them, Archer trod the stairs down to the first floor. His hammering resumed, louder than before.

'What do they say?' Horatio did his best to sit forward in his chair.

William sniffed. He was crying, Horatio thought, but trying to contain it.

'They say it was you,' William said. He began to cry openly. James put his hand on his brother's shoulder.

Horatio tried to sit up, to see William's face, but his body betrayed him. He boiled hot, and when he looked at his boys he saw two black ravens bearing down on him with glassy eyes.

'They are wrong,' Horatio said. 'They are mistaken. Do you hear me?' His voice was a useless whisper. 'It was the miasma from the river that killed them both.' The room swam around him. The ravens had gone. The room was filled with sunlight and the boys were still there.

'Grandfather doesn't believe that,' James said.

The hammering from upstairs seemed to bear down on his bones.

'There are scientific journals confirming the dangers of miasma. It is well recognised,' Horatio said to his son, his firstborn. James, the boy who had made him so proud, who had an aptitude for science; who stood tall and handsome by the window. 'My letter on the subject was printed in *The Times*.' Horatio tapped his finger on the paper folded on the table at his side. 'It was printed in full.'

James said nothing. Beside him, William cried pitifully.

239

'Grandfather wrote to us at school,' James said. 'He has asked that we spend the summer with him in Kent.'

'In Kent?'

James exchanged a glance with his brother. 'We should like to accept.'

Horatio went to reply, but footsteps came down the stairs and then the door opened. Archer stood there with his head bowed. This was the reason they had come, Horatio realised. Their grandfather had sent them. No one had told them of his sickness.

'You must not believe what they say at school,' Horatio said. He felt the itch again in his chest, and he coughed as his boys were led from the room.

'I hope you will feel better, Papa,' William said, turning back at the door. He had managed to stop his tears.

'You must not believe it,' Horatio said, but his voice was weak. He let his eyes close. The words he needed were too difficult, and he feared they would be misconstrued. 'She loved to bathe,' he said, which wasn't right, it wasn't the point. 'I wanted only to deserve her affection.'

'I know, sir.'

Horatio opened his eyes and Archer was there, adjusting his blanket over his knees. It was dark, and on the mantelpiece the lamps were lit.

'I am to blame,' Horatio said. 'The boys know the truth of it. They know it was my doing.'

'Don't upset yourself, Mr Lloyd,' Archer said. He held a cold cloth to Horatio's head.

'They are lost to me, Archer.'

'They will come round, sir. They are young.'

Horatio tried to sit up. Archer was in his shirtsleeves, and his body was strong and well; his skin was flushed from the sun.

'But they know, Archer.'

Archer shook his head. 'You need to rest.'

'They are talking of it at their school.'

'That's enough now. Quiet.'

'Have you told them? Was it you?'

Archer stood by the fireplace, his features made strange by the glow of the lamps. 'I gave you my word, Mr Lloyd, that I would tell no one. I have not told a living soul.'

Horatio felt sleep take him over. He felt the disease swell and burn inside him, the disease that he carried from the rookeries, that he smelled in his clothes, in his skin. He wanted to tell his boys that he adored their mother, he had loved her terribly. She had loved to bathe. He called for William to come back, to sit beside him, but the boy did not reply.

33

17 November 2008

Seb stood on the concourse in front of Canada Tower and checked his watch. He'd done his best to arrive exactly on time, or even a bit late, but the trains had been punctual for once and now he had ten minutes to spare. He felt observed in the shadow of the tower, and uncomfortable in his suit and tie, freshly shaven. Nobody gave him a second look but he still felt ridiculous, in a suit for the day but not part of the club; a hopeful hanger-on. He went and sat at a table outside a café where he could watch people emerging from the Tube exit. Someone had left their *Financial Times* on the chair so he picked it up and glanced at the headline: *Gloom Deepens on Economy.* Nothing new there. He turned to the stocks and shares index, checked the performance of the assets he used to manage. Then he folded it back up and threw it down on the table. A group of women he recognised walked out of Canada Tower and strode across the concourse, heads bowed in conversation, their breath white with the cold. A gull pecked at a discarded Danish pastry under the table.

He hated it here. He hated the tall buildings with their reflective glass and steel cladding, the shock of them and the farce of pretending it wasn't shocking for such wealth to exist. The rushing around, the excess, the bullshit of it all. He'd always hated it, although he might not have said so if you'd asked him six months ago. Six months ago he'd been up to his neck in it and he'd thought he was happy. He'd found a woman whom he loved, who had told him after a few months that she loved him back. It was the first time for him and it had scared him half to death. He'd wanted to be what she wanted. She was bright and ambitious and for a while he'd thought he could hold on to her; he'd thought he could suffer the bullshit if she was in his life.

The clock on the concourse said five to ten. A text came through from Maxine: *Good luck in your interview.*

He stared at it, unsure if it was a peace offering or something else. She didn't believe him, he knew that. She'd refused his calls last night, and he'd slept on the sofa in the living room with the blankets over his head so he couldn't hear it if the shower came on in the early hours. He must have slept through, because he'd woken to the sound of the dustmen wheeling the bins out of the gate, the slow creak of the lever that tipped it all into the truck. He'd watched the sunlight brighten at the window and he'd thought, Today I throw my life away.

A second text came through: *Did you see Colin this morning?*
Yes, he replied. *Didn't speak to him. Why?*

He wants to start on the plumbing.

He put his phone down hard against the table and looked up at the cloudless sky. She was pushing him, trying to get him to talk. He mentally composed a text admitting there was no interview, no money coming. But that wasn't how he wanted it to end with Maxine, not when he had loved her so much, when he'd hoped they might get married. He wanted to tell her all of it and apologise to her face. She deserved that, at the very least. So he waited a minute, then he replied: *I don't want Colin in the house any more. I never liked the guy.* He was debating whether to send a follow-up when his phone rang.

'Jason.' He could feel the panic on the end of the line.

'Where the fuck are you?'

'Nearly there.' Seb looked up at the tower, which still said Lehman Brothers across the entrance. 'Don't stress.'

'We were meant to meet beforehand.'

'Were we?'

There was a pause in which Seb imagined Jason taking his phone from his ear and staring at it in disbelief.

'It starts in three minutes,' Jason said.

Seb pictured them sitting around the long boardroom table waiting for him. He had an urge to laugh.

'Listen, just stick to what we agreed.'

The gull at Seb's feet took off, flying low over the heads of two men standing at the concrete wall, looking out over the dock.

'Remind me what we agreed?'

'Seb, don't do this now.'

'Oh yeah, you want me to throw myself under a bus for you.'

'You're already under the bus. You've been under the bus for months. That's the whole point.'

'How am I ever going to get myself out of this if I—'

'This is a way out for you. I'll write off your debt and you can walk away.'

'I could be arrested.' Seb stood and walked towards the Lehman's tower.

'You're not still worried about that?'

'Of course I'm worried about that.'

'They're not going to call the Plod.' Jason lowered his voice. 'These guys are stretched to the limit, since the crash. They've got more exposures to look at than hours in the day. It's going to take years to work through it all. They'll be there forever if they start throwing the book at the likes of you.'

Seb pushed through the revolving doors. He stood on the marble floor of the glass-fronted foyer, the whole space bleached in sunlight. Last time he was here it had been chaos, people leaving the building with whatever they could carry, standing out on the forecourt in shock. Nothing to do but go home. Grown men and women crying. 'I'll see you up there.' His eyes adjusted, and he went to the reception desk. 'I'll be with you in a minute. Going through security.'

They gave Seb a visitor's pass and he was escorted past the grand piano, the low glass tables and leather seats. He smiled at the security guy, who he recognised, and passed through the turnstiles. In the lift he looked down at his shoes and flexed the muscles in his knees to the tune in his head, the Christmas song that had been there for weeks. He was as terrified as he'd ever been in his life.

245

On the twenty-fifth floor he followed the corridor around the core of the building. Jason was waiting at the door of the meeting room, looking like he might be on the verge of a heart attack. He'd put on weight, Seb noticed. Buttons straining against his paunch. Perspiration at his armpits.

'Are we good?' he said to Seb as he held the door open.

'I'm good, thanks.' Seb smiled, buoyed by Jason's nerves, by the vast, light-filled meeting room. The long table had been laid out with several bottles of mineral water, still and sparkling. White bowls filled with glacier mints. There were croissants and Danish pastries on a tray at the side of the room alongside the coffee machine and the tea urn. Seb knew from experience that nobody would touch them. He exchanged niceties with a blonde woman in a cream business suit, and shook hands with the dark-suited men who sat alongside her. Behind them, the Thames made its wide loop around the old docks and stretched on towards the City. Buildings and containers and boats, all of it razor sharp. The sky was a bright, flawless blue.

'Where do you want me?' Seb asked.

'Anywhere at all.' The blonde woman smiled at Seb as he sat down facing her. Jason sat at the far end of the table and poured himself a glass of water. There was a pause as the suited men did the same: carbonated water sparkled and fizzed. 'Thanks for joining us today, Sebastian.'

'My pleasure,' he said, which was the wrong thing to say, but he coughed into his fist and managed not to laugh, to focus on the woman opposite who was talking.

'Now, as you know, I'm here today to conduct this disciplinary investigation in respect of your time at Lehman Brothers.' She nodded down the table at the suited men beside her. 'My colleagues are here on behalf of the liquidators, who uncovered some discrepancies in the aftermath of Lehman's going into administration.'

Seb nodded. The room was still and bright. Through the sheet-glass panels behind the blonde woman, every roof and window across London shone back at him. He felt a pressure at his temples. He wondered if his hands would shake if he reached for water.

'I'm sure you understand the gravity of the situation,' the woman said. 'The discrepancies in question amount to gross misconduct, as well as financial fraud.'

Seb nodded. 'I do. Yes.'

'We've already had a brief chat with your Head of Desk, Mr Jennings,' she said, pointing her pen in Jason's direction. 'But this is your opportunity to set out for us exactly what happened, from your perspective.'

'Absolutely.' He reached slowly for the nearest bottle of water and unscrewed the cap, poured the water into his glass and put the bottle down on the table. The whole operation went smoothly. He sipped the water and cleared his throat. 'I've come here to tell you the truth about what happened.'

'Thank you.' She clicked the end of her pen. 'Go on.'

'In the spring of this year, my girlfriend bought a house. She invested a lot of the money she'd inherited from her father. The house means a lot to her.' He put his hands on his legs, palms down, and gripped his thighs to stop the tremor. 'I told her I'd fund the renovations. The house needs a lot of work; it's a Georgian townhouse, never been renovated. I needed a cash injection to fund the project.'

Everyone nodded at this. The suited man furthest from him met his eye and tapped the end of his pen against his open page. Seb wished he could remember any of their names. They must have introduced themselves, but he had no recollection of that moment. He couldn't remember walking into the room.

'My bonus was coming up, but I was still short of what I needed.'

'Why was that?' The man who'd caught his eye spoke for the first time. 'You were earning a good salary.'

'I'd made a high-risk investment. A margin account, where I'd make a lot of money if the value of the securities went up. If the value fell, I was in trouble.'

They all wrote this down. He saw Jason in the corner of his eye, felt the weight of his expectation. His fear. It was exquisite. Seb had no intention of sticking to the plan – Jason's plan – of how this meeting should go. But he spun the moment out, like he was agonising over it, like he might still play along. He toyed with a coaster, crossed his legs and twitched his foot. He felt Jason's agony and he thought this was worth going to prison for, if it came to that.

'When you're ready,' a suited man said.

'A few months before the crash I got a margin call,' Seb said. 'I'm sure you know, it's the call you dread, with an investment like that.'

'You were expected to find a lump sum,' the blonde woman said. 'Because the value of the securities had fallen.'

'Yes.'

'How did you find the capital?'

'I went to Jason,' Seb said. 'He bailed me out.'

'I don't see how this is relevant,' Jason said, his voice too loud for the room.

'I'll decide what's relevant,' the blonde woman replied. 'You're telling us you were in debt to Mr Jennings, on account of a margin investment that ran into loss.'

'That's right. I had money tied up in Lehman's stocks that hadn't vested. But in the short term I had a problem. I needed to pay for these renovations and get myself out of debt, so I figured I'd make my books look a bit healthier.'

'Can you tell us how you did that, please?'

'I took a large number of non-liquid assets onto my books. Most of them were priced at around 10p. But I valued them all at one pound or more.' Everyone wrote this down. 'Jason said he'd make sure I got away with it. I'd have been in line for a decent bonus at the end of this year, if the bank hadn't crashed.'

Jason made incredulous noises. The blonde woman ignored him, clicking the end of her pen.

'Are you able to tell us the total amount by which you overpriced your books?' she said.

'I believe it was just over two million.'

She raised her eyebrows. Jason was silent, and Seb knew that he had done it, he had broken away. He felt weightless. A plane made its way across the sky.

'Two million pounds?'

'That's right. Just over.'

Nobody wrote this down. Jason went to speak, sat forward in his chair, but was interrupted by one of the suited men.

'Are you sure of that figure?' he asked Seb.

'I am,' Seb said. 'I also want you to know that I've been under a lot of pressure to lie about it.'

He watched the plane cross the sky and he thought of Maxine, the night he'd met her in that bar in Waterloo. Sitting there with her coat on, nervous and sober. She was as scared as he was; she had been from the start. They had been trying to love each other all this time but the fear had been bigger than them, and they had not faced it. His head cleared as the plane flew out of sight. He felt entirely lucid for the first time in months.

'Your manager – Mr Jennings – has given a different version of events.' The blonde woman glanced at Jason at the far end of the table. 'A different number.'

'I'm sure he has.'

'He led us to believe the figure was closer to thirty million.'

Seb looked directly at Jason for the first time since the meeting began. He was staring back at him, sweating at his hairline. 'Jason asked me to take the blame for all the fraud across the desk.'

'What are you talking about?' Jason leaned forward.

'He said he'd write off what I owed him if I took the blame for the whole lot. He said I'd lose my licence to trade either way, so this was my best bet.'

Jason laughed, and sat back in his chair. Along the far side of the table, papers were shuffled. The three suited men conferred in low voices.

'He's been calling me every day,' Seb said. 'Hassling me for money.'

'For God's sake. I wasn't hassling you.' Jason said this to the ceiling, his head thrown back. 'This is ridiculous.'

'You wanted me to use Maxine's inheritance. You wanted me to get my hands on her money. Get her up the aisle, you said.'

Jason snorted. 'I thought you should marry her. She's a nice girl. Nothing sinister in that.'

'You've never met her.'

'All right,' the woman opposite said. 'I think we've heard enough. Perhaps you could leave us now, Mr Jennings.'

'Gladly.' Jason stood, and took his jacket from the back of his chair. 'All I ever did was cover for him and bail him out. He was a disaster, always took risks to the limit, always wanted the higher return. He'd have crashed a long time ago if I hadn't looked after him.'

Seb found his knees bouncing to the tune of the Christmas song in his head, which was more frantic now than it had been. He heard Jason making denials, saying that he had been a friend to Seb, a mentor. Seb looked past the blonde woman at the river and the cold blue sky and he heard Jason say that Seb had known the risk of those margin accounts, that he had been free to say no. Which was true. It was also true that Jason had taken him on knowing that he had nothing and no one; he'd met him in a snooker hall where Seb had been playing for money on a Tuesday night, on a winning streak, doubling what he earned in a single shift at the call centre where he worked. They'd got talking and in the early hours Jason had offered him a job. No interview, no need for a CV. He'd seen something in him, he'd told Seb, and Seb had known what he meant before long. The stock market was a global game of roulette, an epic card game where the odds were big enough to blow the world up. Seb had slotted in perfectly.

'Is there anything you want to add?' one of the men was asking him. They were all looking at him, their pens poised. The meeting was over and the room felt restless. Jason appeared to have gone.

Seb went to stand, then sat back down. 'One thing,' he said. 'But I think you know this already.'

'Go ahead.'

'I'm glad to be out of here,' he said. 'I don't know how I would have found my way free of it. I was out of control, but I wasn't the only one, and it wasn't a secret. It was insane and terrifying but also normal.'

They all murmured. One of the suits said that they would discuss this between themselves, that Seb should expect to hear from them. He stood, and they thanked him one by one. The room was a white box of light. The river shone silver at the edge of his vision. He found his way back to the lift and as he descended he thought that he would tell Max all of it when he got home. He couldn't go back to lying now. He would lose her, when she realised he was a no-hoper like the other guys she'd got rid of. But in a way it was easier to have nothing, and no one.

On the escalator down to the Jubilee line Seb checked his phone before the signal went. His hand was clammy. He opened a message from Maxine as he stepped onto the platform: *Why did you take him on then?* He looked at it uncomprehendingly. He scrolled through her previous messages and saw his own, telling her that he didn't want Colin in the house, that he'd never liked him. He still couldn't make sense of her reply. His head was still in the meeting room, all that glass and light, the slow curve of the river.

A train pulled in, the doors opened and Seb stepped back. He turned and walked out to the escalator, waiting for his phone signal to return. He typed a quick reply: *I didn't!! You did.* Then he went back to the platform to wait for the next train.

34

14 December 1994

'We're not friends,' Cookie said to Mrs Lloyd's back; to his dad, who was beside him on the stairs.

'This is what I was afraid of,' his dad said. 'You were right.' He said this to Ruth, who was behind him, on the landing. 'You said this would happen.'

'Didn't I tell you she had her claws into Cookie,' Ruth shouted in reply. 'Didn't I?'

Lee said nothing, but Cookie knew his dad was appalled at what he had done: he had blabbed to Mrs Lloyd and now the police were on their way.

'Dad,' Cookie said, his voice a whine. 'We're not friends.'

'Stop that,' Lee said. 'Stop saying that, for God's sake.'

Cookie stepped forward. His ears rang with his dad's words, his dismissal. The colours of the stairwell streaked before his eyes and he moved in a slowed-down lurch as Mrs Lloyd took her hand from the bannister; she lifted a slippered foot. He thought of how he'd cried against her, the soft cushion of her body; the things he'd said. He needed it not to have happened. He needed it gone.

He reached out and pushed her. His hands were flat against her back, high enough to send her pitching forward, hard enough that she would lose her footing. He heard his dad's shout of outrage behind him. He watched her fall.

She went head first, her shoulder hitting the wall and rebounding from it, sending her legs over her head in a somersault that her body was not agile enough to perform. Her feet hit the stairs and her head followed behind her body with huge momentum, reeling through the air and landing with force against the shoe rack in the hallway, with its exposed sharp corner. Cookie heard the crack, the moment her skull fractured. Her feet lifted and settled again against the bottom step. One fleece-lined slipper rested on the stair a few feet away from her body, the other hung from her toe. He knew she was dead.

Cookie stayed where he was, holding the handrail near the top of the stairs. He became aware of his mum screaming. He didn't know how long she'd been screaming for. A while, he thought. His dad was telling her to stop.

'We aren't friends,' he said. He held the handrail and noticed the grain of the wood, the curved underside. He ran his thumb along the curve and thought it was smoother than you'd think; it was well made. He thought he might fall. The new place where he was sorry, where he'd made a huge mistake, was bright and close at the edge of his vision and the only thing left of him, the person he had been, was here in the carpentry of the handrail, the smooth grain.

His mum was still screaming.

He let go of the handrail and the moment rushed up to meet him. He saw the patterned carpet, its fading colours. Below him, at the foot of the stairs, Mrs Lloyd lay motionless.

'What have you done?' His dad pushed past him. His voice was not familiar. He didn't stop to look at Cookie, to speak to him. He crouched down beside Mrs Lloyd at the foot of the stairs and he said, in a low voice: 'Jesus fucking Christ.'

Cookie sat down on the stairs, let his head rest against a spindle. Behind him, his mum said, 'Did you check for a pulse?' She was half-screaming. 'Check her pulse, Lee!'

'Don't be stupid,' his dad said. He stood, and looked down at the body. 'She's dead.'

'I'm going to check,' Ruth said, passing Cookie on the stairs. 'She might be alive. Sometimes you can't tell.'

'I can tell,' Lee said. 'Don't touch her.'

'Let me check!'

'Did you hear me?' He grabbed Ruth by the arm. 'I said, don't touch her!'

Cookie's stomach heaved. He bent over and vomited over his socks, over the next stair down. He recognised the toast and honey from that morning and he retched again.

Ruth walked backwards up the stairs until she was a few steps down from Cookie. She was making a high-pitched sound which rose and fell and when she turned to look up at him her eyes were round, her hand over her mouth.

'Mum,' he said.

She started to cry. She kept her hand tight over her mouth and she cried noisily, her eyes bright and scared. She took a step closer to Cookie, looked down at his vomit-splashed socks and back at his face. She leaned back against the spindles and slid slowly downwards until she was sitting on the step below him, the hem of her coat in his vomit. She reached out with one hand but he didn't take it. Her fear reached him and his head spun with it; he was sitting still but his head was moving very fast, spinning in the wrong direction.

'It's all right,' she said.

Cookie stared back at his mum. His head slowed as he met her eyes. 'I killed her.'

'Shh.' She leaned closer to him. 'You don't know your own strength. That's all.'

Cookie found he was shaking all over. His mum didn't seem to understand. 'I killed her,' he said.

'Shh,' she said again. 'Don't say that.'

'I did.'

'Don't!' She moved closer to him and held his calf. 'Don't say that. You mustn't say that.'

'Listen.' Lee pushed both hands up over his face and into his hair. He looked up at the ceiling, his elbows pointing outwards. 'Both of you, shut up and listen.'

They were all quiet. Rain fell hard against the front door.

'Don't move,' Lee said. 'Give me ten minutes. Just stay here and keep calm. When I give you a shout, I want you to call for an ambulance. Tell them you got home and found her here like that.'

Cookie looked at Mrs Lloyd's feet, the ridge of hard skin around her heel. His mum gripped his calf.

'Do you hear me?' Lee said.

Ruth and Cookie replied: 'Yes.'

'Whatever you do, don't touch her. Don't move.' Lee ran up the stairs, turned onto the landing and ran up again to the loft.

'They won't believe she fell,' Cookie said. He felt horribly lucid, looking at the body below him. The angle of her head.

'What do you mean?'

'They'll be able to tell, that she was pushed.'

Ruth crawled up a step to sit beside him. 'I don't think so,' she said. 'She's an old lady. I don't think—'

'Velocity,' Cookie said.

Ruth shook her head. 'What?'

He couldn't answer her. His body was shaking and the smell of his own vomit filled his nose. His school shirt clung to him, tight around the arms. Overhead, his dad was moving from room to room. A door slammed shut.

'She wouldn't have fallen that way if she'd tripped,' Cookie said, eventually. 'She'd have had a softer landing. Probably would have gone feet first.'

Ruth lifted her backside from the step and looked down the stairs at Mrs Lloyd. 'Oh God.' She sat down heavily.

'I'll tell them,' he said.

'No, you will not.'

'They'll know.'

'Let me think.' She wrapped her arms around her knees. 'Be quiet a minute.' Overhead, Lee was swearing to himself, charging around. Ruth was quiet for a while, her head on her knees, a low growl in her throat. 'Oh God.' She lifted her head. 'I think I've got it,' she said, holding out her hand.

'Where are we going?'

'Come on. Quick.' She led him down the stairs and stepped over Mrs Lloyd's outstretched legs, glancing down at her as she reached the hallway. 'Don't look down.'

Cookie copied her movements. He looked down, although she'd told him not to, and he saw Mrs Lloyd's face, just for a second. Her mouth was slightly open, her neck twisted. There was blood in her hair, a small pool on the floor under her head. He made a noise. Looked away. He nudged her foot as he stepped over her, and it dropped down onto the tiles.

Ruth clamped her hand to her mouth, stifled a scream.

Cookie took his mum's hand. She held it tightly, and pushed on the door to the living room. She shut the door behind them and crossed to the coffee table by the window, where the telephone sat on top of the Yellow Pages. Cookie stayed where he was, by the door. The room was big and gloomy, with a rug on the floor and a large marble fireplace. Mrs Lloyd wouldn't like it if she knew they were in here. He almost said so, and the knowledge that she was dead crossed the room in a cold wave towards him.

'You don't know your own strength,' his mum said, lifting the receiver. Her hand shook as she put it to her ear. 'That's the trouble, Cooks.'

'Are you calling the police?'

She nodded. 'Keep quiet and let me deal with it.' She put

her finger in the dial and turned it, let it reel slowly back, turned it again and again. Overhead, the noise continued. She looked him in the eye as she spoke. 'Police,' she said. Her voice came out high, and she rubbed her throat as she spoke. 'My landlady was pushed down a flight of stairs. I think she's dead.'

Cookie went to stand beside her. She gave the address, and he cried as she repeated that it wasn't an accident.

'That's right,' she said. 'She was pushed. Yes, I'm sure.'

Ruth put the phone back in its receiver: the chime was sharp and bright, and they waited for it to fade. 'Will I go to prison?' Cookie said.

She put her arms around him and he howled into the damp fabric of her coat.

35

17 November 2008

Seb went straight home after the disciplinary hearing in the hope that Maxine would be there. She wasn't answering her phone. He called her again from the top deck of the bus as it turned down Rye Lane and listened to her recorded voice saying she would call back if he left a message.

'Max, where are you? Call me, would you?' The bus stopped and the top deck emptied. 'I need to talk to you, Maxine,' he said. 'I don't want to argue with you. I hate arguing with you.' He found himself talking to Max as if she were beside him, cracking her knuckles against her jeans. 'We need to talk,' he said. 'There are some things I need you to know.'

He kept the phone to his ear as the bus moved forward. From the window he caught sight of the common; its sodden grass, the low slant of the sun.

'The money's dried up, Max.' He pulled himself up to his feet. 'I won't be able to pay for the plumbing. I'm sorry.' He stood at the top of the stairs, gripping the handrail. He could see the house now, the dark windows and the dirty brick. 'Listen,' he said, remembering the text message she'd sent him. 'What did you mean, about Colin? I didn't—'

A voice in his ear told him he'd run out of space for his message. He put his phone into the pocket of his coat and swung on the narrow stairwell as the bus slowed. He waited for the doors to open and he stepped onto the pavement at the edge of the common, turned and looked up at the house. A siren started at the junction as he tried Maxine's number again.

'Max,' he said, when she didn't answer. 'I know you're angry but please call me back. I want to apologise but I don't want to do it like this.' He stepped backwards onto the wet grass and stared at the upper floors, where the curtains were parted and the rooms beyond were black. 'I'm outside now,' he said. 'Please don't work late. Come home and talk to me. I want to tell you what's been going on, all of it.' He pushed his finger into his ear to block the sound of another siren. He stepped away from the sound and waited for it to pass. 'I love you, Maxine.'

He tried to pick his way back to the pavement through the mud. There were deep puddles everywhere he turned. He jumped over a patch of water, then another, until he reached the pavement with the hems of his trousers soaked. The house seemed to lean in towards him. He broke into a run and leapt up the steps to the front door.

In the hallway he stood and listened. Colin was hitting something hard with a hammer, somewhere on the upper floors.

The house was full of dust. He took a quick look in the kitchen but there was no sign of Maxine. Likewise the living room: the blanket he'd slept under was folded on the sofa where he'd left it. Upstairs, the hammering stopped. He heard Colin moving slowly, his footsteps quiet. He listened, and he thought again of the text Max had sent him earlier, the one about Colin that he hadn't understood: *Why did you take him on then?*

He wished she would pick up the phone. He needed to talk to her about so many things. They'd hedged around their problems these past few months. Max had been defensive about Colin from the start. And he'd been put out, offended that she had gone ahead and found a plumber, when he'd said he would do it.

But maybe she hadn't. He stood still and tried to think. What if she hadn't found him, if he'd just turned up out of the blue? There was a skip outside. And the house was clearly falling over. The idea of this grew, then receded. He shouted up the stairs: 'Colin?'

No reply. He loosened his tie, his eyes on his wet shoes, and trod slowly up the stairs. He took his phone out of his coat pocket and checked to see if Maxine had replied, but there was nothing. He hoped he was wrong. He thought of what he would say to her when she called, and in his head she laughed at him, in a soft way, and told him he was nuts. The conversation spooled on. *Don't come home*, he said to the Maxine in his head. *Stay where you are.*

The bannister was grey with a fine covering of dust. He noticed it as he reached the landing: the dust was dense up here, the air was thick with it; he could barely see. He took a step towards the bedroom, his eyes still adjusting, and his foot met with nothing. The ground had gone. He grabbed at the air and fell blindly forward into a space where the landing had been. His hand met with something hard, then his chin, his hip. He waited. He felt pipes and wiring under his hands and knees, the exposed mess of the house, the dark innards of it. He managed to sit up, hands resting on a length of pipe. Some kind of old wooden joist under his feet. The house creaked. What the hell? He felt pain in his knees, his jaw. He crawled backwards, found his feet again and managed to stand at the top of the stairs, holding the newel post. He caught his breath, stared down at the dark space. Jesus Christ. Every single floorboard was gone.

From the second floor, Colin whistled through his teeth.

Seb pushed his glasses back up his nose. There was no way he could get to the bedroom. 'Hey!' He shouted in the direction of the second-floor stairwell. He tried it again, louder. 'Colin?' He waited; he thought he heard a voice, then it stopped. He edged his way along the landing, holding on to the balustrade, his feet between the spindles, then he gripped the handrail and swung himself onto the next flight of stairs.

The floorboards were gone on the second floor and every door was ajar. From the top of the stairs, two long floorboards reached across the landing into the largest room, the one where he'd stripped all the paper from the walls. He looked down at the exposed pipes, the dark opening, the wires and decaying timber. He went to call out, then he heard Colin's voice through the open door.

'I told you,' Colin said. 'Didn't I tell you?' He was quiet a moment, then he said, 'I know. I was close to giving up.'

He was on the phone. Seb waited at the top of the stairs. He would wait for him to end the call, then he'd go in there and ask him why he'd taken up all the boards, if that had been strictly necessary. And how had he wormed his way into this house, exactly? What the hell did he want? He felt his blood rising, an urge to charge in there and shove him to the ground. He took a step forward and stood on the narrow strip of floorboard, holding the newel post with one hand. The board creaked under his weight.

He landed heavily at the open doorway. Colin was on the far side of the room, standing at the window facing the common. He had his phone pressed to his ear and he wore a pale blue T-shirt, a patch of sweat between his shoulder blades. He had on a baseball cap, his shaved head visible through the opening at the back.

'I wanted to call you right away.' A pause, as Colin stared out at the common. 'I love you too, Mum.'

The seconds passed slowly. There was no other sound up here: no birdsong from the Rye, no sirens, nothing.

'I was calling you,' Seb said. 'From downstairs. I didn't expect all the boards to be up on the landing.'

Colin turned from the window and looked at Seb without surprise. 'Sorry about that. I was on the phone.'

'Didn't you hear me?'

'It's always very quiet up here.' He looked around him at the room. 'Have you ever noticed that?'

Seb gestured out beyond the door. 'I nearly broke my neck. I stepped out onto the landing and—'

'I love the view from this floor.' Colin spoke over him, pointing out of the window. 'Sometimes you can see the Peck. It crosses the common, then continues north-east. Meets the Thames at Rotherhithe.' He nudged the peak of his hat. 'Rye means waterway. Old English.'

'I don't see how—'

'Did you know that?'

'What?'

'Did you know that? About the River Peck?'

Colin looked at Seb questioningly, leaning back against the window frame. The quiet was strangely attentive. Seb realised he'd had a headache all day. It had been there in his temple, over his right eye, but the pain had only just made itself known. He still felt the glare of the meeting room, the long glass table, the sparkling water. His anger left him and he knew with a growing unease that he should not have come up here, that he should leave.

'No,' Seb said. 'I didn't know that.'

'Should have asked me, shouldn't you? I could have helped you out with your research. You didn't think of that.'

Seb pressed his fingertips against the pain in his head. 'How do you know about the Peck?'

'I grew up here.'

'Did you?'

'I remember the pub on the corner, the Kings Arms. Never could get my dad out of there.' He paused, thinking. 'They pulled it down, that pub. But otherwise things are the same.'

Seb stared at Colin's profile. He knew something about that pub on the corner, something Clare had told him. The lodgers. One of them had been a regular there, a known criminal. He waited for Colin to look at him, and when he did he knew he was right.

'I never liked it here,' Colin said. 'This house. I felt the same way you do. Couldn't sleep. Couldn't relax.'

Seb felt the creep of fear. 'Is your name Delaney?'

'Very good. I wondered if you'd find me. Your project.'

Seb held his chin up, tried to stay calm. There was something in Colin that set him on edge, something just beneath the surface. It was almost audible: a tight quiver of rage.

'Why did you come back here?'

'Something got left behind when we left. Took me ages to find it.' Colin took a step away from the window.

'What was it?'

'What?'

'What was it, that you came back for?'

'That's not your business.' Colin straightened to his full height. 'None of this is your business, is it?'

'I want you to leave,' Seb said. He shouted, to mask his fear. 'I want you off the property.'

'Do you?'

They faced each other. Seb had never won a fight; he'd lost a few, but mostly he talked his way out of them, distracted his opponent, reasoned with him. He knew, looking at Colin, that he wouldn't talk his way out of this one. At the edge of his vision, Colin's toolbox was open on the floor at his feet. A hammer, and the crowbar he must have used to lift the floorboards. He felt rigid. He went to move but Colin stepped closer, nudging the crowbar with his foot.

'Do you remember the first time we met?' Colin said. 'In the park that day? Remember that? I heard you on the phone.'

Seb shook his head. His mind raced. And then he remembered: the guy who'd stood behind him as he'd talked to Jason by the pond. He stared at Colin and his head rushed with disbelief. The room was utterly, impossibly silent.

'Did you follow me home?'

'Not that day,' Colin said. 'But that day was interesting. I enjoyed your phone call.'

'I think you should leave. Take whatever you came for and go.'

'I think it's you who should leave,' Colin said. 'Do you know why?'

Seb felt the familiar oblong of his phone in his coat pocket. He turned it around in his hand. There was a way to make a call without unlocking it, but he couldn't remember how. His fingers were huge and clumsy, his head stupid with shock.

'I think you know why,' Colin said. 'You know what you are.'

'Get the fuck out of here.'

'You're nobody,' Colin said. 'You're hot air. Bullshit. I knew it the first time I saw you. I could smell it.'

'I could say the same for you.'

'I don't think so.'

'You lied your way in here. You're a fraud,' Seb said. He saw Colin's face change: a chink in his armour. 'You're a total fraud.'

Colin snapped then. He moved quickly, pushing Seb backwards, and in the same moment, on the ground floor, the front door slammed shut. Seb landed halfway across the room. Before he could stand Colin pushed him again and he staggered, falling backwards, and the two of them rolled on the floor, Colin stronger and bigger, more practised. He felt Colin reach for something. He grunted with its weight.

Seb drew breath, shouted as loud as he could manage for Maxine to run.

'Don't think she heard you,' Colin said, pulling up onto his knees with the crowbar in his hand.

Seb lunged forward, almost stood, staggered a few paces before he felt the blow to his back.

From the foot of the stairs Maxine called out for him again. Her voice was distant, and he knew from her tone that she hadn't heard him. He shouted but his voice was stifled, her name was quiet in his mouth.

'Lovely girl,' Colin said, his knee at the base of Seb's neck. 'If you call her again, I'll have to kill you in front of her.'

Seb found himself filled with a new pain: a crack to the skull that blew out in clouds of red and black, sliced down his spine and took the breath from his lungs. He heard Maxine's feet on the stairs. He saw the bare walls, the floorboards, the fireplace. Then nothing.

36

14 December 1994

In the living room, Ruth held Cookie tight against her and felt him shake, crying fitfully, his body slumped. He smelled sharply of vomit. She made soothing sounds into his ear. 'Mummy's here,' she told him, like he was a baby, like he'd woken in the night. 'Don't be scared, Mummy's here.'

It was raining hard against the window. There was no movement out on the Rye, just the Thames Water van and the men in high-vis vests staring down into the hole in the street. The only sound was the rain. She held her boy and thought, This is the end of the world. It was the end of the world and it was just her and Cookie, alone. There was something almost soothing about it, to be reduced to this primal thing of protecting her child. This she could do. She had always known it.

Overhead, Lee was making a huge noise, banging and crashing. God knows why. He might have told her – had he?

– but she had no memory of the hours before this happened. This moment was the only thing: her boy was in trouble and nothing else was real.

'I'm sorry,' Cookie said.

'Shh.' She held his face in her hands. He might puke again, she thought.

'I killed her,' he said.

'No, you didn't.'

She smoothed his hair down, wiped his tears with her thumbs. The rain hit the window, rattling the pane. They heard the sirens, distant and then close, more than one of them. They'd be finding their way through the barriers at the junction, dealing with the workmen.

'I'm sorry,' Cookie said again, straightening up.

'I'll deal with it.'

He stared at her: his nose was running, his eyes bright with fear. From the street they heard the rise and fall of the sirens. They grew close, lighting the room, turning the net curtains blue.

'Don't say anything when they come inside,' she said. 'Let me deal with it.'

'Are they going to arrest me?'

'It's all right. Stay quiet.'

'Will they send me to prison?' He moved away from the window as the sirens filled the room. 'Mum? Will they?'

Ruth put her finger to her lips. 'Shh,' she said. 'Try to stay calm.' She opened the door, caught sight of Mrs Lloyd and pulled it shut again. Jesus Christ, the blood had spread out across the tiles. When she opened it again, she kept her head down but she had the image in her head of that creeping red pool; her blank eyes and her open mouth.

Out on the street, the sirens fell quiet. Car doors slammed.

'What the—?' Lee was halfway down the stairs, one hand on the bannister, sweaty in his donkey jacket. 'What's going on?'

'I called them,' she said.

'I told you to wait!'

She looked at him, his panicked face. His arms wide across the stairwell, his legs bent, ready to bolt. She went to the front door. 'Let me deal with it,' she said.

Outside, the gate opened and closed, then footsteps, the buzz of police radios.

'Ruth, wait—'

She lifted the latch and opened the door. Rain blew into her face. She counted four police and two paramedics. An ambulance parked a bit further down the street, and two police cars right outside.

'We had a phone call.' A female officer climbed the steps with another officer behind her. 'Was it you, who called the police?'

'That was me, yes.'

'Could you let us in?'

Ruth stood aside as the police filed into the house. She looked up at Lee, who was standing on the stairs behind the body, his face incredulous. She was scared now of what she'd done. It was less clear in her head, now the police were here with their noise, their bulk; she thought she might have got it wrong. She felt movement in her chest, the race of her heartbeat.

'What's happened here?' A female voice. A dark uniform. Someone behind her speaking into a radio.

'My husband pushed our landlady down the stairs,' Ruth said to the officer, quickly, before she lost her nerve. She looked at Lee as she said it. 'She surprised him while he was searching the house for valuables. You'll see he's turned the house upside down.'

A paramedic pushed past her and squatted down alongside the body, avoiding the blood. Behind her, in the doorway of the living room, Cookie made a low whine. There was a long pause as the paramedic checked for a pulse. A plane passed overhead. Someone coughed. 'She's dead,' the paramedic said, looking up.

'Lee Delaney.' The female officer spoke. 'We've been wanting to talk to you for a while.'

The paramedic stood aside and Lee climbed over the body, holding the newel post at the foot of the stairs. He stood in the crowded hallway where the rain was blowing in through the opened door; two police waited outside, talking into radios. Ruth reached behind her for Cookie's hand and he stood at her shoulder, looking at his dad.

'What's happened here?' the officer asked Lee.

Lee looked at Ruth questioningly. 'Ruthie,' he said.

Ruth saw in Lee's face that he didn't understand, it wasn't obvious to him that this was the right thing, the only thing. He thought she'd turned on him. She felt herself sway sideways, and the female officer caught her by the arm.

'It's like my wife told you,' Lee said, his voice hesitant. He searched her face and she gave him a small nod. 'I shoved her from behind. It was me.'

273

The police at the door spoke again into their radios. Ruth felt Cookie drop her hand.

'We'll need to clear the area,' the female officer said. 'Get the cuffs on him and put the other two in the car.'

'Dad?' Cookie stepped forward. 'Dad!'

Ruth reached for Cookie but he pulled his arm from her grip, kept his back to her.

'I want the house thoroughly searched,' the female officer continued. 'He's wanted for armed robbery, besides this. We've got a warrant. Give all the living areas a good going over.'

Lee leaned backwards so he could see Cookie through the dark mass of police. 'It's all right, son,' he said.

'Are you going to prison?'

'Listen,' he said to Cookie, leaning closer. 'Remember what I told you. About the river.'

'Why?' Cookie said.

'It's important. Can you remember?'

Cookie was crying, rocking back on his heels 'I think so,' he said.

Lee held his arms outstretched as a male officer handcuffed him.

'You do not have to say anything,' the policeman said. 'Anything you do say may be given in evidence.'

'Come on,' the female officer said. 'I want this area clear.' She stretched her arms out wide and Cookie stepped away, his back to the wall. Lee turned around in the doorway, the rain falling in sheets behind him, and he caught Ruth's eye before the officer led him down the stairs to the car. Ruth saw all their years together packed into that backward glance. She had loved him for a long time. And she had sacrificed him, because the alternative simply was not possible. Beside her, Cookie coughed and choked and wiped his nose on the back of his hand.

'Don't step in the blood,' the female officer said. 'I want the kid in the car with his mother. Don't move anything. I want this door shut before the rain washes the whole lot away.'

37

17 November 2008

Maxine left work early that afternoon in mid-November. The trees on the Rye had just a sprinkling of leaves, lit up gold by the slant of the sun. She was half frozen in the dress she had borrowed from Lin, and Lin's shoes were too smart, and slightly too small. She looked like an actual grown-up, Lin had said that morning. Maxine had promised to follow her advice: to give Seb a chance, to let him explain himself before she jumped to conclusions. He'd sent her a text earlier that had got her back up – something with exclamation marks that had seemed childishly argumentative – and she'd used all her willpower not to fire off a reply. She was ignoring his calls. They needed to talk, and she didn't want to do it on the phone, walking down the street, angry and bothered. She wanted to see his face when he told her how his interview went.

The house was freezing cold and full of dust. She called out for Seb at the foot of the stairs. She thought she heard movement at the top of the house. She called again, but there was nothing. His coat wasn't on its hook by the door. It seemed odd to her, that he wasn't here ahead of her. It wasn't the way she had expected it to go. For a minute she stood there, running the toe of Lin's shoe over the lip of the bottom step, thinking of Seb and the things she wanted to say, which were banked up in her chest now. Where was he? She started climbing up towards the first floor and then she remembered that she needed to charge her phone. The charger was in the kitchen. So she turned around and went back down the stairs in Lin's painful shoes, sat down at the kitchen table and kicked them off.

She rubbed her feet, one by one. Seb's laptop was open on the table next to his coffee cup and his spiral-bound notebook with the pen through the top. No sign of his wallet or his phone. No sign of him. She flicked the heater on. The tap dripped. She listened to a bird out in the garden. The shoes had given her a blister; there was blood at her heel, sticky against her tights, and a ladder running up her calf. She was too tired to go upstairs and change. She pictured Seb on the top deck of the bus, his long legs turned out into the aisle; his bag in his lap and his knees together, his glasses steamed up. She wanted to give him hell, to shout at him until he told her what was going on. At the same time, she wanted to forgive him, to put her arms around him and take him to bed. She rubbed her sore foot and listened to the movement upstairs. It struck her that she was scared, sitting here in this cold room. There was something in the quiet, a threat that hung there.

It was only Colin, moving through the rooms, that was all. His green bomber jacket hung on the back of a chair, pushed in against the table. She felt in her bag for her phone, down at the bottom as usual with the receipts and loose change. The battery was almost gone. She stared at the screen – four missed calls – and put the phone down on the table because she was too scared to think straight, to move or speak. It was something about the cold kitchen, the time of day. It had been cold like this when the phone rang in her mum's kitchen, in the house where she'd grown up. Maxine had answered and a colleague of her dad's had asked to speak to her mum. There had been something in his voice: an urgent formality. Maxine had handed over the receiver and she had seen her mother's face change as she heard the news. An overloaded crane; dead on impact. It had been a cold, clear day like this one. The kind of day when the sound of the telephone could set your teeth on edge, it could put fear in you that would never leave.

Overhead, Colin's footsteps came closer. She stared into the room, at the mess of newspapers and unopened post, the unwashed coffee cups next to the sink. It was getting dark, the room lit by the weak orange glow of the heater. She picked up her phone and hit play on the first of her voicemails, held it close enough to her ear that she could make out Stella's voice, asking her how the feature was going, offering to read it. She sounded concerned, slightly exasperated. Maxine deleted the message. The next one was from Seb, asking her to call him. She smiled at the sound of his voice, so relieved that she barely heard what he said. They needed to talk; he hated arguing with her. It looked like he'd left the message almost an hour ago. The next one was the same, asking her to call him. Sirens in the background, but she heard him say that he was outside. That he loved her. She could cry, she was so glad and so sorry that she hadn't answered at the time, that she'd been too stubborn and mean. She tried to play it again but her phone ran out of battery.

There was nothing to be scared of. He loved her and he wanted to talk. From the stairs, she heard Colin's footsteps, light and quick, reaching the hallway. He put his toolbox down by the door. She looked at her lifeless phone and tried to remember the rest of Seb's message. He'd said he wanted to apologise. As Colin walked towards her, she thought, he said he was outside. She was sure he'd said that.

'Hi, Max,' Colin said. He flicked the light on, and she blinked in the sudden glare. He had a blue T-shirt on, blue jeans, but no hat, despite the cold. He looked drained, his T-shirt filthy, his jeans hanging loose from his hips. Something edgy in him.

'Busy day?' she said.

'Could say that.' He looked around the room. 'I'm going to head off home. I've done what I can up there.'

He took his jacket from the back of the chair and held it in one hand. She noticed how tightly he gripped it, the tendons standing out in his wrist. On the inside of his arm, near the bicep, he had a single tattoo: a line of cursive writing that ended at the sleeve of his T-shirt. She couldn't make out what it said.

'You look nice.' He moved his hand over the stubble at his crown.

'Do I?' She looked down at herself in Lin's dress; the tailored cut which clung a bit tighter than she would have liked. 'I had to borrow this from my sister. She said I could keep it, but I don't think it's really me.'

She felt his eyes on her, his approval. She couldn't look at him. There was a charge between them and she didn't want it, not today. He was a long streak of blue in the corner of her eye and she thought of Lin, saying that fear was helpful.

'Did you hear Seb come in?'

'Don't think so,' he said.

'I was hoping he'd be home by now.'

He ran his fingers along the top of a chair. 'You two patched things up then?'

'Not yet.'

'He won't be too far away. You know how it is. Rush hour.'

She stood and went to the counter where the phone charger was plugged in beside the kettle. 'He left me a voicemail. I thought he said he was outside.'

'Outside where?'

'He didn't say.'

'Well, then.'

She stared at her phone, its blank screen. On the far side of the room, the heater ticked.

'You'll be better off without him,' Colin said.

'I don't think so.'

'No?'

'I'm hoping we can work things out.' He didn't like that: she could tell without looking at him. She tapped the screen of her phone and forced a laugh, just to break the silence. It sounded strange, tinny. 'I think my phone's finally died,' she said.

He crossed the room and stood beside her, close enough that she smelled the dried sweat in his T-shirt. He reached out and turned on the power switch at the plug. 'That should do it,' he said. She saw the veins in his arms pushing up through dense black hair, and his tattoo stretched out thin over the muscle: *Remember the river.*

'Thanks,' she said. He stayed where he was, beside her.

'Aren't you cold?'

'I can take it,' she said. 'I grew up in a draughty house like this.'

'So did I.'

'Did you?'

'For a bit. It was exactly like this,' he said. 'I was always cold.'

She looked down at her phone and for a second could not remember how to turn it on. She knew that if she looked at him he would kiss her. Even now, she halfway wanted it. She wanted the toxicity of it, the harm. From the minute she had seen him she had wanted him to blow her life up.

She held the button down on her phone, turning her thumb white.

Something moved upstairs. A creak in the beams. She put her phone down, moved away, and his gaze burned the back of her neck. It was only a few steps across the room but she felt that she had changed, she had shed her skin.

She stood beside the heater in her stockinged feet and she met his eye. He was gaunt and wired and angry. She needed him gone.

'I don't think there's much more for you to do here,' she said.

'I think you're right.'

'Let me give you what I owe you.' She reached for her bag, fumbled blindly inside for her purse. 'I went to the bank earlier. I think it's right but you might want to check—'

'I don't want your money.'

His voice was dismissive. He was visibly trembling.

'But I owe you for—'

'No, you don't,' he said. 'It's not about the money. That's not the point.' He pushed his arms into his jacket and zipped it up. 'I wanted to thank you, before I go.'

'Thank me?'

'For letting me in that day. I wasn't sure that you would.'

She stared at him. 'That's OK.' She put her bag down on the table. Another creak came from upstairs, making her jump. 'God. What is that?'

'Full of spooks, this house,' he said.

'Seb always says that.'

'Yeah?' His neck twitched. 'Have you seen my hat?'

'Which one?'

'Baseball cap.' He stepped backwards, away from her. 'Must have left it up there,' he said, turning.

She listened as he sprung up the stairs, long-legged, rushing. She thought of him standing at the front door, holding a toolbox, the first time she met him. Tall and lean in a black woollen hat. He'd said, *You must be Maxine.* And she'd said, *You must be here to quote us for the plumbing.* He'd known her name. He'd been friendly and polite and she had let him in.

He had known her name.

She remembered Seb's text from earlier, the one with the exclamation marks which had annoyed her. It took on a new meaning as she reached for her phone, found his message: *I didn't!! You did.*

The phone rang in her hands, loud in the quiet room. She didn't recognise the number. She answered it just to make the noise stop. 'Hello?'

'Maxine?' A woman's voice.

'Yes. Who's this?'

'June. From the bookies. You remember?'

She searched her mind. She heard Colin's footsteps move through the house, from one floor to the next.

'June! Yes. How are you?'

'Did you get my message?'

'No. Sorry.'

'I left you a message earlier,' she said. 'I couldn't stop thinking about you, after you went off with him yesterday.'

She couldn't focus on what June was saying. She couldn't reply.

'You there?'

'Yes.'

'I'm glad you're all right. I just thought you should know, that's all. Hope you don't mind me saying.'

'I didn't hear your message. I don't know what you mean.'

June cleared her throat. 'Colin Delaney,' she said. 'He's been in prison. A long stretch. I thought, maybe you knew that already. But if you didn't, maybe you'd want to know. That's what I thought.'

Maxine stood very still with the phone at her ear. She said, 'I didn't know.'

'He's not been out long. I think he got released early,' June said. 'Maybe he's a reformed character. Miracles happen and all that.'

Her phone became heavy in her hand. Clare's dog barked from the garden next door. She thought, Seb should be home by now.

'I had all sorts going through my head last night,' June said. 'But the good news is, you've got plenty of material for that article you're writing. If Colin Delaney can't help you with that, no one can.'

'Thanks,' Maxine said. She forced herself to ask it: 'What did he do?'

'You could find out if you have a look on the internet, I'd have thought.' She coughed, and Maxine heard her thumping her chest. 'I wouldn't recommend it, personally.'

June coughed again as she ended the call. Maxine put her phone down, brought her hands to her face. She remembered showing Colin around, the day he'd turned up at the door. He'd been enthusiastic about the huge rooms with their original features, saying how rare it was to find a house as untouched as this. And then he'd led the way up to the loft. It had stayed with her, the way he'd gone up there ahead of her, the way he'd drawn breath as he stood in that room. It had been something more than shock in his face. He'd gone white. She'd stood by the garret window and she'd told him, *Seb finds it creepy up here.*

Colin's footsteps were close and he was there at the foot of the stairs with his hat on. It pulsed in her as he turned towards the kitchen. She thought, Seb didn't ask him to quote for the plumbing. That's what he meant.

'Right,' Colin said. 'That's that.'

She held her face in the position of someone who is not afraid. 'I'll see you out,' she said.

He stepped towards her, leaned forward and held the back of a chair with both hands. 'I need you to know something, Maxine. It's important.'

She nodded. She couldn't speak.

'My dad took the blame for what I did.' He looked past her at the kitchen, the cabinets and the stove, the window that looked out onto the old fence where the builders' materials were stacked. 'I didn't want him to do that. But that's what he did, he took the blame for me and I had to keep up this act. I had to go back to school after the Christmas holidays and act like I was this nice, normal kid. Lunch queues and break-times and maths and physics. People were nice to me because my dad died. They made allowances. But the whole time, I knew I wasn't normal. Or nice. You see?'

She nodded again. If he moved she might scream.

'I had to hide it, Maxine. But I knew I was a fucking monster.'

Maxine held herself still. Her head fogged. She didn't dare look away, although he was looking past her again, staring at the back of the room, the floor. She held her fists tight inside the sleeves of her coat and tried to think about the back door, whether she could get out that way, whether she

285

could jump the wall into Clare's garden. But all she could think was, Seb said he was outside. He should have been home by now.

'Did you hear me?' He looked at her then, and raised his voice. 'It was me. It wasn't him.'

'It wasn't him.'

'I killed her,' he said. 'And I got away with it.'

Something about the way he said it. The way he projected his voice, speaking into the room. It cleared the fog. She thought of Clare, the first time they'd met, telling her that the previous owner was killed in the house. Maxine had changed the subject, she hadn't wanted to know; she had pushed it away, this knowledge. But she knew it now. It was looking back at her; it had tracked her down.

'Somebody told me once, it's important to know who you are,' Colin said. 'Did you know that?'

'Yes.'

'Important to know that about yourself. Not to be a fucking fraud your whole life.' He waited for her to nod in agreement. 'Do you know who I am?'

'I think so,' she said, hoping he would leave it now, but he was gripping the back of the chair and he was waiting for her to speak. 'You killed the woman who lived here before,' she said. He stood up, letting go of the chair. 'Maybe you carried on killing people after that. You went to prison and you just got out. You're a killer. That's what I think.'

He considered her across the length of the room. He was quiet, and his jaw worked. The house was silent around him.

'Thank you,' he said.

'I'll see you out,' she said, brighter and higher than the first time. She moved towards the door, past where he stood, and after a moment he followed. She heard his footsteps close behind her as she reached the hallway. She flicked on the light and she thought, I'm scared now, this is happening to me. Her fear was dense around her, slowing time. The coats on their hooks and the shoes by the door were strange in their normality. The tiled floor was clean and bright; her umbrella was where she'd left it, leaning against the wall. Beside these things her fear was huge and grotesque. She reached for the latch and wondered, if she stepped into the street and screamed, would anyone hear her? Would anyone stop?

He stood beside her as she opened the door, his arm touching hers. She forgot how to breathe. Her blood rushed in her ears. She thought, He's going to kill me now, that's why he's here, that's who he is. Then the door was open wide; she felt the cold night air against her skin. A fox appeared from behind a bin, assessed her briefly, then slipped out through the gate.

'Where is he?' She half-screamed it. 'Where's Seb?'

Colin reached down, picked up his toolbox and slowly straightened back up, the box heavy in his hand. He brushed past her and stood out on the step.

'He's upstairs.' He moved his toolbox from one hand to the other. A motorbike revved behind him. 'Second floor,' he said, shouting over the noise. 'Watch yourself on the landing.'

She shut the door. Behind her, out on the Rye, a car horn sounded for a long time, then another. She ran up the stairs.

38

19 December 1994

'Just a few items of clothing,' the policeman said. 'Leave the rest where it is.'

Ruth looked around at the poky loft room and tried to keep her head. She'd barely slept or eaten in the five days since the murder. She was living through her worst nightmare, coping one minute at a time. She saw Cookie's pyjamas on the sofa and his school bag on a chair. The huge slice of quiche she'd brought home from work was still on the plate where she'd left it on the table, blue now with mould. Her hairbrush and her coffee cup. It all had an innocence to it. The before-times, when she'd thought they had problems and she hadn't known she was born. Those pyjamas of Cookie's looked like they belonged to a little boy. She sat down on the sofa and lifted them onto her lap.

'I could see if Colin wants to come up and help you,' the policeman said. 'Should I go back to the car, see if he'll change his mind?'

'Cookie won't come up here. He's in shock. He feels terrible.' She felt him looking at her, and she stared down at the pyjamas in her lap, her head rushing. 'He wants his dad. Misses him.'

'I bet.'

She didn't dare look up. She felt like she'd blown it, like if she met his eye now he'd know all of it; her son would be handcuffed, he'd be locked up for life. She focused on the tartan pattern in the pyjamas. She remembered buying them from C&A on the high street, thinking they'd last him a year or two. But he'd shot up, growing out of everything in the space of six months. He'd need a new pair.

A gust of wind blew rain against the window.

'What will happen to our things?' she said. 'The things I don't take back with me.'

'They'll be left here, I'd imagine. It looks like the deceased had no living relatives, so the house might be empty a while.'

The deceased. The word took on meaning slowly, filling her body with heat. She folded the pyjamas and put them aside.

'I'll have to hurry you, Mrs Delaney.'

A bus passed along the street outside and Ruth thought of Cookie, asleep in this bed as she got ready for work. She could taste it, that feeling she'd had that something was going to happen to him, something bad. There had been fear in this room from the day they'd moved in.

'Do you have a suitcase?'

Ruth looked at the policeman. She couldn't for the minute think what a suitcase was.

289

'To put your things in,' he said. 'I'm only supposed to let you stay up here a few minutes.'

She stood. There was a suitcase under the bed, she remembered. A big grey one with buckles that they'd used for their clothes when they'd come here. She knelt down and reached under the bed for it. There was a sock under there, one of Lee's, grey with dust. She left it where it was. Lee was being held in custody and when she thought of him she could not see his face. She could picture his shape, the way he'd looked across the street when she saw him going into the bookies with his head down, hunched over in his donkey jacket. Sometimes in her dreams she saw him with a full head of hair, young and nice-looking, and she woke up with the memory of him for a second or two. A bit of her would always be nineteen years old, mad about Lee Delaney, the eldest of the Delaney brothers.

But today she was sitting on the floor of a cluttered loft room, staring into an empty suitcase. She had nothing. This was where her faith in Lee had got her.

It came to her then: the Quality Street tin.

'Sorry,' Ruth said, smiling at the officer. She pulled a chair out from the table and dragged it over to the broom cupboard in the corner of the room. She stood on the chair and saw the pipe that ran close to the ceiling, the usual cobwebs and dust. But the tin wasn't there.

'I'll need to hurry you now,' the policeman said.

She stared at the space where the tin should have been. Lee had said something about the tin, that day in the kitchen. Something about money; that he'd had a win, and he'd put the money aside for them. She tightened her ponytail, wrapping the hair band three times around. Her brain felt like a shrivelled pea, hard and calcified. She wasn't sure now that Lee had said anything like that. The small flame of her nineteen-year-old self wanted to think he'd said it; that he'd taken care of them in his own way, he'd at least tried.

Ruth would always wonder about this. Especially as Lee died that day, as she was standing on a chair looking at the cobwebs and the pipe that ran across the ceiling, trying to remember what he'd said. Lee had owed his cellmate a lot of money, it turned out, and that cellmate had strangled him with his bare hands before the guard could break it up. Cookie was the one who believed his dad; he would grow more convinced by the year that Lee had had one last bet, that he'd taken the rent money and the savings from the tin and he'd put the whole lot on a horse. And for once he'd struck it lucky. He'd known he was going to prison, and he'd hidden his winnings somewhere in the house. The idea of it would become the thing that held Cookie together, the thing he lived for. He would develop theories as to where the money might be concealed. He would tattoo his dad's last words to him across his bicep.

'Maybe you could put your laundry into the case,' the policeman said helpfully.

Ruth stood down from the chair. She considered the clothes airers, where her underwear was hanging out: knickers and bras and tights, all of it grey from being mixed in with the coloured wash. She hated that the policeman had seen it. She felt herself growing hot, a huge internal heat, sending a sweat up her back.

'Do you want a hand with it?'

'No thanks.' She stood, opened up the case on the bed and took a big handful of laundry off the top of the rack. One of her bras fell to the floor and she burned hotter at the sight of it, the small cups and the girlish bow in the centre. She picked up the bra, threw it into the case and lifted her shirt away from her skin, discreetly flapped at it to cool herself down a bit. She had never been so hot in her life.

She filled the case with clothes, a few towels, toiletries. She didn't know if she'd chosen the right things to keep, the right things to leave behind. It was too sad, to make those decisions. She did it ruthlessly in the end, leaving Cookie's jeans and trainers because they were old and filthy and a size too small. She didn't notice his school tie, which had slipped onto the floor behind the sofa, but she found his school textbooks and put them in the case. He had done well in his latest test, he'd said. The memory seemed distant, years ago. She closed the case, and she thought that this house had wrecked everything for her family. She had to get out of here. In the urgency of the moment she swung the case off the bed and led the way out of the room, leaving the policeman to follow behind her.

He stopped on the first-floor landing and cleared his throat. 'Just one thing,' he said.

She put the case down. 'What's that?'

'Where was he standing? Your son?'

'Sorry?'

'When your husband pushed your landlady down the stairs. Where was your son at the time?'

She shook her head. 'Haven't we been over this?'

'I just wanted to check. To be sure I understand.'

The policeman was holding the newel post, looking down the stairs at the black and white tiles and the shoe rack. There was bright yellow tape all around it; they'd had to lift it to get up to the loft.

'He was standing here,' she said, nodding down at the thinning carpet, the underlay visible in places. 'He was right here, beside me.'

'You sure?'

'Yes.' She blew a strand of hair out of her face. 'Sorry, but Cookie's waiting outside.'

'So he was on the landing, looking down. And your husband—' he stepped down onto the stairs. 'Your husband stepped forward, like this.'

Ruth nodded. Her head swam.

'And you and your son were standing a little way back from him, where you are now?'

'That's right.' The front door shook in the wind. The sweat on her back had turned cold now and her clothes felt damp. 'Me and Cookie were on the landing,' she said. 'I told you that at the station.'

'Only your son described something to me, which made me wonder if I'd got it right.'

She coughed, to disguise her fear. 'What did he describe?'

'It was the way your landlady's head struck the shoe rack.'

'The shoe rack?'

'Colin said it was the sharp corner of the shoe rack that cracked her skull open.'

'Did he?'

'He was quite clear about it.' He pointed down the stairs. 'Quite precise.'

Oh, Cookie. Jesus Christ. 'He has a dark imagination,' she said. 'Always has had.'

He stared down at the shoe rack for what felt like a very long time. 'He was right,' he said, turning back to face her. 'We found blood on the shoe rack, and a strand of hair.'

'I'm glad he was able to help you,' Ruth said.

'Your husband didn't mention it. The shoe rack.'

'No?'

'Mr Delaney seemed to think she cracked her head on the tiles there.' He pointed down at the floor. 'I'd have thought he'd have been the only one who'd know. He'd have been obscuring your view, wouldn't he?'

Ruth stared the policeman hard in the eye. 'My son is a very bright child. I imagine he worked out what happened from the—' she thought of him sitting beside her on the stairs, the word he'd used. 'From the velocity.'

The policeman raised his eyebrows at this. 'Do you think so?'

'I'm certain of it,' she said. She reached down for the handle of the suitcase. She felt all their things sink to the bottom as she lifted it up.

'Are you sure there's nothing else you want to tell me, Mrs Delaney?'

'Quite sure,' Ruth said. The lie folded itself into the history of the house. It was swallowed up gladly, pulled under, so she couldn't have taken it back if she'd wanted to.

'Good, then,' the policeman said, and he held the tape as she stepped down onto the tiles. 'If you want to go out to the car, I'll follow you once I've locked the place up.'

Ruth hauled the suitcase down the steps, through the gate and out to the police car, which was parked on the near side of the road just in front of the bus stop. Cookie sat in the back seat, his head turned away from her, looking out of the window at the common. She opened the rear door and put the case on the seat next to him. He turned, looked at the case without interest. There was no space for Ruth in the back, so she walked around the front of the car, opened the passenger door and got in.

'Did you find it?' Cookie said.

She looked at him in the rear-view mirror: dark blue eyes, their shine gone. 'Find what?' she said.

'The tin.'

'No. It wasn't there.'

'Where did you look?'

'On top of the cupboard.' She looked up at the house. The policeman was still inside, the front door ajar. 'That's where I used to keep it.'

'You didn't look anywhere else?'

'No.'

'Why not?'

'Because he was watching me.' She turned in her seat and faced Cookie. He seemed to have changed again since she last looked at him: his face was lean, and his eyebrows met in the middle. His top lip was dark with a growth of soft hair. 'He asked me a ton of questions just now,' she said. 'Wanted to know where you were standing when your dad pushed her. How come you knew she hit her head on the shoe rack.'

He sat up straighter. 'Does he know it was me?'

'You shouldn't have said that, about the shoe rack.'

'Why?'

'Because you couldn't have known that, could you, if you hadn't—'

'Pushed her.'

She hissed: 'Don't say that.'

Cookie sat forward, knees in the back of her seat. The car was steamed up, the windows fogged. 'I pushed her,' he said. 'Why can't I say it?'

'Because it's best you don't.'

'Why?'

Ruth reached for his hand but he snatched it away. He was agitated, jumpy. She'd known it was a mistake to bring him with her, but he'd said he didn't want to be on his own, he'd pleaded with her. Now she wished she'd stood her ground. He was getting himself in a state.

'We've been over this,' she said.

'I don't see why I can't say it, when there's nobody here.'

'I'd rather you didn't.'

'Why?'

'For God's sake.' Over Cookie's shoulder, through the rain at the rear window, she saw the dark shape of the policeman locking up the house. 'You know why.'

'No, I don't.' He raised his voice. 'Why can't I say it, when it's only you and me in this car, and you already know that I pushed her?'

'Cookie, don't—' She held him by the arm.

'Let go of me.'

'He's coming back. He'll hear you.'

'I don't care.'

'I'm serious.'

'I don't care if he hears me. He knows anyway.' He wrenched his arm from her grip. 'I'm going to tell him.'

'You are not.' She couldn't hold on to him, he was bigger than her, and stronger. He was too big for the car. 'What are you doing?'

Cookie reached for the door handle then; he did it before Ruth could reach him, before she understood. The rear door flew open onto the road. There was a rush of noise and rain, car horns and tyres against wet tarmac. At the edge of her vision: the huge red bulk of a bus, too close, too fast. Another horn, louder, then another.

Somebody shouted over the noise. A screech of tyres, a crash. A moment of improbable quiet.

Ruth opened her own door. The traffic around them had stopped. The bus was blocking the road, turned sideways, and all Ruth could see was its red flank; it was blocking the sky, she could not see beyond it, she could not see Cookie. She stood in the street. A motorcyclist was sitting next to his bike, its wheels still spinning, his head between his knees. A car was facing the wrong way behind the motorbike, its rear end on the pavement. Ruth walked in front of the stationary bus, her hands at her face, waiting to see Cookie there under the wheels. Her life would end once she saw it. She stared down at the road, the bare stretch of it. She said his name, she screamed his name. But there was no blood, no sign of him.

She swung around. On the pavement, alongside the common, a man said, 'What the hell did you think you were doing?' His voice was loud, furious. Beside him, standing upright, unharmed, was Cookie. 'You could have killed someone,' the man said. He was the bus driver, Ruth realised: he was shouting in her son's face.

'I know,' Cookie replied.

Ruth threw herself at her boy. She put her arms around his neck and cried. She hung off him. Cookie staggered backwards and she went with him onto the grass of the common, away from the road. He was shaking. She sniffed and heaved and held him tight against her.

'They should have locked me up,' Cookie said, quietly, so only she would hear it.

She stood up straight then and let go of him. She wiped her nose with her sleeve. 'You are twelve years old,' she said. 'You are just a child.'

'I should be the one in prison.'

'You should not.'

The policeman who'd taken her into the house was in the road, helping the motorcyclist to his feet. People were standing around, looking at them, staring with open curiosity. She stared back.

'Move along,' the policeman said. He waved the onlookers in the direction of the junction. Nobody moved.

'I want to be locked up,' Cookie said.

'Don't say that.'

'I don't want Dad to go to prison. I want to be the one who—'

'Listen.' She held him by the jaw, gripped him hard so he looked at her. 'That's not going to happen. I don't want to hear that from you again.' When he tried to speak she tightened her grip, tight enough that she knew she was hurting him; she felt his molars under the pressure of her thumb. 'You can't do that to me,' she said. 'Do you understand? You can't do that to me.'

He resisted her, his eyes wide, but she didn't let go until she felt him nod his head. The rain had flattened his hair, and she pushed it out of his eyes. She didn't like the way he was looking at her. She looked hard at him, tried to find the boy she knew but he turned away, hung his head, lifted his feet one by one out of the mud.

39

17 November 2008

Maxine stopped at the first-floor landing. She swung on the newel post and stared into the dark mess of exposed pipes, wires, joists; slats of darkened wood. Colin had taken up every board on the landing. It was insane, the work of a lunatic, and she tried not to let this thought flood her because she needed to hold it together, to stave off the panic. She shouted for Seb. She waited to see if he would walk out of the bedroom and tell her he was fine, and she would laugh at how scared she had been, they both would. There was still that small hope. She shouted again, louder, and from the floor above she heard a movement.

'Seb? Are you up there?'

No reply. Nothing.

She edged herself along the landing, her feet between the spindles. She felt the stitching rip at the back of Lin's dress. The wood creaked and rocked against her and she kept her eyes on the tiled floor below, the curve of the bannister leading down to the ground floor. She leaned out to grab the handrail, swung herself onto the next flight of stairs and stopped again at the top where the floorboards were gone and the whole landing was an open space: pipes and wiring and hunks of masonry encased in ancient woodwork. A dark, earthy smell.

It was quiet and cold and she shouted for Seb. She wanted to cry. The light was dim up here and she saw the planks of floorboard leading to the largest room, the door standing ajar. She stepped onto it, testing its strength under her weight. It wobbled beneath her and she stepped back, gathered herself and tried again. She took one step, then another, and at the halfway point the board tipped. She swayed, arms outstretched, recovered. Her next step landed off-centre. Her balance was gone and the board flipped over, sending her sideways into the opening where her shoulder met a length of pipe, a mess of wires.

She lay still and listened. The pipes were holding her weight, lifting her away from the timber and plaster beneath. For a few seconds she thought the whole landing would collapse, that she would fall through the house, that she would die on the tiled floor downstairs. There was a certainty to it, a pull from the floor below. She lay there, and the house creaked.

This time she didn't try to use the floorboards as a bridge. She turned onto her stomach and crawled towards the open door, using the pipes to support her weight. Boards cracked as she moved. A pipe beneath her knee bent and there was a hiss, a clank; she reached the entrance to the room just as the pipe burst open, sending a gush of water across the landing, weak at first and then stronger, shooting upwards. She crawled into the room, into the grey, cold light, where Seb lay on his front with his head turned to the side, his glasses skewed.

The air thickened. She didn't believe it but she knew it was true; it was real and she couldn't bear it. She got to her feet and called his name. His eyes were shut, his hands palm-down, his body perfectly still. His long coat risen up his back. She went to him, crouched beside him, touched his head, his hair. She felt the soft heat of matted blood. He looked thoughtful, like he was choosing his words. She knelt down and kissed his face and the room glowed dully around her.

'Seb?' She said his name again and again, her voice growing shrill. She rolled him gently onto his back, tried to breathe into his mouth, to pump his chest. He was still warm against her hands. She looked into his face and told him she would forgive him everything, whatever it was, if he would only wake up and be OK. His head rolled away from her. Blood ran from his nose.

She knelt beside him. The walls watched. She didn't want him to die here, not here.

Her phone. She patted her coat pockets, then remembered she'd left it in the kitchen, charging. The panic rose up, she felt a scream in her throat and fought to contain it, to be calm. She searched through Seb's pockets and found his phone in his coat; she stabbed at it but she didn't know his code. A picture of her shone brightly out of his lock screen: her smiling, stupid, clueless self. She crouched down again beside Seb, spoke into his ear. 'I'm going to get you out of here. Just hang on. OK? Just hang on.'

He was going to die. She crossed to the doorway, looked at him lying there and heard herself wailing because she couldn't save him. She sealed her mouth with her hand. She considered running back downstairs, but water was gushing from the pipe she'd knelt on and the landing was a dark pool of water.

She went back to his phone. There was a way to make a call. She held buttons down as she paced the room and when the emergency call activated she dropped the phone in shock, fell to her knees to pick it up, found it again and spoke to the woman who was waiting, talking to her, asking her which service she required.

'Ambulance. Police.' She gave the address; she was able to explain, to talk rationally down the phone. Then she went to Seb and breathed into his mouth, pumped his chest, told him to hold on, to stay with her, that she loved him and she would not give up. She said it again and again, and when the para-medics came they found her straddling his body, breathing hopelessly into his mouth. They had to lift her off him and ask her to stand aside.

40

3 August 1843

Horatio took his usual table at the rear of the Kings Arms. He was not long recovered from his illness, and was not sure that he wanted the ale that he set down in front of him. His clothing was loose around his middle. He had wanted to leave the house, to be among people, but now he was here he thought perhaps it had been a mistake. He had the sensation of dreaming. He had noticed as he entered the tavern that nobody stood to greet him, as they normally would. As he took his drink and walked to his table, he had noticed a hush.

He opened his newspaper and took an interest in an article on the Elgin marbles: scientists were working to restore the sculptures, which were deteriorating due to dust and soot. Lord Elgin had lost all his money on these marbles, which he had removed from the Parthenon in Greece and transported to London at great cost. They were extraordinary, the article said. There was something alive in them which would speak to people down the generations.

Horatio took his time over the article, although he had read it earlier that day. He had read the entire newspaper before noon, in fact. He had hoped to find company and perhaps to mention, in passing, that one of his letters had today been printed in full, on the subject of the miasma rising from the River Peck. His second letter to the editor published on this subject. He had hoped he might be able to pass the newspaper to anyone who was interested, to read it for themselves. Perhaps he might even be asked to read the letter aloud.

The opportunity could yet arise. He could see Mr Pearce at the bar, a neighbour whose cottage faced onto the Peck, on the stretch of the Rye where the weeping willows gave onto the river. He knew that Mr Pearce's cellar had filled more than once with flood water, and that his wife had complained of the offensive smell rising from it. Old Mr Delaney stood not far from him, his overalls dirty from the kiln where he worked making clay pipes. It was a pleasant evening, high summer, and not yet dark. Horatio felt sure that Mr Pearce was aware of him, that he would have seen him at his usual table with his copy of *The Times*. He thought he saw Mr Delaney look up, then look away.

Horatio drank his ale slowly, and turned to the page in his newspaper where the letters to the editor were laid out. He read his own again. The joy he had initially felt on seeing it had not lasted long. He feared that very few people would read it, or take it seriously. And it was plain that nobody would accept the miasma as the cause of his wife's death, nor that of Alice. Despite his understanding of the science, he was finding it harder to believe it himself.

The ale had reached his head. He closed his newspaper and folded it. The thoughts he had tried to banish were often present these days. This evening he was flooded by them. Sitting alone at his favoured table, he knew that he was to blame for the typhoid that had killed Isobel, and then Alice. It was not the miasma which was to blame, but his own low birth. He had brought the disease with him from the rookeries, where he was born, and he had infected the house. He had killed them both and he could never forgive himself.

The disease of the poor.

He took his handkerchief from his breast pocket and ran it over his face.

Archer had been there when the physician gave his verdict. And Archer had been loyal, he had told no one, at Horatio's insistence. Isobel's memory would be protected from that shame. In the days since his own illness had passed, Archer had persuaded him to write to his boys, to make his case that he had loved their mother terribly; that he would gladly take her place in the grave if he could. That he loved them both. The letter had been plain, charged with the truth of his words, with all of his love and hope. He had sent it one week ago, and had heard nothing.

The ale tasted strange. He found he did not want it. Nor did he want to sit here alone, while Mr Pearce continued his conversation with the men at his side, a growing crowd now that the brick factory had closed for the day. When Horatio stood he allowed his chair to scrape noisily against the floor, and he looked around him as he returned his tankard to the bar. He paused there, turned to Mr Pearce, nodded his head in greeting. Mr Pearce did not respond; he turned his shoulder, Horatio thought. He stood a moment, to be certain. Mr Delaney averted his eyes.

'Good evening,' Horatio said. There came no reply.

As he made for the door someone called out: *Killer.*

Horatio swung around to face the men at the bar, all of them turned now towards him. He saw the knowledge in their eyes, their disgust. They knew, somehow they had found out. He stepped backwards, holding his newspaper under his arm.

A man he did not know, on the far side of Mr Pearce, spoke up: 'Did you strangle them both?'

The men waited, and Horatio shook his head. 'Strangle them both?' He repeated the words before he understood them.

'He doesn't deny it,' another man said.

'I do,' Horatio said. 'I would never—'

'Looks guilty to me.'

Horatio stood silent as the men grumbled in agreement. They were pink-faced with the ale and the heat. He thought of dear Isobel, his one love and companion, who had loved him despite his background. She had told him a hundred times that it meant nothing to her. For the first time since she died, he recalled her saying this. He thought of her dignity, and her warmth.

He turned his back. The men at the bar roared as he left. He held Isobel's memory close and tried not to mind it, to rise above it, as she would have. He passed his neighbours' houses, tall and narrow like his own, built of the finest London brick. The men's voices faded as he walked. He thought, as he went through his gate and up the steps, that his reputation would not recover from this. He would not clear his name, now the rumour had taken hold. But he could bear it. He wiped his feet. At the staircase he held the bannister at its base, where the oak tapered downwards, and thought that he preferred the lie to the truth.

The house heard this thought. It breathed it into its beams and its bricks and its carpentry, its atmosphere.

'Archer?'

His voice sounded strange in his ears. The house was full of echoes, since the auctioneers had taken his best mahogany pieces, his Persian rugs and his grand piano. He called again but no reply came. Instead he heard a hammering from the first floor. He continued up the stairs, pausing to call out again.

'Up here, sir,' Archer said.

Horatio found Archer on the landing, holding his hammer in one hand, a nail between his teeth. He had nailed several boards of timber across the door to the water closet.

'I did not ask for this,' Horatio said.

Archer took the nail from his mouth, and the hammer hung loose in his hand. 'I think it is best,' he said.

'This is my house.'

Archer reached out and placed his hand against the door. 'The disease is in here, sir. I feel sure of it.'

Horatio felt the weight of his mourning jacket on his shoulders, the new weakness in his limbs. A carriage passed on the track outside, disturbing the crows.

'The plumbing is the very best on the market, Archer. We are the only house for miles around—'

'We are the only house with typhoid, sir.'

Horatio tensed. 'I have asked you not to –'

'You must not blame yourself.'

'I would rather this was not discussed.'

Archer softened his tone. 'I know you fear that you carry the disease,' he said. 'That your blood is somehow impure.'

Horatio stood before Archer, awash with shame. He felt his legs might give way.

'You spoke of it when you were sick,' Archer said. 'You spoke to me of the rookeries.'

'Archer,' Horatio said. 'Please don't—'

'Mrs Lloyd used this room, and Alice cleaned it,' Archer continued, his hand flat against the door at his side. 'I think there is a danger in here, some flaw in the pipes perhaps. Mr Jardine is of the same opinion.'

Horatio smoothed his moustache. He drew breath to say that it was preposterous. Of course the disease was not in the water closet, waiting silently in the pipes. But he stopped himself short. 'Mr Jardine shares this view?'

'It is his condition, sir,' Archer said, 'that I board this room up.'

Archer lifted the hammer and tapped its blunt end against the palm of his hand. Horatio heard the apology in the other man's voice. He could not object, since it was his father-in-law who paid Archer's wage. 'His condition?' Horatio said. 'Is that so.'

The birds were noisy out on the Rye, and the light was fading. He thought he heard footfall from the top of the house.

'Mr Jardine left not long ago,' Archer said. He was smiling, holding the hammer still. 'He is here,' he called, lifting his voice.

The footsteps became a run, a shout, a familiar voice rising through the house.

'William?' Horatio dropped his newspaper.

The boy almost knocked him over. Horatio staggered backwards and William clung to him, his head against Horatio's chest, his arms tight around his body. Horatio found himself laughing. He felt the boy's love, his health, the stubborn force of his faith in him, and it gave him strength; it held him upright.

41

4 January 2009

The clock radio said three in the morning. Maxine turned in the bed, reached out for Seb and found his shoulder, then his arm. Cold feet. She held him against her, hoping he would stir. It was a new habit of hers, this waking in the night, wanting his company. She was needy and insecure, scared of waking up to find him gone. She had told him in the hospital that this was an extreme way to get her attention.

'What happened?' he said.

She lay her arm across his chest. 'Nothing.' She found it easier to say this, when they talked in the night. It was always the first thing he said. 'Nothing happened. It's OK.'

He shifted his weight, turned his head towards hers. 'They should have locked me up.'

'Don't.' She said it into his ear, softly, as she always did. 'Don't say that.'

He was quiet for a minute, then he said, 'I'm sorry, Maxine.'

'I know you are.' She put her finger against his lips, because she didn't want to get into this game of sorry, where she joined in with all of her own regrets. They had agreed to talk more than they used to, that nothing was off limits. But he didn't want to hear the truth about Colin; she had tried but it had been too soon. He knew she felt she was to blame. For letting him in, for not seeing through him. But he didn't know how long she had toyed with him; how much she had liked his unsettling presence, his strange beauty.

Maybe he did know. He looked at her in the dark and she thought, maybe he knows everything. It felt that way.

He ran his cold hand up inside her shirt. Overhead, a small movement, just a quiet tap against the boards.

'You were right,' she said. 'You knew there was something wrong with this house. You were right to be scared.'

'Don't,' he said.

'Don't what?'

He kissed her on the mouth, slow and soft. 'Don't talk about me in the past tense.'

'Sorry.'

'I don't like that.'

'I just meant—'

'I know what you meant.' He lifted her shirt up and she helped him pull it over her head. 'I know what you meant, Maxine.'

She took her shorts off. He watched her do it. It was cold but she didn't reach for the covers. She didn't lie down. He sat up and moved his hands over her. She kept her eyes open and saw his hands slide down her body, the pressure of his fingers, then his mouth. She lay back then. She thought that he was making up for all those nights of turning away from her. They both had so much to make good. She had kept her guard up for too long; she should have been braver, and so should he.

He was better at this than she remembered. She let her head hang over the side of the bed, reached down and found his ear, a strand of his hair. He was slow, but not too slow. He held her hips and she moved against him.

For a second afterwards she thought he'd gone.

'You OK?' He crawled on top of her. He said her name in her ear and she tried not to cry.

'I'm great.'

'You seem distant.'

'Sorry,' she said. 'I always feel lonely, afterwards. That's all.'

'Don't be lonely. Talk to me.' He rolled onto his side. 'Come on. Tell me what's going on with you. Tell me what you do all day, when I'm not here.'

'You don't want to know that.'

'I do.'

She put her hand through his hair, avoiding the back of his head where he still wasn't healed, where he would never heal. 'I went up to the high street with your laptop,' she said.

'Did you?'

'I paid them twenty quid to hack into it.'

He propped himself up on his elbow. She couldn't tell if he was angry. It was dark, and he was quiet.

'Don't go,' she said.

'You know I don't like it when you talk like this.'

'You asked.' She sat up, her back to the headboard, and he did the same. She found her shorts and pulled them back on. 'That's what I do, when you're not here. I try to figure out where you came from.'

'Good luck with that.'

A night bus went past, changing the light, and she shut her eyes so that nothing changed between them, so that he would stay. She reached for his hand under the covers and he took it. She had to be careful now, not to lose him. He could easily slip away. In the daytime, searching through his notebooks and his files, she wondered if she had ever known him at all. If he had always been a ghost.

'Are you cold?' he said.

'Freezing.'

He pulled her down beside him and put his arms around her. They listened to the house settling in its foundations, its night noises. She knew that she would have to turn from him soon, that she would never warm up with his cold skin against hers. That he would be gone in the morning.

42

10 January 2009

Maxine was on her morning walk, crossing the common in her wellington boots, when she saw the woman standing at the gate outside her house. She slowed down and looked at her through the mist. It was a bit before eight and the house stood tall and narrow on Rye Lane, the sunrise reflected pink in its windows. The woman was looking at her, she thought. Her shape was unfamiliar: short and boxy in a black coat that reached her knees. A red scarf. As Maxine got closer she noticed her bag: a tartan shopping trolley, the sort they sold on the street near the train station.

A bus passed, and Maxine dashed across the road behind it. The woman came into focus: nervous, holding the trolley close against her body. She was older than Maxine – sixty or so – with greying hair pulled loosely back and a fringe that kicked out to one side. Small, bright eyes.

'Hello?' Maxine said.

The woman drew breath to speak, then she hesitated. She put one hand to her chest and tried again. 'I'm Ruth,' she said. 'Ruth Delaney. I'm Colin's mum.'

Maxine became hot, her skin prickled in her coat. She tried to push past Ruth, reaching for the gate, but Ruth stayed where she was. 'Sorry. I don't want to do this, whatever it is you want.' She felt disgusted by this woman. She didn't want to touch her.

'I know,' Ruth said. 'I understand.'

'You don't.'

'Please. I won't bother you again. Just give me a minute.'

Maxine held her keys in the pocket of her coat. She felt ready to fight if she had to. Ruth looked at her hopefully, her eyes wet. Maxine hated her.

'I read your article,' Ruth said.

'Which one?'

'*The House Always Wins*. It was a four-page spread last weekend.' She pressed her lips together.

'That one,' Maxine said. 'Right.'

'You knew everything. The whole thing. You knew what Colin did, and what Lee did, and—'

'I know.'

'How did you know all that?'

'I researched it. That's my job.' She turned her keys over inside her pocket. 'Seb was researching it too. He'd pieced some of it together, and I figured out the rest.'

They both stood quietly, shocked at the mention of his name. Maxine pressed the serrated edge of the Yale key into the flesh of her forefinger because she didn't want to cry in front of

Ruth, who had cornered her, appearing like a spectre at the gate when her guard was down.

'I didn't cover for Colin this time,' Ruth said. 'I shopped him in, when the police came looking for him.'

Maxine was glad Colin was back in prison, but she still wished every day that she had seen him for what he was from the start. She wished she had shut the door on him and bolted it. And it was hard to live in the house now she knew the whole of its history. She wasn't quite free of Colin, his crimes, his deep internal damage.

'That can't have been easy,' Maxine said.

'No.' Ruth tipped the trolley onto its rear wheels, and the contents slid backwards against the frame. 'He wanted to go back inside, I think. But still.' The sun was bright now and Ruth squinted as she looked up at Maxine. 'I'm so sorry,' she said. 'I really am.'

The hate drained out of Maxine, taking her strength with it. She could have lain down in the street if it hadn't been so fiercely cold.

'Do you want to come inside?'

'I won't, if you don't mind.' Ruth turned slightly so her back was to the house. 'I hope you're managing all right. On your own, I mean.'

Maxine shook her head. 'I'm not on my own.'

'Oh?'

'Seb hasn't left yet.'

Ruth cupped one hand around her eyes. She looked surprised but she didn't laugh, or back away. Maxine hadn't told anyone else about Seb's night-time visits, not even Lin, who called every morning as she walked to Rudy's nursery with the baby strapped to her chest. She had no idea why she had told Ruth this private, precious thing. This cold was sharp enough to open up your hiding places, to make you confess your darkest truths to a stranger. They both stamped their feet, and breathed out white mist.

'Listen,' Ruth said, tipping the trolley back onto its base. 'I've got something for you. It's been sitting on my coffee table for a couple of months and I can't stand the sight of it any more.' She opened the trolley and reached down inside, pulling out an object wrapped in black plastic, square-shaped, as deep as a shoebox. 'This is what Colin came back for. I told him not to, but it's a long time since he listened to me.'

Maxine took the parcel and held it uncertainly in her arms. 'He came back for this?'

'That's right.' Ruth seemed relieved to have handed it over. 'He found it inside the wooden casing in that disused loo on the first floor. Right down under the old soil pipe, apparently. He missed it the first time he looked.'

Maxine shook her head at Ruth. She felt slow, like she had missed something. 'Why didn't he ask me, if there was something in the house he wanted?'

'In case you said no.'

'But if he'd asked—'

'He wouldn't have risked that, Maxine.' She took a small step backwards, pulling the trolley to her side. 'He knew he might have to rip the house apart.'

Maxine held the parcel against her chest. She thought of the floorboards Colin had lifted on the upper floors, the exposed pipes and wiring. She'd got someone in to repair the damage: a quietly industrious man from Poland who had done what he could before she ran out of money.

'It's not—' Ruth lowered her voice. 'Compensation,' she said. 'It's not that.'

'OK.'

'But it's rightfully yours, I think. And I don't want it.' She shook her head, as if Maxine might protest. 'I don't want it.' She stood for a minute looking across the road at the common: bare trees rising above the glow of the mist. The sodden grass had stiffened with the frost and the crows were dispersed across it, sleek and still. 'It's legal tender,' she said. 'I checked.'

Maxine went to reply, but Ruth gave her a small nod and turned away towards the junction, the trolley weightless now behind her.

The house was full of light when Maxine let herself in. She kicked off her boots and pushed the door shut with her foot. Then she went into the kitchen and put the parcel down on the table. *Legal tender.* Money, then. She remembered Colin standing here, sweaty and agitated, telling her it wasn't about the money. His loping movements around the room. When she thought back over that afternoon it seemed that she had been wading through treacle. She had been too slow, too stupid and slow, and too late.

She filled the kettle and took milk from the fridge. She stared into the sink, at the stain in the porcelain, the yellowed streak where the tap dripped. The tap had been dripping for years, endlessly dripping, marking time. Seb had found it intolerable. She thought of him as the kettle boiled: his voice, reading to her from his book. She missed his voice.

It was early, and she didn't know how to fill the day. Hours until she could crawl into bed and wait for him.

She held her hand against her mouth. She saw herself, living a half-life, full of love for a dead man. Full of grief shot through with regret. She could have loved him more if he had let her. He was her should-have-been, her nearly-love. Nearly but not quite, not this time.

She made coffee, remembering to take only one mug down from the cupboard.

The plastic wrapping around the parcel turned out to be several bin liners, and inside was an old, dented tin, purple and white: one of the octagonal tins her mum had always bought at Christmas. The lettering was raised on the lid: *Quality Street*. Inside were dozens of tight rolls: banknotes. Fifties, big and pink. Jesus, so much money, more cash than she'd ever seen. She sat down at the table, pulled the tin into her lap and tried to estimate the number: thousands, she thought. Tens of thousands. An elastic band perished in her hand as she peeled off one of the notes. She stared at its detailed flourishes, held it up to the light and looked at the watermark.

She cried a bit, because this meant that she would move on from here. Seb would understand, she knew that. She knew that he would be glad for her. That he was waiting for her to let him go.

She stared into the room. The fifty curled up and dropped to the floor.

She said his name.

It sounded odd in the quiet room, in the full light of day. But she said it again, and again, until he was everywhere, it was almost too much; the house held him in all its surfaces. She felt that if she brushed the table with her fingertips she might feel the touch of his skin. She half expected him to stare back at her out of the shine in the kettle. He might gush at her from the pipes.

He heard her when she spoke. He listened as she told him about the visit from Ruth Delaney, and the things she'd said; the way she'd held herself, her back always to the house. She couldn't see him but she felt his smile in the room when she showed him the Quality Street tin and the money, all that cash. She said she would give it all to the dogs' home if it meant she could have him back. He cried when she did, when she said she was going to be OK. When she said goodbye.

Later, when she'd eaten and washed the dishes and got herself together, she went through the house opening windows. She lifted them as wide as she could manage, even the ones on the second floor where the paint had sealed the joins in the woodwork, where the light changed as the sash cracked open. For over an hour she stood the back door open with a crate, chasing squirrels and wood pigeons back into the garden. The rooms whistled with cold, and they were simply rooms. Floorboards settled against one another, bricks breathed in and out; the house adjusted and relaxed. It grew dark, and she was alone, and she was not afraid.

Acknowledgements

My heartfelt thanks to everyone who put up with me while I was writing this book, and who helped in various ways to bring it into the world. The initial spark of an idea that grew into *The House on Rye Lane* came from a talk given by Jon Newman and David Western early in 2020, on the subject of London's lost rivers. Jon and David were kind enough to answer my questions about the River Peck while I was researching this novel, and I'm grateful for their input. My thanks also to Tom Bolton, author of *London's Lost Rivers: A Walker's Guide* for helping me to make sense of old maps and for kindly sharing his expertise. Thanks to Paul Talling for his Lost River walks, which I recommend to anyone interested in London's hidden history. Thanks to Loraine Rutt of the Little Globe Company who generously shared her local knowledge. And thank you to the nice people at the Southwark Archive library, who were a big help.

I'm grateful to the friends and family who helped in various
ways. Firstly, for feedback on the early drafts, thanks to my sister
Sarah, my long-time writing buddy Francesca Jakobi, the Book
Square crew Emily, Sam and Tilly, and my author friends the
D20s. You are all the absolute best. Thanks to Simon Hargreaves
for sharing his professional experience and helping me to shape
the 2008 strand of the plot, and for reading an early draft so
considerately. Thank you to Matthew and Elinor Line for the
inspirational tour of their home, which is far lovelier than the
house I invented for this book. Big thanks to Emily Elias and
Rob Turner who gave me a much-needed hidey-hole when I
thought I would never finish my edits. Thank you to my Mum,
who is the best storyteller I know, and has always inspired and
encouraged me. Thanks to Dad and Gillie for all their support,
and for being proud of me, which means a lot.

Thank you to my brilliant agent Nicola Barr, who gently
persuaded me to keep writing through the long periods of
lockdown when my mojo was not always at the desk with me.
My thanks to the whole team at The Bent Agency for pushing
this book into the world. Thank you to my wonderful editor
Suzie Dooré at Borough Press, who saw the potential in this
book and helped me turn it into its best self. Thanks also to
Jabin Ali, Sofia Saghir, Emily Merrill, Sophie Waeland, Francesca
Tuzzeo, Ellie Game and the wider team at HarperCollins in
the UK, and to Ilaria Marzi at HarperCollins Italia for the
Italian edition.

Thanks to all the café-owners who let me write at their tables,
especially Spinach on Lordship Lane, for the caffeine-fuelled

smoothies. Thanks to all the friendly folk at Chener Books, to Roz at Review Books, and to Alistair at Rye Books, for being such champions of my writing.

Finally, most importantly, thank you to my amazing and gorgeous children. And to my husband David, my most trusted sounding board, who can casually resolve a plot hole in a heartbeat and convinces everyone he speaks to that they should buy my books, thanks always for everything.

Author's Note

It's thanks to the lockdowns of the Covid pandemic that I grew interested in the history of my neighbourhood. Like most people, during those long stretches of time spent at home, I walked my local streets and did circuits of the park, and I noticed things that I'd been too busy or distracted to pay attention to. I started thinking about what was here before there were roads and buildings and cars and trains, and planes always passing overhead. For a while, as the world was forced to pause, it was easier to imagine that quieter time. History was closer than it used to be, and I saw it everywhere. It started to obsess me.

The focus of my obsession, once I started writing this book, was the River Peck. I'd always known that a small section of the Peck still ran through Peckham Rye Park, and I'd heard that it had once continued across what is now Peckham Rye common. But where had it gone? And why? What course did it take across the common, and from there, where did it go?

Was it lovely? Was it deep or was it a trickle? What part did it play in people's lives? I felt the loss of it, as I circled the common on my daily walk. I found a book which mapped out its original course, and my husband and I walked the route through the back streets of Peckham and on to Rotherhithe. There was something eerie about this lost river, still running beneath the tarmacked surfaces of the city, a link to another time.

A quick Google search will tell you that the River Peck was enclosed in 1820-23. This date pops up everywhere, in newspaper archives and online. But a deeper search will take you to old maps which show the Peck running across the Rye, and onwards to the Thames, in the 1840s. The London Picture Archive contains watercolour paintings and sketches of Peckham Rye in the 1830s, showing the river above ground, crossed by a footbridge. There are paintings and Ordnance Survey maps which suggest that a waterway crossed the Rye until the early 1860s, when Joseph Bazalgette's sewers were constructed. I started to imagine the rural scene that might have existed when the first houses were built on the Rye, overlooking the River Peck. The old maps and drawings were my inspiration, and my story grew from there.

At some point during the pandemic I found myself several drafts into a book about the history of one of those houses. The River Peck was important, running through the story. Everything I had learned told me the Peck would have been an open sewer until Bazalgette's works were complete; that it would have become less lovely by the year as bathrooms were installed in those middle-class houses, and early Victorian drains failed to cope. But I am not a historian. What if I had it wrong? The whole novel would fall apart if it turned out the River Peck had indeed been enclosed in the 1820s, long before the imaginary Lloyd family moved into their new home. I kept writing, but it nagged at me. Occasionally I woke in the night thinking that I would have to tell my agent I'd wasted all this time, that I was scrapping the whole idea. And I didn't have another idea.

Eventually I got back in touch with Jon Newman, local historian and author of several books on London's lost rivers. He pointed me towards a set of minutes for the Metropolitan Board of Works from 1859, which record that local residents were petitioning for the River Peck to be covered over due to its offensive smell. (The Board apparently refused their request, and provided deodorising agents.) To say I was happy to receive this information is an understatement. It was validating, and slightly spooky, to see my imagined world reflected in this nugget of history. In Horatio Lloyd I had invented a character who complained obsessively about the smell from the River Peck, and wanted it buried. It seemed a version of Horatio may well have existed in Victorian Peckham.

And so lockdown ended, the novel was sold, and the mystery of the lost River Peck was solved. I was glad to move on from my obsession, to get on a train and go somewhere else. But the project had kept me relatively sane during a dark time, and I am proud of the story that emerged: a portrait of a corner of London whose wealth and fortune has fluctuated wildly over the centuries, and a cast of characters whose lives were shaped by it. The book is about more than its location, but it has left me with a deeper connection to the place I see from the window as I write, which for a short time was my whole world.

For those who may have spotted that the house in this book would have been situated on a street called Peckham Rye, rather than Rye Lane, I apologise for this deliberate inaccuracy, which was inserted at a late stage when the book's title was changed. For a stickler for detail like myself, this wasn't easy to do. But it's a good title, and fact needs to bend to fiction sometimes for a novel to work. Beyond this, any errors are unintentional, and entirely my own.